MINE TO SAVE

Also by Diana Gardin

Mine to Save

Rescue Ops Book 3

Diana Gardin

FOREVER
YOURS

New York

Copyright © 2017 by Diana Gardin
Excerpt from *Sworn to Protect* copyright © 2017 by Diana Gardin
Cover design by Elizabeth Stokes
Cover copyright © 2017 by Hachette Book Group, Inc.

Forever Yours
Hachette Book Group
1290 Avenue of the Americas, New York, NY 10104
forever-romance.com
twitter.com/foreverromance

First published as an ebook and as a print on demand: December 2017

Forever Yours is an imprint of Grand Central Publishing. The Forever Yours name and logo are trademarks of Hachette Book Group, Inc.

The publisher is not responsible for websites (or their content) that are not owned by the publisher.

The Hachette Speakers Bureau provides a wide range of authors for speaking events. To find out more, go to www.hachettespeakersbureau.com or call (866) 376-6591.

ISBNs: 978-1-4555-7160-4 (ebook), 978-1-4555-7158-1 (print-on-demand trade paperback)

For Raleigh. I love you.

Acknowledgments

First of all, I'd like to thank my Lord and Savior Jesus Christ, who gave me the desire and skill to write. Through Him I can do all things!

My family is always there for me when I put down my computer and unplug from all things writing. I'm so thankful they're along for this ride with me.

Thank you to my agent, Stacey Donaghy. You are more than an agent. You are my friend, and I'm so very thankful to have found you. I am even more thankful that you're always on my side.

To my fabulous editor on *Mine to Save*, Lexi Smail: I've loved working with you on the Rescue Ops books. You have such an understanding of where I want each character to go, and your love of Sayward especially on this one just made our connection that much stronger!

To the team at Forever Romance: You are all such a well-oiled machine. From editing, to copyediting, to cover design, and all of the other inner workings I don't even get to see, you are all fabulous and I'm lucky to be a part of it all. Thank you for your efforts on my behalf!

To my favorite sounding board and the girl who's become one of my very best friends, Sybil Bartel: I don't know how it happened, but you're like the other half of my writing brain. You're there at all hours of the day and night whether I need to get an idea out or I'm completely out of them. I only hope I help you as much as you help me! Love you, girl.

To the very best group of writers a girl could ever ask for, the NAC: Ara, Meredith, Kate, Bindu, Sophia, Laura, Missy, Jessica, Amanda, Jamie, Marie, and Marnee—you are my very best source of sanity. Without you, this business would have ended me long ago! Love y'all!

To the fabulous author Kennedy Ryan, thank you for offering your thoughts and insights on this particular topic. Autism matters to so many people, and the last thing I wanted to do was get Sayward's character wrong. Your advice was so wonderful!

To the authors I admire so very much and are always willing to help me in any way they can, through promo, visibility for my books in their groups, or just an ear to listen when I need it: You'll never know how much you mean to me! Thank you so much to Rachel Van Dyken, Heidi McLaughlin, Susan Stoker, Willow Winters, K. A. Tucker, Jennifer L. Berg, J. S. Salsbury, Jo Raven, Lia Riley, Megan Erickson, and Brighton Walsh.

To an assistant I've learned I cannot live without, Jessica Shapnaka: You are willing to do so much for me, and all because you love my books. Thank you so much for not only being a fabulous assistant, but for being an amazing friend! I love you!

To the Dolls—the best fan group a girl could ask for. Talking to you guys every day, sharing my fictional world with you, receiving your feedback, it all keeps me going! You all recharge me and refuel me when I need it, and your support and positivity makes this job so much more fun! Thank you all for being you!

To the bloggers who have supported me throughout this journey: There are too many of you to name, but you know who you are. You have read every single book, given me great reviews, and shared my work with as many people as you can. I couldn't do any of this without your help and enthusiasm. A thousand thank-yous.

And last but never least, to the readers who find their way to Wilmington, North Carolina, to hang out with the sexy men of Night Eagle Security and the women who are strong enough to love them. I hope you fall in love with this world as much as I have, because without you I'd be nothing. <3

1

BENNETT

I never wanted this shit.

Adding the lemon on the edge of the glass like the coed requested, I slide the tumbler across the scuffed wooden bar toward her and give the chick the fake-ass smile I've perfected in the past few years. She giggles, fluttering all kinds of long, dark lashes at me while simultaneously pushing her big, fake tits together in front of my face.

My dick doesn't even twitch. I'm so far removed from this type of flirtation it's almost funny. As soon as she slips a wad of folded-up bills into the tip jar I turn away and lift a brow at the next paying customer.

And the night continues.

I wash glasses. I make drinks. I watch as the town's idiots get drunk and make bad decisions.

And all I can think about is, maybe bartending was the perfect job for me when I was fresh out of the joint. But now? After what I experienced over the past few weeks, I realize how motherfucking bored I am.

My fingers twitch, itching to do something. Really do something. My brain flashes back to the night I helped my buddy Ronin Shaw rescue his woman from a mob boss. The explosives. It'd been awhile since I'd made something go boom, but that shit was like riding a bike. Once I started, the rest was smooth sailing.

After pouring the remaining drops from the last bottle of SoCo into a tumbler and pass it to the grizzled old man waiting, I stride down to the end of the bar.

"Be right back. Headed to the stockroom," I mutter to the other bartender, a recent hire named Kandie, who gives me than a nod and a smile in response.

Trying to slide past her is difficult because her ample ass cheeks take up more than half the space behind the bar, and she cuts her gaze toward me.

"You tryna cop a feel, B?" she asks with a smirk.

I would abso-fucking-lutely be trying to do just that, because Kandie is as hot as they come with her sexy hourglass figure. Her brown skin is smooth, and the miles of waves in her thick black hair puddle around her tits tonight, even though she changes her hair up weekly.

But Kandie made it very clear when I hired her that not only does she not sleep with coworkers, I wouldn't be on her list even if she did. But she also doesn't swing my way.

Bumping her hip with mine, I hit her with the Bennett Blacke charm. The fact that she's immune to it doesn't stop me one bit. "Fuck yes, I am. Gotta get my touches in when your hands are full of booze, or else you'll punch the shit outta me."

She laughs, deep and throaty, and I can see the dude she's pouring the house draft for visibly swallow as he stares at her. She purses deep red lips at me and blows a fake kiss. "Kiss this ass, B."

"As soon as you'll let me," I toss over my shoulder as I push through the swinging door toward the back hall and the stockroom.

I pass by the open office door on the way there, and then I backtrack a few steps and pause in the doorway. Glancing around the room, it's like I'm seeing a ghost. Mickey's everywhere in this office. I can still feel his presence here.

Running a bar was never in my grand life plan. Shit, I never even had a grand life plan. Claw my way out of the rural, backwoods town where I was raised in the low country of South Carolina, be the best soldier I could while I was in the army, and that was about it. That was as far as I got before it all went to hell.

When I almost ruined my whole life with two minutes of blind rage.

Continuing on to the stockroom, I pull liquor bottles down off the shelf and place them in a crate, which I haul back out to the bar. After I shelve them and toss the crate under the counter, I scan the bar area and note some familiar arrivals.

Sitting at a couple of high-top tables just behind the row of stools are a group of faces I never expected to see. I school my features so hide my surprise.

My buddy Ronin Shaw wears his usual too-intense expression on his face. The man always looks like he's carrying the weight of the fucking world on his shoulders, and I've told him on more than one occasion that he needs to lighten up. He's seated beside his boss at Night Eagle Security, Jacob Owen. My gaze skates over Jacob toward Jeremy Teague, his long hair pulled back into a bun at the back of his head. Sliding over to the table beside them, my eyes land on two more NES team members, Grisham Abbott and Dare Conners before finally settling on her.

Sayward Diaz.

The woman they call Viper.

I can't help it when my eyes travel from the exotic features of her face straight to the hint of cleavage visible above the vee of her T-shirt. She might think she's hiding the luscious curves hidden underneath her uniform of jeans and a zipped-up hoodie, but there's no running away from how sexy she is. When I force my gaze back up to her face, it's to find her looking at me with irritation-filled hazel eyes. She shifts, her nose twitching with a show of disinterest as her sensuous, full lips roll between her teeth. Her long, black hair is pulled into a messy bun and she's not wearing any makeup, but who the hell cares with a face like that?

When a woman looks this fucking perfect without even trying, she's a danger to society. I've also seen what she can do when she's sitting behind her computer, so the Viper tag? I get it. She's straight-up nasty with her tech. No one can hide.

"Two Coronas with limes please." I don't even notice as

the barely legal girl bats her lashes and slides her credit card across the counter. "And I wouldn't mind if you wrote your number on the back of that receipt."

What the hell are they doing here? I think as I pull two Coronas from the fridge and stick a lime into the neck of each. I grab the girl's credit card and swipe it, offering her a distracted grin as I slide the white slip of paper back for her to sign.

"I'm off the menu, baby girl, but if you keep comin' into this bar I might be persuaded to change my mind."

I don't bring home women from the bar. It's a choice. The last thing I need is some chick hanging around for weeks afterward, searching for a repeat performance that won't ever happen.

I'll flirt with them until the cows come home, though, because it's what they want, and they pay nicely for a little attention.

The girl bites her lip and grabs the beers, making sure to lean over the bar as she does so. I look, because I'm not blind, but then I glance at Kandie when she elbows my side.

"You know that bunch?" She inclines her head toward the Night Eagle team, and I nod.

"Yeah, I do. Just not sure what they're doing here. Didn't expect to see most of them again anytime soon."

When Ronin's woman was taken from the parking lot of this bar by Wilmington's most notorious organized crime family, I got involved. Not only because he's my friend and he needed me, but also because Mickey's son, Mick, was at the center of the bullshit. I refused to let Mick screw his dad—the man I thought of like a father—over one more time. I backed Ronin up, worked some of my magic with explosives, and helped rescue Olive safe and sound.

I knew there were a few members of the NES team that didn't like my past or my attitude.

Doesn't matter to me. They can all go fuck themselves, because I don't answer to anyone. Not anymore.

"Well they're a pretty bunch." When I glance at Kandie, her dark brown eyes are locked and loaded on the two high-top tables. "Especially little Miss Converse Sneakers over there. That nerdy vibe she's got goin' on works for her."

Kandie licks her lips as she watches Sayward, and I follow her gaze without meaning to. My cock stiffens in my jeans, growing uncomfortable as hell, and I turn toward the wall so I can adjust myself without looking like an asshole.

Kandie chuckles. "Looks like I'm not the only one who noticed."

With a sigh, I'm getting ready to face the music and find out what the NES crew wants with me, when a commotion at the end of the bar pulls my attention. I turn that way just in time to see one dude's fist slam into another one's face.

And the bar erupts in absolute fucking madness.

2

SAYWARD

I run the side of my straw around the rim of my water glass. I don't even know why I'm here. I don't hang out in bars. Other than a beer every now and then, I don't often drink.

Ronin convinced Jacob that having me here would help make Bennett's decision easier. I can't even begin to understand what that means. Bennett Blacke barely knows me. Sure, he looks at me. But I have tits and an ass, so a guy like him is bound to notice. But other than that? The fact that I work at NES shouldn't be any sort of selling point for him.

When shouts erupt at the bar I glance up. Two guys are shoving each other, and then one of them punches the other in the face. Wincing, I pull back in my chair. But I stay seated while the other members of the Night Eagle team jump up. My eyes track Bennett as he uses one strong, muscled arm to propel himself over the top of the bar and thrusts himself between the two fighters. But now, each man's friends have thrown themselves into the melee, and the shouting grows louder as the violence intensifies. Girls scream and leap out of the way, and suddenly the fray shifts in the direction of my table.

No, no, no.

This is why I avoid bars. Being in the middle of a brawl is something that my personality just doesn't handle well. My mind racing a million miles a minute at the same time that my body removes itself from my chair, my legs take steps to get me out of the way. In one hazy moment, my eyes lock with Bennett's. Then, turning, I push my way through the crowded bar and flee through the front doors.

Cool night air drifts against my skin, and I sigh in relief as gooseflesh rises on my exposed flesh.

Dark night surrounds me, only broken by the yellow glow of the gravel parking lot's streetlamp. I lean against the wall beside the wooden door, sucking in deep breaths to calm myself.

I don't like conflict. In fact, I hate it. The prospect of someone touching me, especially in a way that will harm me, sets off an eruption of fireworks inside me. And not the good kind. The kind that burns me up from the inside out and threatens to engulf me in flames.

I could blame it on the fact that I was diagnosed with autism at age two. I'm on the lowest end of the spectrum, but it's always *been* there. It's something I have to deal with every single day, trying to overcome and understand the differences that separate me from everyone else.

But some of the aversion to raised voices and violence comes from a childhood spent in a conflict-filled village in

Colombia. It's where I was born and partially raised, until my father was forced to send me away.

I clamp my mind shut around those distant memories, forcing myself to forget. Just like I do every time they try to surface. I don't go back to that time in my life. Not for any reason. What's the point? Colombia, and everyone associated with it, is behind me.

An unexpected pang of sadness stings my heart, bringing with it a wave of loneliness that, if I'm not careful, could drag me under and drown me.

Beside me, the wooden door creaks open and a tall, broad body appears. My shoulders tenses, but when the yellow wash of light spells out his facial features, I release a breath.

"It's just you, Jeremy."

Jeremy Teague, or "Brains" as we call him in the field, thanks to his gadget-geared mind, leans against the wall facing me. He folds big, tattooed arms across his chest, so much like the rest of the men I work with. They're big, they're bossy, and they rock tattoos. It's just their thing.

"You know, 'it's just you' sounds like you don't know I'm a badass, which we both know is complete bullshit."

Rolling my eyes skyward, I hug myself and glance around. "The fight over in there?"

He studies me. "Yeah. Blacke's got both guys by the collars, and that chick who works the bar with him poured a bucket of ice over all of them." His lips pull into his signature grin. "She's feisty, that one."

As if on cue, the door opens and Bennett shoves the two men who were throwing punches before out the door. "I hope neither one of you are stupid enough to drive home."

But their buddies, about six other frat-boy types, stream out of the door and grab hold of their respective friends, pulling them into the parking lot. I watch them go, my arms tightening around myself as I sidestep out of the way. Avoiding any of them touching me.

Jeremy's gaze flicks toward Bennett. "Rowdy crowd."

Bennett blows out a breath through lips unusually full for a man. "Gets that way in here lately. Especially on a Friday night. Comes with the territory."

Bennett's eyes land on me. "What are you doing out here?"

I force myself to lower my arms and straighten my shoulders. "Just getting some fresh air."

Jeremy nods to back me up, knowing full well the reason I fled. "Bars aren't really her thing."

Bennett pushes back against the door, crossing his feet at the ankle and folding his thick arms. His eyes, dark in the shadows of the night, hold mine. My natural instinct is to look away, but maybe the darkness that cloaks us both keeps the impulse away. "What *is* your thing, then?"

Feeling my face heat, I shrug one shoulder and snap, "Not watching a bunch of Neanderthals get drunk and beat each other up."

Pushing past him, I make my way back into the warm, now much calmer, atmosphere of The Oakes.

Both men follow me, and as I take my seat at the table Bennett stands before us. He reaches out to slap Ronin Shaw's—or "Swagger" as we call him—palm and glances around the table at the rest of us.

"To what do I owe the pleasure of an NES team visit?"

Jacob Owen, our boss and probably the closest thing I have to a father, clasps his hands together on top of the table. He inclines his head toward an empty chair. "Sit for a minute."

It's evident to me that Bennett wants to refuse. His eyes narrow just the slightest bit and his biceps flex even though his arms don't move. With an exaggerated sigh, Bennett glances toward the bar. The beautiful girl working it seems to have it all handled, and when he lifts a brow at her, she gives him a thumbs-up. Bennett turns a chair around backward and straddles it.

His whole I-don't-give-a-shit attitude is probably attractive to a lot of women. To me, it just screams that he's more trouble than he's worth. But as my eyes travel down his muscled arms, corded with veins and tracing the lines of the tattoo sleeve on his left arm and across broad, hard shoulders, I can't help but think he might have some qualities worth exploring.

If I were interested.

Which I'm not.

Bennett shakes his thick, dark blond hair out of his face as he focuses on Jacob. "What's this all about?"

Jeremy and Dare stare him down hard, but Bennett acts like neither one of them are even at the table. It's no secret they aren't fans of his. I'm pretty sure it's a guy thing, but I don't know exactly why they don't like Bennett. All the NES guys respect each other because of their military service and the brotherhood they've formed as a result of working for NES. They complete secretive, black ops missions together on a regular basis, and they also protect important people who pay well for discretion and for the guys' willingness to lay their lives on the line for them.

It's never easy for them to accept someone new to the group. They've welcomed me because I'm important to Jacob and I proved myself with my computer skills when Jeremy's wife and son were taken.

But when it comes to Bennett, his background is something that some of the guys take real issue with. They don't really know him, only Ronin does, but digging into peoples' backgrounds is what NES *does*. We know that Bennett Blacke, although he served in the army and performed his Special Forces duties exceptionally well, he's also served time in prison. The charges were aggravated assault. Bennett nearly beat a man to death.

But according to Ronin we should give him the benefit of the doubt. He insists that there were extenuating circumstances behind Bennett's crime, and that he's learned and grown from his time spent in prison.

Maybe Ronin's right. I have no idea. All I know is that Jacob liked what he saw when Bennett helped the team rescue Olive Alexander, Ronin's now-fiancée. And he wants to offer him a permanent spot with the NES Rescue Ops team.

I sit back in my chair, running my straw over the rim of my glass again and again as I wait for the fireworks to start.

"Bennett, we have a proposition for you." Jacob's voice is low, but it commands respect. He didn't get to where he is in life by being anything less than a boss.

Bennett plasters a smirk on his face, leaning his elbows on the table. "Do tell."

Ronin places a hand on Jacob's shoulder, asking him silently if he can speak up. Jacob nods.

"Bennett, man...we all saw how you reacted when Olive's life was on the line. I know that I personally will always be grateful for that. But the team saw something in you that night, too."

Jeremy snorts, and I shoot him a glare over the table.

Jacob picks up where Ronin left off. "Come work on a mission with us. It can be on a trial basis, if that's what will make you comfortable. What we can offer you is a unit of brothers who've been where you've been, who can have your back and allow you to exist in a world where your specific skills can be utilized instead of squashed."

Bennett lifts a brow. "My skills? You mean the fact that I'm a chemist who knows how to blow shit up?"

Jacob's lips tilt in a smile. "We could use your wheelhouse. We don't have anyone like you on the team. And we do good work—exciting work—that'll feed the adrenaline rush you're missing in your life right now."

A shadow crosses Bennett's face. "I've had plenty of adrenaline. And I left that life behind when I landed behind bars. I can't go back to the man I was back then." He pushes back from the table and folds his arms. "I don't want to go back."

Ronin stands, placing a hand on Bennett's shoulder. "Listen, man. No one is asking you to call up the beast of the past that tore you apart. We're here to show you that you can have it all. You can have the rewarding career, the one you were damn good at, in the private sector. All while finding your place in a unit that will value your expertise and help you stay on the path you want to be on."

Bennett's glance flicks toward me, just for a moment, before his eyes land on Jeremy and Dare. "And every member of the team is on board with this? With giving me a trial run?"

He spits the words *trial run* like they leave a bitter taste in his mouth.

Clearly Bennett Blacke is a man who doesn't like to work under anyone. He doesn't trust the camaraderie that these men have formed. He's a man out for himself and himself alone.

And when it comes to protecting yourself above all else? I can definitely relate.

No one speaks, but Grisham glances pointedly at Jeremy and Dare.

"Yeah, that's what I thought." Without another word, Bennett turns around and walks away from our tables. I watch as he nods to the female bartender, and then he disappears through a swinging door heading for the back of the bar.

Jacob tilts his head toward me. "You're up."

Swirling my straw around the rim of my glass, I don't meet his gaze. "Why do you even want him so bad? He obviously doesn't want to have anything to do with us."

Ronin speaks up. "He needs this, Sayward. Maybe he doesn't know it yet, but he does. Working behind that bar is something he's doing to pass the time. There's so much more in him than that shit. Trust me."

And I do trust these guys. Everything single one of them would lay their life on the line for me. So if they're asking me to help convince Bennett to come on board, I can try my best to do that for them.

I rise from my seat and stride for the bar. Meeting the female bartender's gaze, I detect a hint of heat in hers as she stares at me, leaning over the bar. "Need something, sweetheart?"

I place both hands on the bar and lean forward. "Give me a tequila shot. I'm trying to talk to a man, and I'm pretty much the worst when it comes to that. So why don't you go ahead and make it a double?"

Never mind the fact that I've never had a shot of tequila in my life, much less a double. For this? I need liquid courage.

Both of her perfectly arched eyebrows lift, her exotic features twisting into a pretty grin. "Coming right up."

She pulls the stopper out of a top-shelf bottle, and then sprays the contents into two waiting shot glasses. Then she pours a third. "Mind if I have one with you?"

A smile tugs at the corner of my lips. "I'd probably prefer it."

With a flash of white teeth, she picks up her shot and hands me a wedge of lime.

"I'm guessing you're not the kind of girl who wants to lick salt off another person," she muses as she hands me the salt. "But maybe we'll get you there."

I lick the salt off the top of my hand and down the contents of the shot glass. The liquid is smooth rolling down my throat and I stick a lime wedge into my mouth and suck.

The girl behind the bar watches me, her eyes dark and full of something I can't quite place.

I gesture toward her glass. "Your turn."

Her eyes on me, we both pour and then lick the salt off the back of our hands and then we knock back our shots. I stick another lime wedge in my mouth, and to my extreme shock, she leans over the bar and takes the lime from my mouth with her own. Her tongue slides across my lips, and my entire body goes stiff.

"Atta girl," she says with a smile as she wipes the back of her mouth. "Now go get him."

Feeling a bit light-headed from the shots and from the graze of the bartender's lips against my own, I head for the swinging door where Bennett disappeared. I don't feel nearly as reluctant as I did a few moments ago.

Now I see why they call this stuff liquid courage.

3

BENNETT

When I appear at the office door again, my fingers grip the top of the doorjamb hard enough to throb.

At this point in my life, I've been taking shit one step at a time. The only plans I had for the near future was helping Mickey get this bar straight and being there for him through the hell that is cancer. Working on another special ops team? I never thought I'd do it again. Everything shifted when Mickey announced, out of the blue, that he was taking one last trip out west before he died. He left the bar to me. His life's work.

There was a time in my life, right before I went to prison, that I told myself it was all my training, all my military precision, all the knowledge I had of how to hurt a man, kill a man, that made me do what I did. Later, I figured out that it had more to do with the rage inside me that had built up over two tours, seeing things no man should ever have to see. That particular night, when everything in my entire world shifted, tilted, and changed forever, I snapped. I lost my shit. It happens to a lot of vets. I just never expected it to happen to me.

So now, maybe I'm scared. It's true; I *did* feel something when I was on that rescue mission beside Ronin. It felt like I was back in my own skin again, doing shit that meant something. I was comfortable, in my element.

But going back to the man I was before is something I swore to myself I'd never do. Exposing myself to my PTSD triggers, no matter how in-control I feel now, is a door I don't want to open.

Isn't it?

I lift my head and stare at the desk, right at the place where Mickey used to sit. I can almost make out the shape of him sitting there, and I chuckle darkly to myself as I picture not only the knowing expression that'd be on his face, but also the wise old voice that would have come with it.

"What are you scared of?" Mickey's voice would be low and laced with a demanding note that would make me talk.

I sigh, having the conversation with him in my head that I would have had aloud if he'd actually been here with me. *Fuck if I know. I don't even know if half those guys out there want me on the team. They know my past. They don't trust me. And I can't fault them for that.*

I know exactly what Mickey would have said next. *"You have a friend on the team, right? You know how this works, kid. Once military, always military. We're all one and the same. One team member trusts you, the boss wants to hire you ... the rest will come around. They're like one mind when they work to-*

gether the way those guys do. If they're asking, they want you."

Without Mickey, I don't know where I would have ended up. Thinking about losing him, well…it still hurts.

I know the bar is in good hands. Kandie can run the place with one eye shut and her hands tied behind her back. This isn't about the bar…it's about me. It's about whether or not I think it's possible for me to step back into that life without losing myself to the darkness all over again.

Someone with a small voice clears her throat behind me. Whirling, I find myself drowning in hazel eyes, creamy bronze skin, and miles of black, thick hair streaked with hints of red.

Sayward rocks back and forth on her Converse sneakers, her gaze falling to the floor. "Can I talk to you for a second?"

Nodding, I move so she can slide past me. She hesitates, remaining where she stands, eyes cast down toward the floor. I can feel the heat from her body. She's that close. I can tell she's uncomfortable with my proximity though, because she doesn't lift her eyes from the floor.

Taking a few steps back, I gesture into the office. "Come on in."

When she looks up, her eyes lock onto mine and interest finds its way into my brain and straight down to my dick.

"You here to talk your company up?" I drop onto the edge of the desk and fold my arms.

Sayward leans against the doorway and I take a minute to drink her in. She has a tight little body, full of the kind of curves a man can get lost in, but it's obvious she's in shape. I wonder if she works out with the team at NES, even though she's not active on assignments except for making decisions behind her computer screen. Her skin is this deep bronze and it's set off by the long, thick black hair and her deep-set hazel eyes. Her beauty is so damn unassuming, though, because she doesn't have a clue. Or she does and she's never wanted to use it to her advantage.

"Listen," she says matter-of-factly, and my eyes snap back to hers. "I don't know why they sent me in here, but here's the deal."

When she talks to me, her eyes jump around from the features of my face, down to my body and back again, which makes my lips twitch. She's so serious about what she's saying, like she's about to lay down the law.

Yeah, okay, beautiful. Let's have it. My lip-twitch turns into a full-blown smirk. I can't fucking help it.

She's adorable.

"These guys, they're good guys. Trust me, I know the difference between good people and bad people, and the team at NES? They're good."

At those words, I study her more carefully. *What the hell does that mean?* Somehow, the idea of someone like Sayward having to deal with bad people sits like a stone in my gut.

There's something about her...something different from dealing with any other woman. I have an immediate instinct to make sure no one messes with her.

Even though it seems like she does a damn good job of that on her own.

"We've looked you up," she continues. "I won't beat around the bush about it. Despite your past, Jacob wants to give you a chance. He liked what he saw when you worked on Olive's rescue, and he's not the easiest guy to impress."

I school my features, wiping all expression from my face.

"So, if they're all willing to give you a chance, why aren't you willing to give them one?" She finishes in a rush of words, her face looking irritated as she pushes a chunk of her hair behind her ear. Her full lips purse, and my gaze drops there for a second before I answer.

"Don't you mean 'us'?" I watch as her expression becomes confused and flustered.

"What?"

"You said *they're* willing to give me a chance. You're with them, right? So shouldn't you include yourself in that?" My comfortable smirk pulls at my mouth again.

It's just way too much fun, messin' with this woman.

Her gaze widens and then she blows out an exasperated breath. "I tried." Her tone flat, she whirls around.

The sight of her back and the thought of her retreat does something strange to my stomach. It's not a good feeling, and I don't have time to evaluate it before my mouth is working faster than my brain.

"Wait."

She pauses before she turns around again, her eyebrows lifted.

"I'll come tell your boss I'm willing to give it a try. Trial basis. I still run this place, you know."

I can't explain why I'm saying yes. The idea of working at Night Eagle is exciting as hell, but it also scares me to death. It was one thing when I helped out my friend Ronin a

few months ago. But the last time I really allowed that part
of myself to come out to play—the black ops, bomb-loving,
soldier side—more than one person ended up dead back in
the desert. And one person ended up in the hospital fighting
for his life when I returned home.

That kind of work...it brings out a darkness in me I
never want to see again. Can I control it if I go back to work
in this field?

I don't know.

She doesn't try to hide her smile, which is a surprise and
something I find refreshing. There're no games with Sayward; she puts out exactly what's going on inside her head.
Her face is expressive and her smile is fucking contagious.

"I did it?" Her voice lifts with pleased surprise.

I chuckle, pushing up from the desk. "Don't get cocky,
Diaz."

Her chin lifts with pride. "They call me Viper." She spins
and walks out of the office.

Following her back down the hallway toward the bar area,
I mutter under my breath as I think about what just happened. "For good reason."

4

SAYWARD

On the drive back to my apartment, I keep replaying the moments spent in the office with Bennett. I stayed for another hour to allow the buzz I had going thanks to my tequila shots fizzle out. During that time, Bennett accepted Jacob's offer to come aboard NES on a trial basis. I also watched as he worked his magic behind the bar. As much as I tried to keep my eyes from straying toward him, I could never prevent it for long. By the time I left I could be considered an expert on all things Bennett Blacke.

He's friendly with his customers, especially the female ones, but not in a slimy kind of way. There were several overt attempts from women, mostly college coeds but also a few who looked around my twenty-four years who tried to garner an intimate encounter with him. He funneled invitations to meet in the bar bathroom or out in the parking lot. I saw him shake his head each time, pretending he was sad he couldn't take them up on their offers, but now and then he'd throw me a wink, just let me know he knew I was watching.

That drove me the craziest of all. Knowing that Bennett knew I couldn't quite keep my eyes off of him was maddening. I hated the way my body reacted every time his eyes met mine, or slowly roved their way down my frame. It made me feel like I was completely naked when in reality I was more fully clothed than any other woman in here.

I pull up to my apartment, which is on the top floor of a big old duplex. Starting up the exterior stairs to my front door, the first thing I notice is that my porch light over my entrance isn't on.

There's never been a time I've left my apartment, knowing I'd be back after dark, that I haven't left my porch light on. It's one of the many routine tasks I do before leaving my place, something that makes me feel a little more in control of my world. So the shroud of darkness at the top of the landing has me frozen, staring in trepidation up at my darkened front door. At least my living room lamp is on inside, something else that I make sure to do before leaving in the evening.

Damn lightbulb must have burned out. Taking a deep, calming breath, I clutch my keys tight in my hand and hurry up the steps.

My apartment is located in a safe area. The beach is only six blocks away, and my neighbors are all very friendly, despite the fact that I'm not exactly the get-to-know-you type. My landlord lives on the first floor of the duplex, a nice lady in her fifties who's kind enough not to inquire about my unconventional social graces and brings me baked goods at least twice a month. There are no lights on in her apartment, which lets me know she's in bed for the night.

Chills skate across the back of my neck and creep down my spine as I shove my key into the lock. I pause, confused. Glancing at the key in my hand and to the lock, I frown. I know I locked the door this morning.

Everything looks the way it should, but I can't help the distinct feeling of *not-rightness* that hovers over me like a thunderhead. Remembering my training from NES, I quickly walk to my bedroom, keeping my eyes wide open and watchful as I go. Walking into my roomy closet, I crouch down in front of the safe and turn the combination lock with steady fingers. I'm pulling out my small handgun when a voice behind me draws a startled yelp from my throat.

Standing, I aim my weapon at the person standing there in the shadows, because I didn't turn on the light in my bedroom when I entered.

"Don't move," I say, steeling my voice with resolve I don't feel.

I didn't even register whatever he said to me. All I can see is a tall figure standing at the entrance to my bedroom. My stomach bottoms out, just like it would if I were on an amusement park ride. Only this isn't even a little bit fun. Terror is turning the blood in my veins to ice.

All I want to do is drop the gun and run, but I've been trained better than that.

You are strong. My hands shake, a direct contrast to the thought.

I can just make out that he's slowly raising his hands in the air, and I take that opportunity to reach just outside of the closet door and flick a wall switch. My overhead bedroom light floods the room with a sunny glow and I suck in a breath at the sight of the man before me.

A man I haven't seen in thirteen years, but one with a face I'd recognize anywhere.

"Marcos." I breathe, just before placing my gun carefully on the floor and lifting my hands to my chest.

He steps close enough to hug me, and even as I stiffen I allow it.

Because this is *my brother.*

"Jesus, *hermanita.*" He and holds me at arm's length. "*Qué pasa?* A gun?"

Whereas I've been living in the States since I was eleven years old, as far as I know, Marcos has been in Colombia all that time. My accent is minimal if anyone hears it at all, but his is thick, and it immediately fills me with a sense of home so strong I almost collapse under the weight of it.

He gives me a stern glare. "I thought you were supposed to have the kind of life here where guns were not necessary. What the hell?"

He shakes my shoulders a little, and I snap back to attention. Every ounce of fear that had turned my body into an autopilot machine a few moments ago has melted away, instead leaving me with a pure sense of happiness and a slight bit of confusion.

"Marcos? What are you *doing* here?" Turning away from him, I retrieve my gun and place it back inside my safe.

When I turn around again, my brother is watching me with a mixture of emotions in his eyes. It's been so long since I've seen him, I can't read any of them, and that realization nearly brings me to tears.

Clearing my throat, I walk past him, gesturing that he should follow me. "I'll fix us some coffee. And then I want to hear about why you're here."

I retrieve my phone and my keys from the floor where I dropped them near the front door. Placing my keys on the appropriate hook, I pocket my phone and follow my usual route, the one I walk each and every day when I come home, toward the kitchen and the coffeemaker. I peek out at Marcos over the counter pass-through. He's staring at me, a wistful smile on his face.

"What?" I shove a mug under the one-cup machine and press a little coffee cup into the slot. As I press down, the machine hums to life and prepares the hot, steaming brew.

Marcos shakes his head. He drops down onto my tan suede couch and leans back. "I'm glad you seem to have a good life here. But you're still...you. You know, the little things you do over and over again the same way?"

I glance down at the coffeemaker. "You mean the thing that makes me a weirdo? My autism?"

He shakes his head. "That's not what I mean. I mean, I'm proud of you. It could have held you back, but it didn't. You're smart and you seem to have made a life here in the States that's so much better than the one you would have had..." He trails off and a lump forms in my throat.

While he's looking away, I pull out my phone and shoot

Jacob a quick text to let him know that Marcos is here. I'm not sure why I do it; I trust Marcos. He's my family. He would never hurt me. I know that there's probably a lot of things he's done in his life back in Colombia that are less than savory, but he's my blood. My only sibling. If he's here, maybe he needs my help.

And maybe Jacob's help, too.

After the second cup of coffee is brewed, I grab both mugs and hand one to my brother. Kicking off my sneakers, I carefully place them inside a compartment of the bench beside the door. Returning to the sofa, I tuck my feet beneath me while Marcos grips his mug. Sipping deeply, he eyes me and I cast my gaze downward. It doesn't matter if he's family. Looking someone in the eye for a prolonged period of time makes me want to jump out of my own skin, and it probably always will.

"So," Marcos begins. "Tell me about your life here. What do you do for a living?"

"I work for Jacob Owen. He runs a private security company here in Wilmington, and I do research and investigation for them." I don't elaborate on exactly what NES does. The fact that the men who work there often participate in covert, black ops missions and contracts for the government isn't something I'm at liberty to share. As far as the public knows, all the company does is private security for the rich and famous. And sometimes, that *is* what the guys do. They're pros when it comes to making sure someone is safe and protected, whether it be while they're on the move or in their own home or office.

My brother's eyes narrow when I say Jacob's name. "Are you sure that's the best idea?"

Disbelief colors my tone as I shake my head. "You know what he did for our family. He is the only reason I'm able to have a life here. I wouldn't want to be anywhere else."

Jacob Owen goes way back with my family in Colombia. The past there is deep and dark, and not something I like to revisit. When I turned eighteen I left the foster parents I'd been placed with when Jacob brought me to the United States. I made a living as a hacker, doing all kinds of things I shouldn't on the dark web. But Jacob got wind of that, straightened me out, and brought me into the fold at NES.

My gratitude for that man is endless.

"Sayward, I have something to talk to you about." His tone softening, Marcos turns toward me, his hands folding in his lap.

My stomach plummets. Nothing good ever comes after those words.

Standing, I shake my head and pace the room. "You know what? I think I have some shortbread to go with the coffee."

I dart back into my small kitchen. Cooking is something I do when nothing I'm doing technologically is clicking, or when my brain needs a break from it all. It's so simple and fun, something no part of my life has ever been.

I read a recipe and follow it. It's a comfort to me.

"Sayward—" Marcos starts, but I quickly manage to talk over him.

"No, I know I have something somewhere. Something

sweet to go with the coffee. Just give me a minute, okay, Marcos?"

On the inside, my guts are churning, my heart is racing, and my brain is in total denial. It doesn't matter what he wants to tell me, all I know is that it isn't good and I'd rather distract the hell out of myself rather than face it alone.

I've been pretend-searching through the kitchen cabinets, making enough of a racket that Marcos doesn't bother coming into the area to check on me, when there's a sturdy knock on the front door.

Jacob.

All the breath leaves me and I sag against a counter in relief.

I hear the front door open as Jacob Owen lets himself in, and Marcos rises from the couch. His whole demeanor is wary, and he glances toward where I'm now standing in the kitchen doorway before zeroing in on Jacob.

"You called him?" he asks me with accusation in his voice.

Jacob closes the front door behind him and squares off with Marcos. "Marcos. It's good to see you. What brings you into town?"

Jacob glances at me, his eyes checking me over to make sure I'm okay. It's what he does. It's what he's always done. He takes care of me. And there's nobody I'd rather have with me to ride out whatever news Marcos is about to drop.

"Marcos was just about to tell me something." My voice barely exists as I scurry into the room with a plate full of already baked shortbread. I'd known exactly where it was the entire time, but Marcos doesn't need to know that.

I perch on a chair in the corner, needing my own space. Jacob and Marcos sit on the couch, Marcos darting wary glances toward Jacob the entire time.

"Sayward... it's *Papa*. He's dead."

I suck in a breath as the pain rockets unbidden through my chest.

No. No, no, no.

My father, the one person who made sure I made it safely out of Colombia all those years ago. When my life was in danger, my father made sure I made it out of Colombia into safe hands... Jacob Owen's.

I grip my stomach as the pain lances through me, sagging. I don't glance at either Jacob or Marcos as I ask the only question I need the answer to. My voice is nothing but a ragged whisper. "What happened?"

Marcos's answer is blunt and honest. "Cartel."

I suck in a deep gulp of air even as my insides threaten to collapse in on themselves.

Jacob is speaking then, asking Marcos more detailed questions about what happened to my father, but I tune them both out. All I need to know is that my father is dead. A man I loved more than life itself, the person who sacrificed everything so that I'd be safe.

Dead, gone. Dead, gone. Dead, gone.

Just like that.

But I was made to compartmentalize. I can feel the heavy, stifling hand of sadness, of devastation really, pressing down on me. But I shove it away and focus on what I can control.

On what I can handle.

I look first at Marcos, then at Jacob. "I have to go home."

Jacob's stance goes rigid. "Home?"

I nod, my features as calm as undisturbed waters while a storm swirls inside of me. "Yes. Home to Colombia. My family needs me."

Along with Marcos, I have a few aunts and uncles back home in Colombia. Just because I haven't been able to be with my family for years doesn't mean that they're not still just that—my family.

"No."

Both Marcos and I glance at Jacob, Marco's head snapping while my gaze slides over in reaction to his defiance. This, I expect.

"No?" Marcos' voice rises with heat. He bristles with anger. "You can't keep her from her family!"

Jacob doesn't move. He's like stone, standing completely still and watching us. But I can see one muscle in the hard line of his jaw ticking dangerously, and I know that Marcos should watch his step.

"There's a reason Sayward lives here. She cannot go back to Colombia. It isn't safe. Her security is the most important thing." He turns his cool blue eyes on me. "Sayward, I understand why you want to go home. What your family must be going through . . . But they will have each other. And you will have us. The team at NES will be there for you." His eyes are full of comfort, but nothing is going to take away the pain of this loss. Except maybe helping my family get through it.

I shake my head. "Jacob...I have to go."

Silence stretches between us, taut with tension, before Jacob finally speaks again. He looks at Marcos. "When is the funeral?"

Marcos spits the words. "There is no body. There will be no funeral. But there will be a service to remember him in a week."

Jacob, still stoic, approaches me. He places his hands lightly on my shoulders. I close my eyes and inhale at the touch, but I don't flinch away. Not from Jacob. He releases me quickly, though, knowing me well. "I'll spend this week educating the team on what we're dealing with in Colombia. When you go, we go. Understood?"

He must note the confusion on my face, because his expression softens. "If you want to do this, I won't let you do it alone."

I know there's no point in protesting this, but Marcos isn't aware of how serious Jacob is right now. "She has me. She doesn't need bodyguards."

Jacob, who knows how sensitive I am to the touch of others, leans in and does something he's never done before. He kisses my forehead gently, with the soft love of a father, and the tears I've been fighting against well up in my eyes.

"I'll see you at the office tomorrow. An NES operative will be stationed outside all night. I'll feel better if you have around-the-clock supervision from the Rescue Ops team until all ties from your past"—he flicks a glance at Marcos— "are gone."

With those words he walks out my front door.

Marcos almost splutters he's so mad. "Rescue Ops team? What the hell is he talking about?"

With a shaky breath, I pull myself together and start painstakingly making the couch for Marco to sleep on. "I told you that I work for Jacob and that he owns a private security company. The most elite team there is called Rescue Ops. And that's all I can tell you."

"Why does he feel like there should be someone watching you?" Marcos runs his hands through his dark, thick hair. Agitation crawls off of him in invisible waves.

My answer is simple. "Because he loves me."

With that I escape to my room where I allow the lump of emotion fighting for purchase in my throat to be free, and my pillowcase becomes soaked with my tears.

5

BENNETT

W hat do you think? Think you can find your way around now?" Ronin leans against the desk in the front lobby of the Night Eagle Security building.

The desk is where Jeremy's wife, Rayne, sits busily typing information into her computer while she ignores us completely. Her swollen belly is hidden, but I know it's there.

Running my tongue over my teeth as I try to recall everything Bennett just showed me as we toured the building, I nod. "Yeah, think so. We're having a meeting this morning, right?"

I'd arrived a half hour earlier than the rest of the men, in order to complete the paperwork that Rayne had prepared. Then Ronin was cool enough to come in early and show me around. There were still iron-fisted nerves in my stomach, though.

I haven't been in an environment like this for a long, long time. Even though the sight of the state-of-the-art workout facility and the conference room set up with military-grade tech gives me the drive to work, I'm still nervous as fuck.

What if I don't measure up to this kind of life anymore?

Sure, the atmosphere at NES is more relaxed than the army, but I could still fail at this. And now that I'm here, it's becoming pretty clear that this isn't something I want to fuck up.

Jacob Owen is giving me a chance, despite my record, just like Mickey had. And as much as I hate to admit it, that means something to me. Proving myself to him and the other guys is gonna be work, but I'm willing to put in the time.

Now that Mickey's gone, The Oakes belongs to me. And the first thing I did was promote Kandie to manage it. She'll hire someone else to help her behind the bar, and I'll check in often. But she's running the place, which leaves me free to put in full-time effort here at Night Eagle.

"So," I glance at Rayne, who's still typing away. She's so used to the men around her invading her space that she can completely tune us out and still do her work, which I think is impressive. Her long, dark hair forms a curtain around her while she works.

"You guys are called the Rescue Ops team?" I continue, looking at Ronin.

He nods. "Yeah. It just made sense to give us a name, because the same guys work together on almost every mission. There are a lot of other people who work here, other teams of guys who can get a job done, but we've been clicking for a couple of years now and Jacob decided that we'd be better off staying together."

"And that's the team he wants me on?" I lift a brow, still doubting it.

But Ronin claps a hand on my shoulder. "You've earned the chance. We don't have anybody on the team with your kind of skill with explosives. All you have to do now is prove you deserve to be here."

The front door to the building closes behind Dare Conners and Grisham Abbott as they enter.

Jesus. Are those two joined at the hip or what? I try to think of a time I've ever seen them apart, and fail. Grisham moves at a pace that would never make the fact that he's working with one prosthetic foot obvious. Ronin once told me that he and Conners used to hate each other, but damned if I can tell by the way they have each other's backs now.

"Proving yourself to us should be your first order of business." Dare's voice grates against my nerves.

He didn't like me from day one, and normally I wouldn't give a fuck. But now I have to work with the guy, and if he wants my respect he needs to know that shit goes both ways.

"Not really in the habit of jumping through hoops to make people happy." My words, easy with an undertone of hard, are directed at Conners.

"Well, you better learn how to make exceptions, then." His retort is just as smooth, but there's an edge to his voice that I don't appreciate.

Grisham and Ronin exchange looks, and I take that as my cue to leave before my desire to put my fist in Conners's face grows any more. "Coffee?"

Rayne looks up, like she's heard every word we've said.

"Break room. Go grab some, Bennett, and then head up to the conference room." Her smile is kind and understanding, and I immediately get why Jeremy Teague put a ring on it.

Without looking at Conners's cocky-ass face again, I turn and walk down the hallway toward the break room.

I rummage around in the cabinets, looking for a mug. When I find one, I put it under the coffee dispenser and adjust the settings. Just as I press START, the door swings open and I turn to see who's walking in.

Sayward pauses when she sees me, her eyes locking with mine, before she averts her gaze and changes trajectory. Instead of heading toward the coffeemaker where I'm standing, she instead strides to the round glass table in the corner and drops into a chair.

She doesn't say a word.

She met my gaze for less than a second, but it was enough to send a jolt of awareness through my chest and to my dick, which stirs with interest.

What the hell? Why can't I be in the same room with this woman without getting hard?

Watching her without trying to make it obvious that I'm watching her, I note the change in her almost immediately. Sayward doesn't usually come off as the kind of woman who cares what people think, but she doesn't carry herself with the posture of an overconfident woman. She walks like she's aware of herself more than she's aware of anything else, because she probably is. Ronin let me in on the fact that she's struggled with autism her whole life, and even though she's on the low end of the spectrum, it's probably more natural for her to turn inward.

But right now, she's hunched over the table like she wishes she could literally crawl inside her own little cave and never come back out again. Her hair, usually pulled into a smooth ponytail or a messy bun, is loose around her shoulders. It's wavier than I thought it would be, thick and cascading for miles down her back. But it's not styled; it's just natural. There are dark circles under her eyes, barely noticeable with the bronze tone of her skin.

But I notice.

Everything about Sayward says she's exhausted.

What the hell happened to her?

The question shows up in my head without permission. Because, why do I care? It's not my business. *She's* not my business. But for some mysterious reason, I do care. I can't stand the fact that she looks like she's been kicked emotionally.

That tightens my chest ... and my fists.

There's a connection here, between this woman and me that I can't explain.

"Jesus. Are you just going to stand there staring at me, or are you going to grab your coffee and get the hell out of my way?"

My head jerks back to my mug, which is now full, and Sayward rises from her chair and comes to stand beside me. I don't miss the space she leaves between us, though. When she reaches up to the upper cabinets to grab a cup for herself, the hem of her light-blue hoodie rides up, exposing smooth, caramel skin. That one, brief flash of flesh is all my cock needs to come to full attention.

Her waist is tiny, flaring out into hips that my hands are suddenly itching to squeeze.

It's like my body is thinking for me right now, instead of my brain.

When I force my gaze back to Sayward's face, her deep, dark eyes are narrowed on me.

Oh, shit.

"Are you done staring at me like I'm something to eat?" Her tone is full of hostility, but she can't hide the pretty flush in her cheeks as she speaks.

Not sure if she caught her own double meaning, I grin. "Well hell, I might not be done. *Are* you good enough to eat?"

Her lower lip falls away from the top, parting her luscious mouth in surprise. "What?"

Chuckling, I sip my coffee and lean a hip against the counter. Letting my eyes do what they want, roving up and down her body in a slow, lazy perusal, I speak again, digging myself in a little deeper. "I mean, you sure look like you are. But I might need to find out the old-fashioned way."

She slams her mug down under the coffeemaker and glares at me outright. Somehow, it just makes her sexier. She even taps the toe of her gray Vans on the floor. "Who talks like that? Are you for real?"

My grin widens. I can't help it. She's so damn funny. "I do. And I'm real, sweetheart."

Her lip curls and she takes a step closer when I expect

her to retreat. She jabs a finger in my chest. "I'm not in the mood for this today, pretty boy. Why don't you just stay out of my way?"

Liking how close she's standing to me way too much, I lift a brow and glance toward the door before looking back at her face. "I was here first, beautiful."

Her eyes widen. There's a pause. I watch as shock swims in her gaze, followed by utter confusion. "Why did you just call me beautiful?"

Now *I'm* completely thrown off by the abrupt change in where I thought this conversation was going. So the only thing that comes out of my mouth is the God's-honest truth. "Because you are."

She stands there for almost a full minute, like a statue, just staring at me. Then her lower lip trembles.

Fuck.

Instinctively, I reach for her, but she steps out of my reach. My arms fall back to my sides, and I stare down at her. "Hey, Sayward...you know that, right? That you're beautiful?"

Without another word, she snatches her coffee—black, no cream or sugar—off the counter and spins around. She leaves the room without looking back at me.

What the fuck just happened?

When I show up in the conference room just a minute later, everyone else is already there. Jacob Owen is standing in front of an enormous touch screen mounted on the wall, and he turns to face the door as I close it behind me.

"Blacke. Welcome." He nods at me, and that's it.

When it comes to Jacob Owen, I'm learning fast. The dude is not about the bullshit. He's gruff, but he's straight to the point. There's no extra drama with him, which means I actually might like working for him.

"Thanks." I settle into the only empty seat around the table, and thank fuck it's next to Ronin and not Conners.

I glance at Sayward, who's sitting on my other side, in a seat behind a laptop. Her fingers are busy on the keys, and she doesn't look up at me. I wonder what it was about the word *beautiful* that changed her so completely.

Has she really never heard that before? The thought's pure insanity, but I guess it could be possible. She definitely doesn't ever *try* to look pretty. Everything about that girl is natural. It's the kind of beauty that other women are jealous of.

And the kind that every man dreams of.

But maybe, because she doesn't try, she doesn't even realize that she's gorgeous.

That thought unsettles me more than it should. More than I want it to.

Tearing my eyes away from the woman who's beginning to fascinate me, I focus on Jacob.

"I just declined a contract." He lets the words drop like hammers, and that's the impact they have on the room. Every person goes still in their seats, staring at their leader like he's just lost his ever-lovin' mind. Everyone except Sayward. She stares down at her hands folded in her lap.

It's clear to me that Jacob dropping a contract is something that doesn't happen very often, if ever.

Finally, his tone cautious, Abbott speaks. "Which one?"

It might be because he's about to become his son-in-law, but Abbott seems to be more comfortable questioning the boss than anyone else.

Jacob's cool gaze lands on him. "Not the government op for the rescue in Mexico. That still goes down in a month. But as for the private event next week, accompanying the heiress, that's out."

Silence again. Then Conners breathes a sigh of relief. "Not that I'm disappointed we're not going to be taking over the heiress's security for her event, but we've never declined before. Want to tell us why?"

For some reason, my gaze is drawn back to Sayward, and I notice that she hasn't moved. Although she's not looking directly at anyone in the room, her cheeks are burning red.

Jacob places his hands on the table, looking around at each person in turn. Conners, Abbott, Sayward, Ronin, Teauge, and me.

"When I say 'declined' I don't mean NES isn't going to take the contract. We've already agreed, and Abbott already put the plans for her into place. The Rescue Ops team just won't be the ones carrying them out."

Grisham's expression changes. "Oh...got it. So which team will you put on it?"

"Delta Squad."

Every man at the table nods except for me, because I'm new here and I don't know what the fuck team Delta Squad is.

"We're taking another assignment," Jacob continues. "And this one involves a member of our team."

Another heavy silence descends, and every man at the table glances at one another, trying to figure out what the hell Jacob is talking about.

Sayward clears her throat. She glances up at Jacob, and then darts a quick glance around the table. "It's me, guys. And I hate it that Jacob is using NES resources for this." She glares at Jacob, but there's also a tenderness in her gaze that shows her love for him despite her frustration.

My mind wanders for a split second, wondering what it would be like to have Sayward looking at me with tenderness. And *fuck*, the idea is appealing.

Immediately alert, Ronin levels his gaze at Jacob. "What's going on?"

Whatever tension exists between me and this team of men, it doesn't matter now. Sayward is someone that I already know I'd protect with everything I have. I don't know why, but it's true. When I have time to sit down and analyze that, it's gonna scare the shit out of me. I never want to be vulnerable to another person again. It's the very reason I lost my freedom for two fucking years. But right now?

I'm all in.

6

SAYWARD

I feel like dropping into the floor. Or blending into the walls. Or crawling under the table.

Anything so that the focus of this meeting won't be on me.

I came into work this morning, after staying awake most of last night emptying buckets of tears onto my pillow, knowing that this was going to happen. That Jacob was going to have to finally share my story with the team at Night Eagle. I thought I was prepared for it.

I'm so not.

It's not that I don't trust these men. I do. Even though I've never had to before, I realize now that I can trust them with my life. I've seen them during a rescue mission. They don't hesitate, they're smart, and they don't lose. They're the strongest men I've ever met in my life, and I know that going to Colombia with their protection and support means I'll be safe.

But I hate going back to the scariest, most confusing time in my life.

All the emotions that I've learned how to fight against over the years, the feeling of wanting to completely retreat into a cave of my own making, rise to the forefront. Even though I'm trying desperately to beat them back I can feel myself slipping.

There have been times in my life when my autism has protected me. It's kept me from having to deal with social situations that make me uncomfortable, or from feeling things that might break me.

But it's also been a cage.

Something that holds me hostage when I really wish I could just be like everybody else.

The urge to get up from the table and flee the room is overpowering.

Just as I'm about to shove my chair back, there's a nudge on my foot. I glance up and to the right, straight into Bennett's stare. His eyes are an unusual color—such a deep blue I'd call them ocean. The combination against the tan tone of his skin is striking. His jaw is square and set, and thick scruff covers it. Even though the structure of his face isn't perfect: there's a small scar just above his left eyebrow, his mouth is wide, his eyes set a little too far apart. But the combination of his features work together to make up a perfectly sexy specimen of man. His stare is intense, where I've previously observed it to be light and playful. And instead of jerking my gaze away like I normally would when someone's eyes meet mine, I'm held captive by him instead.

After a moment, Jacob begins talking, and I realize that I've been so preoccupied and transfixed by Bennett's gaze that I stayed rooted to my spot at the table.

And I no longer have the urge to run.

Like an anchor, Bennett kept me here. Grounded to this place. I have no clue why, or how, he has that effect on me.

"When I was a Ranger, I was on a mission in Colombia. We were extracting a U.S. diplomat who was being held captive by the cartel. At that time, the cartel's leader was a man named Philip Suarez. Suarez was a nasty fucker, and he terrorized the villages in his territory like a dictator would. We had a contact in one of the villages, a man who gave us information on Suarez when he could. Our contact wasn't cartel, but he did a lot of work around the village and knew a lot about what went down."

Jacob's tone is somber, but his gaze is steady as he relays the story to the team in front of him. I want to squeeze my eyes shut, but instead I just keep them locked on Bennett. His gaze darts back and forth between Jacob and me, so I know he's listening intently to the story, but he mostly stays focused on me.

It's like he knows I need him in this moment. Suddenly, I find myself wishing I could hold his hand in mine.

It's the first time *in my life* I've ever wished for someone else's touch.

"I was the main point of contact for the informant in the Colombian village, since I was the commander of my Ranger battalion at that time. It was near the end of my military career, and after months of communication, the man became a friend. His name was Ricardo Diaz."

The team members' eyes flicker with recognition, and Jeremy's glance flits toward me with concern. My gaze immediately returns to my hands in my lap, as does the lump in my throat, the one I thought I'd gotten rid of last night.

As Jacob continues with the story, that gentle nudge presses against my foot again, and I know that Bennett wants my eyes on him. But right now I'm fighting so hard against the tears I just can't look up.

"When we arrived in the village, it was under the cover of night. Diaz met and led us to the location where the diplomat was being held. It was at great risk to himself, but he was willing to do whatever he could to get our man home safely. Diaz was a good man."

The best. My words are silent, but it doesn't mean they have any less meaning.

"At the time, Diaz had a wife, a fifteen-year-old son, and an eleven-year-old daughter. You've all already figured out that the little girl was Sayward."

Every eye in the room lands on me. But then, knowing me as well as they do, the guys immediately look back to Jacob. They don't want to embarrass me, and I'm extremely grateful for their effort.

Except for Bennett. He doesn't leave me alone without his gaze. And I'm holding on to it like a tether.

"It all happened fast that night. Every single one of you knows what a situation like that is like. You have orders, plans, strategies in place. Every contingency has been thought of. But sometimes, nothing works the way it's supposed to."

I attempt to bore a hole into the table with my eyes.

"After Diaz pointed out the location, we holed up in the jungle to wait for the right time to make our move. Diaz returned to his home a few miles away. But when he got there...he found his family, held at gunpoint, by the devil himself. Suarez."

Unbidden, a strangled breath escapes me. Because as soon as Jacob says the words, the memories come flooding back like a wave of salt water you try so hard not to swallow but can't help it. I'm suffocating on the memories, choking on the emotions they evoke.

"Somehow, Suarez had intel that we never anticipated him having. He knew we were there, he knew what we were there for. And he knew that Diaz was the one who'd sold him out. Instead of killing Diaz's family right then and there, Suarez used them as incentive for Diaz to go back to us, tell us to call off the rescue and the raid. Suarez's whole operation would have gone down that night, and he knew it."

I suck in a deep, shuddering breath as the horrific memories, the gruesome images I never wanted to remember bombard me. I bury my head in my hands, trying to keep the thoughts out. But they're seeping in, despite my best efforts.

The gun. I remember how big and shiny it looked. I'd seen plenty of them before, growing up where I had, but never one so close to the head of someone I loved. So close to my own head. It seemed so much shinier and more solid than it did when I saw them from afar.

Suarez, shouting at my mother in a way that my father

never would. My brother, Marcos, as a skinny fifteen-year-old, trying to shield us from the worst of it. But he was no match for Suarez. Suarez used the butt of his gun to knock Marcos to the ground, and I remember my mother pleading with him to wake up.

The blood, streaming from the side of my brother's head? That's what started it. The buzzing in my brain. The only way I was able to block it all out. I kneeled in a corner of the room and began to rock. I was vaguely aware of Suarez shouting at my mother, asking her what was wrong with her freak daughter. The strong resoluteness with which my mother refused to answer him.

Shuddering, I take a deep breath to try to calm my heartbeat.

Jacob continues. "Diaz ran straight back to our location, telling us what was happening at his home. I immediately decided that the mission still needed to go on. I knew the U.S. Army would never reconcile saving one family versus bringing down an entire cartel family's operation and saving a diplomat. But I promised Diaz I'd save his family, along with bringing down Suarez and his crew."

Jacob stops talking after that, leaning back from the table and pacing toward the windows. Grisham's voice rises in the oppressive silence.

"What happened?"

I won't look at Jacob's face when he relays the next part of the story. I can't. I stare at Bennett like he's the only thing in the room, and somehow his eyes, burning into mine, seem to understand how much I need him.

My hands are wringing so hard in my lap I'm in danger of cutting off my own circulation.

But I stay.

Jacob's voice gets rough, granules of sand scratching against the,weathered stone of his memories.

"The mission came first. It had to. I had orders. So we followed the procedure we'd planned and went in after the diplomat. After we got him out, with plenty of cartel casualties but none to my team, I sent three of my men to the pickup point without me, and took one man with me to Diaz's home. The cartel took a big hit that night, but not all of them went down. One key member in particular, Suarez's son, escaped."

I suck in a deep, rattling breath. My lungs can't seem to fill with enough air. All I can do is keep taking shallow ones because the breath going in and out of my body right now is the only thing keeping me upright.

That, and Bennett's stare.

"By the time we got there, a gunshot sent us into overdrive. When I looked in a window, Diaz's wife was bleeding out on the floor. Suarez yanked the little girl to him by the hair, holding her in front of him. The son was sprawled out on the floor, and I couldn't tell if he was dead or alive. Diaz was pleading for his daughter's life."

Despite my best efforts, I can't turn off my brain. Because of my autism, I can usually shut out any and everything that makes me uncomfortable. Block it off, tear myself away, whatever it takes. But this is my job; it's a professional setting and I don't want a single one of these men to think less of me because I need to leave the room when shit gets hard.

I squirm in my seat, and the next thing I know, there's a warm hand squeezing mine under the table. I look up, startled, and Bennett gives me the smallest of nods.

He's encouraging me. He's here for me. Like I need him to be.

I squeeze the shit out of his hand, hard enough to hurt, but he doesn't even flinch.

He just *squeezes back.*

My heartbeat takes off, my stomach takes flight. The smallest, most shredded pieces of me start to slowly thread back together again.

"We didn't have time for a plan. I went around to the back of the house and snuck in through the back door. The little girl's screams...Sayward's screams still haunt me to this day."

And that's when it all comes rushing back. Every last detail that I didn't want to remember.

My mama falls down, the loud pop *still echoing through our small house. I'm right beside her, and as soon as she falls I place my hands on my ears and my mouth opens to scream.*

But the scream never comes, because someone's big hand lands on top of my mouth before I can make a sound. My heart beats so fast. Like I've just run a mile. I know what running fast and far feels like; I've tried to keep up with my Marcos more times than I can count.

"Please." Papi's voice is low, but it's so full of pain and sadness that I want to close it out. I want to close everything out, this entire night. I don't want to remember any of it.

A man I've never seen before creeps out from the kitchen, a gun aimed on the awful man holding me close to his chest. The man who yelled at my papi and shot my Mama.

My eyes skirt over to where my mama lies on the floor. Her head is bleeding. My stomach rolls, and I feel the need to throw up, just like when I'm sick from eating bad food.

The man pulls out his cell phone. "Pablo. Are you safe?" He listens, and then nods. Relief blazes in his dark, dark eyes. "Good. Yes, I have the man responsible for everything that happened tonight. He'll pay. I have the loveliest little thing here, Pablo. I'm sure you'll enjoy training her. And one day, she will be your wife. Her name is Sayward."

His smile is what I later came to know as pure evil as he places his phone back into his pocket.

"Please. Don't hurt her." Papi's voice is begging. "Don't take her, too."

There's a mean growl behind me. "I'm not going to hurt her. I'm going to take her with me. Your daughter is going to make the perfect drug runner. Quiet, innocent–looking, unassuming. And then one day, she will make the perfect wife for my son, Pablo, who will take over my entire operation. And you will have to watch, watch her while she belongs to me. That will be your punishment."

My papi lunges then, reaching for me with both arms as I hear another pop, pop, pop *of gunfire. The clawing hands release me, and I drop to the floor. I want to rush to my mama, but instead I crawl toward the wall and curl into a small, tight ball. I cover my ears and I sing. Sing every single song I know, as loud as I can, until the noise is over and the horrible scene in front of me melts away into nothingness.*

"Together with Ricardo and Marcos, we moved Suarez's body and made sure it looked like a rival cartel encroached on their territory. It was the best we could do with what we had, and I told Ricardo he needed to take his family and run. We knew Suarez had gotten the call in to his son, and that he'd used Sayward's first name. We had no way of knowing if the cartel would buy the cover-up or if they were already looking for Sayward, since that's the only piece of information they had."

Jacob's voice sounds like it's traveling from somewhere far, far away. "Ricardo and Marcos refused to run. He wanted to stay, make sure that the cartel never caught wind of the fact that a bull's-eye had been placed on his daughter's back. He wanted to know if and when chatter started up about Sayward. He thought he could protect her better by staying in Colombia and keeping his ear to the ground. I promised him, at that moment, that I'd take his daughter and hide her. Make sure she couldn't be found by the cartel. I brought her back to the States. Found her a family nearby to raise her. I knew I couldn't do it, not when my marriage was falling apart and I was still on active duty. But I made sure that I could check in on her as often as possible."

A heavy silence falls. No one speaks, and every single man in the room has eyes on Jacob while they digest our story. But I can only look at Bennett. I have the strangest feeling that if I look anywhere else I'll lose it. I'll start crying or screaming or rocking like when I was a child, and I'll never be able to stop.

I've never allowed myself to relive that night.

Never.

And now the entire team of men I work with know exactly what happened to me, to my family, all those years ago. The fact that the truth has come out should be a comfort, but it isn't.

My past is catching up with me; between Marcos showing up in my life here and Jacob having to share all of my deepest, darkest secrets... it's all too much. Finally, I allow myself to break contact with Bennett, just as Dare speaks.

"What do you need from us?" he asks, his voice thick, rough.

These men, even though I haven't known them long, have become like big brothers, and I know that whatever pain I'm suffering, they'll suffer it right along with me.

"Sayward's brother, Marcos, just showed up in town." The dark cloud of suspicion in Jacob's voice is something he's unable to hide.

But I don't want to hear it. The mention of my brother, the one connection to my past—to my family—that I have left, sends me running. I need air. I need quiet. I need *solitude.* I push up from my chair.

"Bathroom," I mumble to the room as I scurry around the table and finally out the door.

Making my way downstairs, I find the bathroom just outside the lobby where Rayne's desk is set up and lock myself inside. I slide down against the wall, and hold in my sobs as tears streak silently down my face.

7

BENNETT

When Sayward gets up and practically runs from the room, it takes everything I have not to rise from my seat and go after her. But when I glance around the room, it seems like no one else is inclined to do so.

"Is she gonna be okay?" I ask the room.

I don't know Sayward the way these guys do, but I can feel the sorrow evident on all of their faces mirrored inside me. It hurts, thinking about what happened to her all those years ago. It's almost like I can feel what she's feeling, and the desolation is a goddamned force trying to knock me backward.

Conners shoots me a sharp look, while Jacob levels a shrewd one on me. Rather than answering me, Jacob begins to speak about how Marcos showed up to tell Sayward her father died. Jacob says we'll be traveling to Colombia next week so that Sayward can attend her father's memorial.

"Wait...is that even safe? Is the head of the cartel still

after her?" I stare around the room like every man there has lost his fucking mind.

"Suarez is dead." Jacob's tone is flat.

I stare at him, my eyes narrowing with suspicion. "But you don't think the danger to Sayward has been eliminated. It's why you've been hiding her all these years. And why we're going with her?"

I sit back in my leather chair and fold my arms. On the inside, I don't even know why words are coming out of my mouth right now. This is Day One on a brand-new job. A job in which I'm participating on a trial run, for shit's sake. All I wanted to do was sit back and learn the ropes.

Only now, because of a woman I feel a strange, unexplainable pull toward, I'm sticking my nose where it doesn't belong.

Jacob's eyes cut toward me. He's silent for a beat, before he answers. "I've kept tabs on the situation in Colombia. It appears that Suarez's son, Pablo, did take over as head of the cartel. If a Suarez is in charge, I don't trust anything that happens down there while Sayward is in Colombia. Even if she's with her brother. As far as we know, Pablo bought into our cover-up, but he knows Sayward's name. That's enough for me to be concerned."

He glances at Grisham. "Ghost, I don't know how focused Sayward is going to be right now. I'm going to need you to handle planning and strategy with me. We don't know what we'll run into, and it very well could be nothing. But I have a schedule for the memorial and we can assess the lay of the land. I need Brains on tech and weaponizing us as we see fit

once we find out more. You can handle doubling up, right?"
He turns his attention to Teague.

When he starts using the team members' field nicknames,
I know that Jacob is in mission planning mode.

"Yeah, Boss Man." Both men nod, but Abbott's the one
who speaks up.

Jacob nods. "The rest of you can go train. Rayne has information about the way guerrillas in the cartel are most likely
to fight. Use that intelligence and train accordingly."

Abbott glances at us. "We should have the bones of a mission strategy in place by tomorrow afternoon. We'll start
practicing maneuvers and how we're going to implement
them then."

We all nod as we file out of the room. Glancing around, I
don't see Sayward anywhere, and *damn*...I'm worried about
her.

Something inside me pulls, tugs, urges me to find her,
put my arms around her.

As soon as we're in the hallway, I stop Ronin with a hand
on his shoulder.

"Nicknames. If you're all gonna use that shit all the time,
I need to know who's who."

I have a general idea from when I worked with them to
save Ronin's fiancée, but the names are fuzzy. I figure if I
hear the stories behind the names, I'll be more likely to remember them.

Ronin chuckles. "We don't use them all the time, mostly
in the field. But yeah, guess you should know that." He
heads for the training room, and I follow. Conners is already

a few steps ahead of us. "Jeremy is Brains because he's always the first to know about the new weapons and techy gadgets we can use on missions. He's into it in a way that none of the rest of us are. And he outfits us accordingly. There's a whole room here dedicated to all his shit. He's also damn good with a computer, even though Sayward wears that hat better than he does."

I nod, thinking that makes sense. I don't know Teague that well, but he geeked out over some of the devices we used during Olive's rescue.

"And Dare up there..." Conners glances over his shoulder, one eyebrow lifted. "We call him Wheels. Apparently when he was in the field as a Ranger, they called him Cujo. But no one drives like him. He's really into cars, like rebuilds them and shit. And in the field, no one drives like he does. So to us, he's Wheels."

I call out to Conners. "You rebuild cars?" Despite myself and my less-than-friendly feelings toward Conners, I think that's cool as shit. "Like old ones?"

He gives one short nod before pushing through the training room door. "Bikes, too."

As Ronin and I file in, he points to his own chest. "They call me Swagger."

He doesn't elaborate, and I pause. "Why?"

A few feet away, Conners fits his hands with hand wrap. "Because he's so cool and confident when he's interrogating a target. It doesn't even affect him like it does the rest of us. Doesn't matter what he has to do to a guy, he gets that shit done. He's a machine."

I glance at my friend, one brow lifted. "We talkin' about torture?"

His lips set in a firm line, his eyes narrow. *"Interrogation."*

I nod, understanding completely. "Got it."

Conners continues. "And we call Sayward—"

"Viper," I interrupt. "That one, I know."

And speaking of . . .

I jerk a thumb over my shoulder. "No one checked on her after the meeting. She looked . . . I'll be right back."

Ignoring the questioning glances and the curiosity behind them, I turn and jog back down the hallway. Heading downstairs, I round a corner just in time to see Sayward exiting the bathroom. She spots me and freezes, glancing down at the floor.

Not pausing until I'm standing in front of her, I keep my voice low. "You okay? Damn . . . that was rough. Sayward . . . Jesus. I'm sorry."

She shakes her head, still studying the smooth gray floor. "It's in the past. I'm usually just fine. But today . . . having it all brought up in front of everyone like that . . ."

Sadness courses through me, pulling down the corners of my mouth at the same time it seizes up my chest. "One thing I've learned? That kind of negativity always rises to the surface, sooner or later. But I'm sorry you had to deal with it in a roomful of coworkers."

She glances up then, her eyes meeting mine in a glance that jacks up my heart rate. It doubles when her mouth twists into a small smile. "Thank you. For understanding."

I nod. "You gonna be okay?"

She turns away. "I'm always okay, Bennett."

I watch her walk away, knowing that she believes that's true.

But everyone breaks, at one point or another.

When I walk back into the gym, Ronin and Dare are standing near the door. Both men eye me, Ronin with curiosity and Conners with suspicion.

"What?" I can't keep the irritated growl out of my voice.

Conners folds his arms across his broad chest. His dark brown hair almost reaches his collar, and his eyes are such a light green they're almost colorless. They're similar in color to Ronin's, but where Dare's looks like the foamy part of the ocean, Ronin's are more forest-deep.

"Make a move on her and Boss Man will fucking castrate you. Unless Viper does it herself first."

Irritation prickles inside me. Dare Conners might be my new teammate, but he's not my friend and he's definitely not about to tell me who I can spend time with.

Instead of answering, I wrap my hands and start warming up on a speed bag. But as my body becomes coated with sweat and my heart rate increases, the same gorgeous face keeps running through my head.

Sayward Diaz is under my skin, and I have no idea what it's gonna take to get her out.

As the workday winds down, my head is swimming. Not because I'm overwhelmed with the work. No, this shit is coming as naturally to me as breathing. Even though I thought I'd lost my heart for it, keeping people safe is what used to drive me to wake up every single morning. When I lost that, I lost a part of myself.

After today, I feel like I have at least part of that back.

I lean back at my new desk, in a large open room where all the security specialists at NES have workspaces, one thumb drawing across my stubbled jaw as I stare down at the plan Grisham and Jacob have sketched out. We'll basically be functioning as Sayward's bodyguards for the two days we're in Colombia.

"How much danger do you think she's really in? If the man who originally threatened her is dead?" I throw the question out to Ronin and Teague, who are leaning over the plans with me.

Ronin's eyes narrow. "Not sure. You never know with these crime families. It seems that one vendetta can be passed down from generation to generation. Especially if the son has a suspicion."

I know he's thinking of the recent past, when his fiancée was taken by an organized crime family here in Wilmington. "Yeah. No one there has known where she is since she left Colombia? Jacob has managed to keep her hidden all this time?"

Teague nods. "Yeah. He and his wife weren't doing well at the time, and they ended up divorcing, but I think another reason he placed her with another family was because he didn't want anyone to connect them in case Pablo ever found out who really killed Suarez. Jacob was just keeping her as safe as he possibly could."

Leaning back in my chair, I commit the plan to my

memory. "Tomorrow we'll talk about what we're bringing with us?"

Knowing that we have only a week to prepare, I want to be as ready as possible. This will be my first mission with NES, and the desire to prove myself gets stronger with every hour I'm here.

When I was first offered this position, I thought it might bring me back to the dark place I worked so hard to crawl out of when I ended my military career. I didn't think I'd want this.

But I can't deny the fact that I do.

We all walk toward the lobby, and the rest of the team is standing just outside Jacob's office. As we walk past another open door, I glance in and notice Sayward leaning back in her chair behind her desk, her gaze aimed out the windows. Being that the NES building is directly across the street from the ocean, I can imagine the view is something to look at. But something tells me her mind isn't on the pretty sight in front of her.

My steps falter, and I end up pausing right in front of her office door. Something in my chest twinges, and I inhale as thoughts swirl through my head.

I'm guessing she hasn't seen her dad in years, but when you lose a member of your family, that shit hurts. No matter how much distance has been put between you.

"You doing okay, beautiful?" Maybe I'm supposed to be thinking about her as one of the team instead of paying attention to the fact that she's a goddamn knockout.

But I find that really fucking hard to do.

Her hazel eyes, so damn clear and full of all the things she doesn't say, turn on me. "I'm fine."

Jacob appears at my side in the doorway, leaning against the doorjamb. "Quittin' time, Sayward. I've assigned Lawson Snyder as your security detail for the next few days while we're still in town." He sidesteps me into her office, and for some reason I follow, standing just inside the door.

Sayward scowls, and stands up from her desk. Her hands go to her hips, and there's a sassy flare to her stance that makes a small grin tug on my mouth. "I don't need a detail. Plus, Marcos is staying at my place."

Marcos? Who the fuck is Marcos? Then I remember that Jacob mentioned the fact that her brother showed up here last night to tell her about her father.

Jacob stands firm, his expression unwavering as he squares off with Sayward. I'm learning pretty quickly that they have a father-daughter type of relationship. He speaks slowly, enunciating each word. "Your brother isn't trained to keep you safe. Lawson Snyder is."

Her eye roll makes Jacob set his jaw, and my gaze ping-pongs back and forth between the two of them.

Then some dude I haven't met yet pushes past me. There's no uniform at NES, but all the guys who work here dress casually, in clothes they're comfortable in. This guy is no different, except he wears his T-shirts too fucking tight. The black fabric stretches over biceps that he must spend six hours a day working on.

His head is shaved like he's still military, and his light brown skin is only a shade darker than Sayward's. His voice is a deep murmur as he walks up to Jacob and stands too close to Sayward.

"Ready to escort her home, Boss Man." He glances down at Sayward. "You ready to go?"

She opens her mouth to speak, but I'm striding forward before she can get a word out. "I'll be her security detail."

Sayward turns her big eyes on me, wide with surprise, while Jacob faces me directly. Lawson looks me up and down, and if he isn't careful I'm going to end up showing him exactly what he can do with his cocky-ass attitude.

Jacob's tone is half-suspicious, half-amused. "I already gave out this assignment, Blacke. You aren't needed here."

The hell you say.

I aim for a respectful tone of voice. "Sir, with all due respect, I'd really like this assignment. It'll give me the chance to prove myself until we leave for Colombia. And I ... personally ... want to see to it that Sayward is safe."

I don't even know where the words come from. I only know they're true.

Sayward's bottom lip disappears between her teeth at the same time her expressive eyes narrow, and if it's even possible, Lawson sticks his broad chest out even farther than it was before.

The sight makes me want to grin, but I keep my face blank.

Jacob scrutinizes me while he thinks it over. Sayward taps her sneakered foot.

"Is anyone listening to me?" she snaps. "I. Don't. Want. Security."

Ignoring her, Jacob makes a decision. He gestures to

Lawson. "Sleuth, you can return to your team. You have your hands full right now anyway. We'll keep Sayward with Blacke."

An irritated expression ghosts across Lawson's face when he glances at me, but he nods at Jacob and leaves Sayward's office.

She groans in frustration and walks to her desk. Shutting down her laptop, she stuffs it into her backpack and brushes past me.

"Coming?" she grinds out through gritted teeth.

Jacob's lips twist in what I can only assume is his best imitation of a smile. Damn, the dude is gruff as fuck.

"Good luck." He keeps his voice low. "She better be in one piece tomorrow morning."

He pats me way too hard on my chest, but I don't flinch. Instead, I turn and follow Sayward out the front door of NES.

She walks straight to my big, red truck. I unlock it before she pulls the door handle, and she climbs up. Her stiff, robot-like movements indicate she's still pissed, so I let her do it all by herself and climb into the driver's seat.

I pause with the keys halfway to the ignition. "Where's your car?"

She keeps her gaze aimed out the windshield. "My brother has it. I let him drop me off this morning so he wouldn't be stuck at my condo all day."

I start the big engine.

"How'd you know which car was mine?" I ease out of the NES lot and head down the road.

Sayward glances at me. "I'm a hacker, Bennett. I know everything about you."

Her tone is blunt and unashamed, and I swallow hard.

"Don't know how I feel about that," I admit.

She shrugs. "Don't really care. It was my job to research you before you were hired."

"You take your job pretty seriously, don't you?" I keep my eyes on the road, but I'm very aware of the woman sitting next to me.

"It's all I have."

Her tone is so low, so full of *truth*, that I study her profile out of the corner of my eye while I drive. "I can relate."

I can feel her eyes on me. "Yeah, I guess you can."

Silence stretches out between us, but it's not uncomfortable. It's actually kind of nice. I've been around people who can't shut the fuck up, so Sayward is a change of pace that I can really appreciate.

When I make a left turn, Sayward turns to face me. "Where are we going? You should have made a right to get to my apartment."

I keep my gaze glued to the road, my voice easy. "Gotta stop by my bar first. I just want to check in with Kandie, make sure everything's running smooth."

After a beat, Sayward speaks up again. This time, her tone is curious. "*Your* bar?"

My hands tighten just slightly on the wheel. "It is now."

She doesn't say anything else, and I'm grateful for that. The last thing I want to do right now is talk about the fact that I've now lost the only other person in the world who gave a shit about me.

No matter what Mickey said, I know he left so he could

die in peace. Without anyone hovering over him. Without anyone having to watch him weaken and wither away. It's the kind of man he is.

But damn if it doesn't hurt like hell.

When I pull up in front of The Oakes, Sayward and I exit the truck and walk in through the front doors. The place is steady, but not packed, on this weekday night. I glance around as we walk toward the bar, and everything looks like it's in order.

"Head above water, Cotton Kandie?" I ask her with a playful wink.

She leans over the bar, her black corset top accentuating her curvaceous figure. "Do I know you?"

I lift a brow. "Yeah...I'm your boss? That's something you shouldn't forget."

Beside me, Sayward snorts. Kandie glances at her, and a wide grin almost splits her face.

"Oh, you brought the pretty one back. Should we do another lip-lock, honey?"

When I look at Sayward, eyebrows flying up in shock, she's actually *blushing.* The sight throws me so off balance, I just stare at her with a stupid grin on my face. "What the hell am I missing *here?*"

She shakes her head, her thick waves swishing around her shoulders.

"Oh, you wish you knew." Kandie grins and turns her back on us, getting a drink ready for a customer.

I turn to Sayward and tug on a strand of her hair. I just needed to touch some part of her, and something tells me her hair is the safest part of her to touch right now. "You got secrets, beautiful?"

She rolls her eyes, which I'm starting to figure out is her go-to reaction when she's irritated or embarrassed. "If you only knew."

Yeah... if only.

She looks up at me then, and I'm caught in those deep, deep eyes of hers. Her face is so innocent, yet there's a wisdom there. I'm guessing it comes from everything she's been through in her life. But as I take a step closer to her, drawn like a goddamn magnet, I'm also wondering how deep the innocence goes. She tips her head up to look at me, refusing to back down from our mutual stare, and the electricity growing between us, and my cock stirs to life wondering the same thing.

I have no idea what the fuck this is between Sayward and me. All I know is that it's been happening, slowly, since the first time I saw her. And the more time I spend with her, the more I want to know. The closer I want to get.

And for a man like me, that's dangerous.

8

SAYWARD

When Bennett speaks, it's like I'm broken from the spell of those damn eyes of his. They're all light and jovial, but when I look into them—really look—I can see the depths of darkness he's trying to hide embedded in the silver flecks in his irises.

Or maybe he's not trying to hide it. Maybe he's just buried it down so deep he doesn't dare pull it out and examine himself anymore. What happened two years ago...what made him unleash on the guy who ended up in the hospital? I know that anyone capable of losing it like that has scars so deep they'll never heal.

I've never been violent, but I have bone-deep scarring of my own.

Is this what makes me feel so drawn to him?

Bennett inclines his head toward the back hallway. "I need to stop in the office and check on a few things. Then I'll take you home."

Without a word I follow him down the hallway. My eyes are glued to his tall, broad form. Muscles ripple and slide under his T-shirt as he moves and there's a grace to his stride that most men don't have. It's like all his pent-up aggression is poured into efficient movements; nothing is wasted. When he enters his office, he drops down in the chair behind the desk. He moves the mouse around, studying something on the computer.

"Do you need help with that?"

The question pops out before I can stop it. I see someone sitting in front of a computer and I automatically want to be sitting where they are. It's where I'm most comfortable.

But Bennett just chuckles, his clear blue eyes glancing up at me with amusement before he shakes his head. "No hacking needed here, superstar. Just boring bookkeeping and accounting."

So while I wait for him, I walk around the office. The walls aren't bare; they're littered with maps and photos from places far away. I've only traveled to two countries, Colombia and the United States, so the exotic locations in the photos draw me in, keeping me transfixed. There's a weathered map of the high terrain in Switzerland, and a photo of palm trees leaning toward one another in a photo labeled Abu Dhabi.

I'm not sure how much time passes while I'm completely engrossed, but I feel him behind me before he speaks.

This magnetism between us, or whatever it is, is unlike anything I've ever felt.

I've never been *with* a man. In my teenage years, I was

way too awkward and socially inept to have dated. I didn't go to college, so I didn't have the opportunities for casual flings the way most women did.

But, in the span of time that I left the home of my guardians when I was eighteen and before I started working at NES about a year ago at twenty-three, I did freelance work—mostly hacking—for several small companies in North Carolina. Many of them were shady as hell and would pay me under the table. But I had access to computers, and my hacking skills became second-to-none. There was one man I worked for, who in order to turn a blind eye to what I was doing behind my screen, only asked for one favor in return.

It was something that was done in his office behind closed doors, and I became really, really good at it.

Sucking a man's cock is like anything else. With research, you can become a pro. And he didn't touch me, being that I made it a stipulation of the arrangement, so I was able to get the job done and get the hell out and back to my computer.

When I feel Bennett behind me, though, a rush of thoughts and emotions and feelings wash over me and I can't pick one to focus on. My body flushes, my nipples tighten, my thighs clench together while wetness pools in my panties. My brain floats to a place where my lips are wrapped around Bennett's cock instead of my old boss's, and my body reacts.

Shit . . . is this what real attraction feels like?

Whatever it is, it makes me more uncomfortable in my own skin than I've ever been. And at the same time, *I don't want it to stop.*

His voice is nothing but a murmur, too close to my ear. I tense as my skin heats to a dangerous temperature.

"Those were all taken or gathered by Mickey, the man who used to own The Oakes. He was in the army most of his life, and he collected a lot of things on his travels around the world. Then when I started working here, I added a couple of my own. I think that when I travel with NES, I'll keep the tradition up. I'll bring back photos or maps just like he did."

He's not touching me, but I can feel the warmth of his skin, can practically hear his heart beating in that broad, solid chest of his. I close my eyes, trying desperately to grab my walls, build them up high enough that he won't be able to get past them.

That's what I do. I protect myself.

But I can't seem to manage it when it comes to Bennett Blacke.

And that's when it hits me.

There's only one way to fix this situation.

I turn around, and he's *right there.* But instead of backing up into the wall, I reach beside me and close the office door. Then I place both hands on his chest and push until he's backed up against his desk.

His eyes go wide, but then quiet amusement makes his face light up. "What's going on, beautiful?"

Beautiful. Every time he uses the nickname for me, I want to believe it.

"What's going on," I snap as my hands drop to his belt. "Is that I'm sick and tired of this tension that's pulling between us. We need to eliminate it, and there's only one way I know of to do that."

Bennett's expression loses all trace of humor. "Sayward—"

"Shut up." I finish with his belt and the button on his jeans and yank down the zipper. Tugging his pants down over his narrow hips, I drop to my knees in front of him.

Now that I'm not looking up into his eyes, now that I've taken control, I no longer feel like I'm at his mercy. This, I can do.

It's clear by the large bulge of the erection tenting his tight gray cotton boxers that he wants this. A surge of power hits me like a bolt of lightning, and my lips curve into a half-smile.

Pushing his boxers down so I can take a firm grip on his erection, I hear him hiss through his teeth.

God. He's...huge. Bigger and thicker than the man I used to do this for. I'm not prepared for the size of him, but I should have realized that not all men are made the same. Fascinated, I lose myself a little bit as my small hand strokes his long, steely length. He's as smooth as silk, but harder than stone.

"Fuck...*Sayward.*" His voice rough, his breathing ragged, he says my name like he's cracking a whip.

I jerk my gaze up to his again. "What?"

He gestures down at where my hand meets his hot, throbbing cock. "What are you doing, beautiful?"

Well, that's an easy one. "I'm about to suck your dick."

Even though my stomach is turning flips inside me and my hands are trembling, my voice is simple and matter-of-fact. The sound of it does something to him. He tenses, a confused expression entering his eyes. Then, with a muttered curse he pulls me up from the floor and, in one fluid motion, turns me so I'm sitting on his desk. Then he's standing in front of me, holding my gaze while he fastens his pants.

When he's finished, he steps between my legs and holds my face in one cupped hand. "What. The fuck. Was that?"

I'm still trying to decide what just happened. Never, in all the times I'd given oral sex to the man I'd previously worked for, had he ever once stopped me in the act. Or before the act had really even begun.

I must have done something wrong.

It's my first thought, because well...Bennett is a man, right? And according to my research, all men love getting head.

Love, with a capital *L*.

I look just to the left of his gaze. "What did I do wrong?"

His fingers tighten slightly on my chin. I can feel Bennett's stare, hot and steady, but I refuse to give in to it. I will not look at him.

I will not look at him.

"Look at me, Sayward."

Without my permission, my gaze strays to his.

"There was nothing wrong about what you just did. I have the hard-on to prove it right now, and it probably won't go away for hours. What I want to know is, *why* were you about to suck my dick?" He speaks slowly and methodically, but his words fall like feathers rather than bullets.

"Because all of this...tension...between us is uncomfortable. That's the only way I know to dissipate it. Especially
since we're going to be working together now. I just decided
to get it over with." The heat rises in my cheeks, I can feel the
warmth just as surely as if I were standing in the sun.

Bennett's either shocked into silence, or he just can't
decide what to make of me. Either reaction would be something I'm used to dealing with.

I move to push off the desk. Suddenly, the office feels way
too small. Too enclosed. Too...*intimate.*

But Bennett isn't going anywhere, and his hand only
moves from my face to clasp the back of my neck. "Listen
to me, beautiful. I've imagined those plump lips of yours
wrapped around my dick more than a few times since I met
you. But when that happens, it's gonna be because you *want*
to do it. Not because you think you have to. And when you
take care of me? I'm damn sure gonna take care of you."

Now I don't think I could stand up from the desk even if
I wanted to. His words turned my legs to Jell-O.

I've never been the kind of woman to appreciate words.
To me, most people just waste them. But every single thing
that Bennett Blacke just said to me held meaning.

And promise.

When Bennett and I walk in my front door, Marcos stands
from the couch where he was watching television. Shutting
off the TV, he scowls at Bennett.

Bennett sets his duffle bag down on the floor. When I
asked him if he needed to stop by his place to grab an

overnight bag, he informed me with a grin that he keeps one in his truck. Just in case. *Who does that?*

"Who is this?" Marcos asks, suspicion evident both in his tone and his expression.

I gesture toward Bennett while placing my keys on the hook beside the front door. "This is Bennett Blacke. He works with me."

Marcos folds his arms across his chest. "Okay. But why is he *here?*"

Facing my brother, I match his stance. "Marcos, I'm glad you're here, but please don't be rude to my guest. He's here because he's been assigned to protect me."

Marcos looks around the room, and then spreads his arms wide. "But *I'm* here."

Bennett steps forward. His expression is unreadable, but he shifts his body in front of mine. It's an unconscious movement, effortless, almost as if he doesn't realize he's doing it. "Are you a trained security professional? Or a trained military operative?"

Marcos's frown only deepens. "American cowboys are all the same."

Bennett barks out a laugh. "Yeah. Whatever you say. But I'm here to keep your sister safe. So hate me all you want, but I'm not going anywhere."

I step around from behind Bennett. I aim a stare at Marcos before stepping up beside my brother. I don't wrap my arms around Marcos, but I nudge his side. "He doesn't hate you, Bennett. Right, Marcos?"

Marcos shrugs. "Whatever you say, *chica.*" He marches

over and holds out a hand to Bennett. "I'm sorry for my rudeness. Thank you for escorting my sister home safely."

With a grin, Bennett shakes Marcos's hand and then brushes past him to drop down on the couch. He pats the cushions. "This where I'm sleeping tonight, beautiful?"

At the nickname that still burns me up from the inside out, Marcos lifts a brow. "That's where *I* am sleeping."

My one-bedroom apartment doesn't afford me much room for guests. And honestly, I hadn't even thought about where Bennett would sleep. Last night, the NES guard stayed outside in his car all night to keep watch.

I stare at Bennett, confused. "You're sleeping here?"

One corner of his mouth tilts up as his sexy smirk goes rogue. "Where else did you think I was gonna sleep?"

Rolling my eyes skyward, I sigh.

Bennett flips the television back on. "Can't protect you if I'm asleep in my truck, now can I?'

He makes a good point. He's actually working tomorrow. He can't stay away all night keeping watch. He'll actually have to sleep here. Which means I have two unplanned houseguests.

Suddenly feeling very tired, and trying very hard not to recall the vivid memory of what Bennett felt like fisted in my hand, I gesture toward my bedroom. "I'll make you a bed on my floor."

Bennett slaps his thighs and stands up. He grabs his duffle bag from where he dropped it by the door and hoists it onto his shoulder. "Where's the bathroom?"

I point down the very short hall and Bennett disappears. When I hear the water running, I turn to Marcos.

"What is your problem?" I hiss.

"I don't like him," he answers simply.

I throw my hands up. "You don't like Jacob, you don't like Bennett. I'm seeing a recurring theme here, Marcos. You're my brother and I love you. I'm glad you're here. But you have to lighten up. This is my life."

He drops his head between his shoulder blades, staring at the ceiling. When he looks at me again, his eyes are sad. "Just because we've been apart for years doesn't mean I stopped being your big brother. I only want what's best for you."

He pulls me into a hug that's stiff with my tense body, and I try hard not to wriggle out of it. "I love you, *hermanita*."

"*Te amo*, Marcos," I whisper in return. "We're family. That will never change."

When we part, I give him a small smile and head to my bedroom to prepare a pallet on the floor for Bennett.

And I try really hard not to panic while I'm doing it.

9

BENNETT

Sayward's coming apart at the seams.

I've been doing some reading on typical behaviors of adults on the autism spectrum, and it's clear to me that having both Marcos and I invading her space is too much for her. She's trying to cope, that much is plain. But her movements are strained, she's repeating certain behaviors more than once, like the routine or the repetition is going to help her feel more comfortable.

I want to pull her into my arms and tell her that everything is fine. That this is only temporary, that I'm here to keep her safe. But that action probably won't help Sayward feel better. It might only push her deeper into herself.

Shit. What do I do here? I can't leave. I'm not leaving her alone in this apartment to sleep in my car, whether her brother is here with her or not.

Giving her the space I know she needs, I throw on a pair of sweats and retreat to her bedroom and lay down on the blankets and pillows she's set up for me beside her bed. Then I make a couple of calls.

When I hear the shower running in the bathroom, I head back down the hallway and face Marcos, who's pacing the small living room. He stops and glances up at me, irritation flickering in his eyes.

"You realize your sister doesn't do well with change, right? Having both of us here in her space . . . it's making her really uncomfortable." My tone is even, steady, but Marcos's nose flares with anger.

"Then you should leave."

I shake my head. "Not happening. I'm here to make sure she's safe. You have no idea who could have followed you here from Colombia, do you realize that? Maybe the cartel killing your father was a way to track down your sister."

Marcos stops, his eyes going wide as he contemplates. Clearly this isn't something he's thought about. A dark shadow creeps into his expression. It's the first time I've seen a shred of doubt in him.

"Right. Hadn't thought of that? I'm qualified to protect her. I'm not leaving. But I called you a car and booked you a hotel for the next two nights. Do it for her. Meet her for lunch tomorrow, have dinner with her. But don't put her in danger by staying at her place."

Until we know more about him, I'd prefer it if she didn't see him at all. But I can't keep her brother away from her. Not now . . . I've got no reason.

With a heavy sigh, Marcos crosses to the corner where his

small suitcase lies open. "Fine. Tell Sayward that I will call her tomorrow."

He's out of the apartment before Sayward finishes her shower, and she walks out as I'm moving my makeshift bed from her floor to the living room couch. I'd already put the blankets that Marcos had used on top of the small dryer I'd found under the washing machine in her kitchen.

She pauses in the hallway, staring at me. "Where's Marcos?"

I turn, and my breath catches as I take her in. Her long, black mane of hair is wet, braided and slung over one of her slender shoulders. There're miles of bronzed skin on display in her gray ribbed tank top and small black shorts. I notice for the first time that her toenails are painted cherry-red.

Fuck. Sayward Diaz is sexy as hell, and she doesn't even know it.

I swallow and realize I'm squeezing the pillow in my hands way too tightly. Sayward's eyes zero in on it, and I relax my hands, placing the pillow on the couch.

"I booked him a hotel room and called him a car." I answer her question honestly. "Having both of us here was too much, and I have to be here. So I made sure he had a place to go."

A series of emotions chase each other across her face, and I'm not sure which one will win out. Irritation grows to anger, and then confusion turns to relief. "You...didn't have to do that. I could have handled it."

I cross the room until I'm standing in front of her, but not so close as to force her retreat. "I know that, beautiful. I'm pretty sure you can handle just about anything."

She looks up at me, and her eyes are darker, muddier, more difficult to read. Finally, she turns toward the kitchen. "It's Tuesday. On Tuesdays I make a Mexican meal. And then every night before bed, I drink tea and watch *The Late Show*."

Chuckling, I pull my phone out to check the screen. "Well, we've got a little while before bed, and we haven't managed to eat yet. But can I propose something?"

I know how important routine is to Sayward. I've noticed little things about her. Every time she gets in the truck, she places her bag between her feet. Then she reaches for the seat belt and pulls the buckle carefully to the top of the strap before she pulls it across her body and buckles herself in. Then she crosses her left leg over her right, reaches for her backpack, and moves it between her leg and the console. Every time.

And the way she runs her index finger or a straw over the rim of whatever mug or cup she's drinking from before she takes a sip. And when she walked into her apartment, even with the chaos Marcos brought to the picture, she'd hung her keys in their rightful place, set her bag down on the corner of a bench against the wall, and put her shoes neatly in the compartment under the bench.

I'd never try to take her away from her routines, but for some reason this woman has compelled me to insinuate myself all up into her norms.

When she doesn't answer, I toss out a suggestion. "I think I need to get to know the woman I'm protecting a little better. You agree with that?"

She chooses her words carefully, sinking into the corner

of the couch. She's like a carefully guarded fortress, and I'm suddenly dying to break down those walls. "What exactly did you have in mind?"

"Why don't we fix dinner together?" Holding my breath, I watch her reaction. Outwardly, though, I'm playing it cool; leaning back on the couch, I cross an ankle over a knee.

Finally, she lifts her eyebrow. "You can cook?"

I spread my arms. "This is your train, Sayward. I'm just along for the ride."

One corner of her mouth lifts and it feels like I just won something big. She stands, heading into the kitchen without looking back.

I follow.

Her kitchen is tiny, with no sitting area and not a whole lot of counter space, so I have to stand close to her if I want to help. The forced proximity works just fine for me, though. The heat from her body bleeds into mine, and when I glance at her out of the corner of my eye she's so focused on laying out ingredients into neat rows that something inside my chest shifts, rearranges.

She puts me to work. She's already seasoned some chicken and she pulls the container out of the refrigerator and opens her back door.

I'm right by her side, slamming a palm against the door to push it shut again. Turning to face her, my expression is murderous. "What the hell are you *doing?*"

She looks up at me, bewilderment apparent on her face. "I'm going outside to get the grill going."

Jesus. "Wait, Sayward. If you're going outside, let me give it a quick scan out there first. Stay inside the door."

She doesn't like being told what to do. I can see it in the stubborn set of her mouth, in the way her eyes sparkle with irritation. But instead of arguing, she nods and hangs back.

I take a step out onto her back patio and glance around at the dark line of trees behind her duplex. My training kicks in as I take in every detail of my surroundings. My mind's eye clicks like a camera, over and over again: the sounds, the smells, the details of what's normal to see here and what's not. The feel of the pistol sitting in the holster at my hip is a hefty weight, letting me know it's there.

Usually, I'd never carry in someone's house. I would have taken my gun off when I came in or left it in my truck. But this is a different situation, and not having it on me isn't an option.

As my eyes slowly scan the yard, the hairs on the back of my neck start to bristle. My breathing slows, my eyes and ears going into overdrive as I try to see or hear whatever it is my sixth sense tells me is there. I don't know if I'm in hyperdrive because this is Sayward, or if there's really an unseen threat.

Rather than scaring her, I spot the little portable grill she's going to use for the chicken and carry it inside with me. As I shut the door, she glances down at the grill.

"That's a grill," she says.

I place it on the kitchen floor and follow with the bag of charcoal. Hauling the large concrete square that had been situated underneath the grill, I put it down carefully on the kitchen floor and move the grill on top of it. Catching Sayward's apartment on fire is the last thing I want to do. "I know that."

"It belongs outside."

"Well, beautiful, today's an adventure. Let's grill inside.'"

I don't look at her, because I don't know if I can without scaring her. As she goes back to chopping onions and tomatoes, I pull out my phone and shoot Jacob a quick text. I know he has connections at the Wilmington Police Department, and I'm going to call those ties into play right now.

Me: Get WPD to patrol the area around Sayward's apt.

His response is quick; my phone vibrates a few seconds later. I knew it would; when it comes to Sayward it seems that Jacob Owen doesn't mess around. His own daughter, Greta, is engaged to Grisham, and he treats Sayward the way I imagine he does his own daughter.

Jacob: Done. Tell me what you saw.
Me: Didn't see anything. Just an instinct. Could be nothing, but I want to be sure.

I slip my phone back in my pocket, knowing Jacob will text me if the police turn up anything in their patrol, and work on lighting a small fire on the grill. I open the kitchen window so the smoke will be able to escape, and turn back to Sayward while I wait for the coals to turn white.

"So why hacking?"

Her knife pauses for just a second before she continues her chopping. "Because I was good at it. And it's solitary. Why the military?"

Maybe if I open up just a little bit to her, she'll be more willing to share. "Because my dad died serving this country. As much as it hurt my mom for me to join up at eighteen, it was something I always felt like I had to do. Pick up where he let off."

I watch Sayward methodically place all of her chopped veggies into a bowl. "What are you making with those?"

She whips out a fork and starts mixing everything up together, adding in something fresh and green as she does. "Pico de gallo."

I'm impressed. Turning back to the little grill, I note the snowy color of the charcoal. "This is ready."

She brings me the platter of chicken, and I realize I'm going to have to throw them on the tiny grill one at a time.

"Did your mother forgive you?"

My cell phone buzzes in my pocket. Holding up a finger to Sayward, I pull it out and scan the words in the text flashing across my screen.

Hey, Bennett...Hoping this is still your number. We need to talk.

I blink, staring at the one number I never expected to see on my screen. Not now.

Not *ever*.

My fingers squeeze the metal on the device tight as I slip the phone back in my pocket and turn my attention back to Sayward.

"Yeah, she did. She lives in Georgia, which is where I'm from, but we talk a lot and she visited me when..." I trail off.

Maybe I'm ready to be open with this woman, but only so that she feels comfortable enough to be open with me. I don't talk about my time in prison. It's an event that changed me, and I never want to go back there. I don't even want to think about how I felt that night, or how I felt afterward knowing what I did.

Sayward stands beside me. "When you were in prison?"

All I do is nod, tensing for the questions.

But they never come. Sayward just goes back to the counter and stretches up, opening a cabinet and trying her damnedest to reach something too high for her slight stature.

My eyes travel the length of her curves, following the line of her bare, toned legs and pausing at the flare of her hips. Something inside me stirs, waking up in response to the natural beauty of the woman in front of me. My gaze continues up, sticking to the bare skin peeking out where her shirt rides up. There's ink visible there, the delicate lines of a design I can't see snaking up over the top of her shorts. My interest in her intensifies, wanting to see what a woman like Sayward would have permanently tattooed on her body. She doesn't make decisions lightly, and I can imagine that she very seriously considered exactly what she would get before she went and had the work done.

Glancing down at my own arm, where a full sleeve winds its way from shoulder to wrist, I want to ask her what she has. But when ink is hidden, it can be a private thing. I'm not going to ask her what it is.

I'm going to wait until she lets me see it for myself.

Crossing the tiny space until I'm beside her, I get in her space. "What are you reaching for?"

She glances at me, notes how close I am, and immediately looks back toward the cabinet. Her voice is just a whisper, and the sound of it makes me feel like she's touched me even when she hasn't. "Flour tortillas."

My hand easily sweeps across the shelf until I find the flat package she's looking for. I place it on the counter in front of her, and she takes a deep breath as she trembles a little.

As I step away, Sayward points to the refrigerator. "Do you want a beer? I drink Coronas on Mexican day."

"Would love one."

Heading back over to turn the chicken, I kneel down beside the grill. "How long has it been since you've seen your brother?"

She doesn't hesitate. "Thirteen years."

Whistling, I glance up at her. "And your father?"

"The same."

Sadness blooms in my chest. "I'm sorry you lost him, Sayward."

She nods. "Thank you, but you can't lose something you didn't really have, can you?"

I switch out the cooked chicken breast for a raw one. "Yeah, beautiful. You can."

My phone buzzes in my pocket, and I pull it out.

Jacob: Cops didn't find anything suspicious in the area. Everything OK there?

So it was just my own paranoia. Thankful, I type a response.

Me: Everything's good. Thanks.

Twenty minute later, Sayward slides a generous amount of chicken quesadillas onto my plate. She tops it with sour cream and pico de gallo and we both carry our food to the small table just outside the kitchen at the edge of the living room.

Sitting down, I stare at my plate. "This smells amazing, Sayward."

She shrugs. "I'm a good cook."

Sipping my beer to cover my laugh at her blunt honesty, I shoot her a look. "What else are you good at?"

If she understands my innuendo, she doesn't let on. I'm guessing she doesn't, which just makes this even more fun. *How far can I push the flirting before she realizes what I'm doing?*

"Other than hacking that's pretty much it."

"Oh, I doubt that very much, Sayward."

She narrows her eyes as she sips her beer. She's drinking out of a straw in a drinking glass instead of straight from the bottle, which I thought was pretty fucking adorable. She runs her straw absently around the rim of her glass. "Are you flirting with me?"

Ah. So she doesn't completely miss all social cues. Atta girl.

I shrug the same way she did a minute ago. "Abso-fucking-lutely."

"Well, stop. You're here right now regardless of the fact that I don't need a bodyguard. You also turned me down flat just a couple hours ago. Let's just get through this." She makes eye contact with me as she fires the last comment with an edge to her voice, and I don't miss how important that is.

I put down my bottle and stare right back. "Sayward, I didn't turn you down. I told you that I wasn't going to let you suck my dick because you felt like you had to. This?" I gesture between the two of us. "Will happen. And yeah, we work together. But there's no rule at NES against it, are there?"

She opens her mouth, then closes it.

Ha. Gotcha there, don't I, beautiful?

There's a stubborn set to her mouth. Seeing it makes my dick hard as fuck, and I can't even apologize for it. The woman is white-hot and she has no clue.

Gesturing between us exactly like I did, she emphasizes each word. "*This* won't happen unless it's on my terms. You got that?"

I smirk. "And what would those terms be, exactly?"

I take my first bite of food, and I was right: it's delicious. She's a good cook, exactly like she said. Wolfing down a quarter of a quesadilla, I wait for her response.

Her eyes are on my throat as I swallow, her pupils dilating as she takes me in. The fact that I know she's getting turned on by watching me eat her food just makes me want to throw everything off of this table and bend her over it. Seeing that perfect, round ass all stuck up in the air as I pound into her from the back is a thought that has my knuckles turning white around the tight grip I have on my Corona.

She points her fork at me. "This is sex. Nothing more. Obviously there's an attraction here, and I want to see it through so everything can *go back to normal*."

My smirk grows. "So you're saying you want me to fuck you, Sayward?" Pushing my chair back, I wipe my mouth and then stand. Placing both hands on the arms of her chair, I lean into her.

Now she's the one who swallows, and my eyes zero in on her delicate throat. *Fuck, I want to taste her.*

No... I need to.

10

SAYWARD

He's leaning over my chair, caging me in, and there's the usual part of me that knows he's too close and the urge to run is just as strong as ever.

But then there's another part of me, and I'm afraid to admit that it's actually a *bigger part*, that wants him closer. Even closer than he is now. And the words he just uttered?

Holy shit. No man has ever spoken those words to me before. It shouldn't be sexy, right? Women don't want to be *fucked*, do they?

But right here, right now, in this moment? With this man, and this man only?

I do.

My breath hitches, and I'm acutely aware of the steady beating of my heart in my chest. It's fast and it's hard, and blood pumps to all the places I thought lay dormant inside me. Squeezing my thighs together as wetness once again pools in my panties, I stare up at him with determination.

"Yes, Bennett. I want you to fuck me."

And then I want you to get out of my head.

His eyes go dark then, and I'm not prepared for how it makes me feel. One second they're light blue and full of the mirth he usually carries and then they're stormy.

Dark.

Dark.

Dark.

The darkness should scare me, because I already know there's a murky place inside of Bennett that he's pushed way down. But it doesn't fill me with fear. It just makes my body react more, makes me want more.

More.

Maybe I need this.

In the next second, he's lifting me out of my chair, our dinner forgotten. My legs wrap around his waist automatically. I don't know how I know what to do, because I've never been like this with a man. But instincts kick in when my back slams against the wall and his lips crash down over mine.

My hands tangle in his hair, surprisingly soft, and I hold his head to me like I never want him to pull away. His tongue presses against my lips, tasting my skin, and my mouth immediately opens for him.

He dips inside, his tongue hot and wet, tangling with mine. He tastes like everything I never even knew I wanted. I moan against his mouth and I have no earthly clue where that sound even came from.

His response is immediate; he grinds his hips into mine

and a whimper escapes my mouth as I feel the hard length of his erection rubbing against my core. I'm like a starving woman who hasn't had food for days. But the only nourishment I want right now is Bennett.

Bennett.

He kisses me like he owns me. Like if he tried, he could take possession of every single part of my body. Maybe even my soul.

And that absolutely terrifies me.

My body trembles, and I'm not sure if I'm slowly drowning in his closeness or because I'm about to combust from the inside out. I'm feeling things I've never felt before. Even when I used to suck my boss's dick, I never felt aroused. It was all about pleasing him so that I could move on with my day. And it always worked out really well.

For him.

Not for me.

But this? This is epically different.

Bennett's barely even touched me, and I already know that this is going to change the way I think about sex.

Sex. The very idea of it used to completely baffle me. I mean, how could I ever want my body plastered against another person's that way? How could I want to exchange air with them, exchange freaking *fluids* with them, without losing my mind? The very thought almost gave me hives.

But that was then.

This is very much *now.*

Bennett releases my mouth, only to plant his surprisingly soft lips on the very center of my throat. The force of it slams my head back against the wall, but I feel no pain. All I feel is pleasure.

"Bennett," I gasp. I've lost my breath.

He speaks between kisses. "I've been looking across the table at you, staring at this fucking spot. I knew I needed to taste you, but this is just the beginning. I want to taste you *everywhere*."

"Everywhere?" My eyes drift shut, my legs wrapping even tighter around him. *Where the hell did my breath go?*

He takes my mouth again, and my back is no longer against the wall. Instead, we're moving; Bennett walks down the hallway with me in his arms like I weigh nothing. It's only a few seconds before he's slamming me down on my bed, and the forceful bounce kicks my brain into high gear.

Fear overrides my body, my physical reactions, and all of the lust roaring in my veins.

Bennett is a violent man.

With that thought, my blood slows it's progression in my veins. Fear prickles every part of me, freezing my limbs and stopping my heart. My breath hitches for a very different reason, and I squeeze my eyes shut just as I feel his hands hit the mattress on either side of me.

What am I doing? I can't do this. I can't be with a violent man. Not after what I went through back in Colombia. A violent man killed my mother.

I can't do this. I can't do this.

"Sayward?"

Bennett's voice sounds like it reaches me from the other

side of a well. I realize that I haven't been able to catch my breath for at least a minute.

Bennett's hands cup the sides of my face. "Hey, beautiful. Come on, now. Talk to me."

I open my eyes and focus on his deep-ocean gaze. His eyes are troubled, wary, worried. Realizing what I've just done, I reach up and grab his wrists, yanking his hands off the sides of my face. Then I shove myself off the bed and escape into the bathroom.

Slamming the door behind me, I lean over the sink as huge, hot tears pour down my face.

Why can't I just be normal? An extremely attractive man was just whispering all the words any woman would ever want to hear while he had his lips all over me, and all I could do was think about the night my mother was killed?

A night I've successfully blocked out of my memory for years. Jacob insisted on my going to counseling as soon as I arrived in the States. I went faithfully for a year and a half, and never said a single word.

Not a single word.

I didn't want to think about it, much less talk about it. So I just forgot. Moved on. Grew up.

Obviously, I can't be with a man like Bennett. Not if it triggers those memories.

I expect Bennett to bang on the door any minute, but he doesn't. Instead, after my breathing has slowed and the tears have stopped, his voice thrums softly from the other side.

"Sayward. Please come out here and talk to me, baby. I need to know what just happened."

His tone is so quiet, so full of patience and something else I can't identify, that my little dead heart begins to thaw. If he was someone capable of hurting me, would his voice sound gentle enough to wrap around me like a blanket? Frantically, I rub at my chest, but nothing changes. He's getting to me. Whether I want him to or not.

Slowly, I reach for the door and turn the knob. I pull it open and stare out at Bennett.

He takes one look at my red-rimmed eyes and splotchy face and his expression crumbles. "Fuck, baby. What'd I do?"

My eyes fill with tears again. How can I tell him? Instead, I hang my head and whisper. "Nothing."

He takes my hand, all of the intensity from a few moments ago long gone, and leads me to the couch. Pulling me down beside him, he turns his body to face mine as I curl into the cushions, attempting to disappear.

Bennett stares at me for a full minute while I try to look anywhere but at him.

Finally, he speaks, and his voice is rough. Like he's been swallowing glass. "Sayward, be honest with me. You've looked into my background. Are you . . . are you *scared* of me?"

I look straight ahead. Needing some distance, I scoot away from him. "Bennett, my mother died at the hands of a violent man. You have a history of violence. In that moment when you slammed me on my bed, those two things merged in my head, which resulted in the panic attack I couldn't control."

I can't help it when my gaze strays to him. His eyes close, and he leans his head back on the couch as he utters a quiet curse. It takes a few minutes of silence before he speaks.

He gets up and then slides down until he's on his knees in front of me, his palms resting lightly on my thighs. His touch makes me stiffen, but I don't push his hands away.

"Sayward...I'm about to do something I never, ever do."

I hold my breath, looking at him. Really looking at him. The darkness in his eyes threatens to take over, but the warmth in his touch and the sincere brokenness in his voice let me know that I don't have to be afraid.

He's beautiful, in his own battered way. And it speaks to something deep inside of me I thought could never be reached.

"I'm gonna tell you about that night."

11

BENNETT

I was deployed. For Special Forces. We don't know where we're going until we get there, and our friends and family aren't allowed to know our location. Or how long we're going to be gone."

I pause, glancing at Sayward to make sure she's paying attention. She only knows what she's read on a computer file. She doesn't know where my head was when I made the decision that almost ended someone else's life.

She meets my gaze, which is still so rare I almost lose my way in the steadiness of her eyes. But I keep going, because Sayward being scared of me?

Unacceptable.

"I was married." I pause after those words, like I just threw a grenade into the room and am waiting for the explosion.

Sayward doesn't respond, though. She just waits, the patience rolling off of her like waves of peace that push me forward with my story.

The story that I'd rather die than tell. But if she's scared of me, I need to change that.

"My last deployment was brutal. We lost two men in our unit, and all I wanted to do was come home and hold her. We'd been together since high school, and sometimes it seemed like she was the only part of my life that saved me from total darkness. Like, the military gave me the structure and discipline I needed and wanted, but it also took me to places inside myself and in the world that I never wanted to visit."

I heave a deep breath, remembering what it was like. "When I left, I wasn't able to tell her where I'd be or how long I'd be gone. At that time, we'd been married for a couple of years and she knew the drill, but she was miserable about it. She worried and had a hard time without me while I was gone."

Standing, because I feel like I want to crawl out of my fucking skin, I pace from one side of the small living room to the other. My hands go to my hair, raking and clawing through it while I relive this pain over again like it just happened. Anger flashes hot inside, boiling and bubbling just like it did that day.

The only difference is, somewhere in the back of my mind, I know I'm here with Sayward, and that she's already scared of me. Whatever it takes, I have to control this rage that still eats me up whenever I let myself think about what happened when I came back to my house that night.

Our house.

"It took about four months to get in, complete the mission, and get out. By the time I was stateside again, I decided that instead of calling to let my wife know that I was coming, I'd surprise her. All I wanted was to wrap myself up in her again, forget about the shit show I'd just experienced. She was the thing that kept me whole, kept me together after a tough deployment. And they were all tough, Sayward.

"I walked into our town house around nine p.m. I was tired, hungry, and horny, and that wasn't a good combination. As soon as I closed the front door behind me, our dog lifted his head from where he was lying on the floor. This is gonna sound so weird, but as soon as I looked at that damn dog I knew something was off. He walked over to me, hanging his head like he was ashamed, and usually the second I walked in the door he was all over me. Jumping up and trying to lick my face and barking and shit. Not that night."

Pausing midpace, I brace my hands against the wall and lean my forehead against cool plaster. I squeeze my eyes shut. and my fingers curl into fists. I want to beat my head against the wall, beat back the memories and the feelings and the anger, but it's like a snowball rolling down a hill now. Can't stop it. It's all gonna come rushing out.

"The house was dark, which was unusual for her. She never liked being home alone at night, and she usually left every single light blazing and stayed up late. Each step I took up those stairs, Sayward, felt like one step closer to something I knew I wouldn't be able to just walk away from. I should have turned around, should have sensed the total chaos that was coming, but I didn't. I just kept going, even though something told me not to. When I opened the door to our bedroom, they were there. My wife, in *our* bed with some motherfucker I didn't even know. Sayward...that's when shit went sideways. I was filled with this sense of overwhelming betrayal. That betrayal is what set me off. It's something I learned later in counseling, but it was a trigger for me. Something inside me, probably the thing that had been tied together with nothing but a thread since I lost two of my brothers back in that hellhole, snapped. I was *shredded*. And the only thing I remember afterward is the way it felt each time my fist pummeled his flesh, each time he grunted or cried out, and even though it was making me sick I couldn't control it.

"I blacked out. And when I woke up again I was behind bars. I pled guilty to aggravated assault as soon as I found out the dude was in the hospital. I'd beaten him to within an inch of his life. I had an attorney, he tried to make me fight the charge. He said I could claim that PTSD made me do it, and hell, part of that could be the truth. But I've never been the kind of guy who runs away from the shit I do. I own up to it, and that's what I did. I was sentenced, I served my time, and I got out. First thing I did was move to another state, next to an ocean. Oceans have always made me feel calm—more steady. And then the old man, Mickey Oakes, gave me a job and here I am."

My words are muffled as they get lost against the wall my head still rests on, but I know Sayward heard me. A heavy silence blankets the room, but it's not like the kind of silence where you can feel a person judging you, blaming you, hating you. No, it's oppressive, but there's something in it that makes me believe she might get it.

Like she might get me.

Those suspicions are confirmed when I feel her small hand press against my back, her fingers kneading the tight, tense muscle at the base of my spine. Then her arms go around me, and I can feel her face pressing into my shirt. My eyes fly open, and my whole body is tight, but then I take a deep breath and relax against her.

I suck in a shuddering breath. "Remember how I said I learned something later, in counseling? Even an emotion can trigger PTSD. For me, it was feeling betrayed. On my last mission, we had an informant that we'd been working with for months. This person gave us some bad intel to save his own ass, and we didn't find out until after I'd set the explosion that was supposed to . . . kill a known terrorist leader." Getting into the specifics of this story is dicey. There's a lot she doesn't know, and will never need to know. But I need her to understand what happened to me that night, so she knows it's never going to happen again.

"Just before the building went up in flames, our sniper saw movement in one of the windows. It wasn't the terrorist, who we were told was going to be inside by himself. It was . . . " My throat closes up, with the memory. I talked about it when I was in counseling as soon as I got out of prison, but I've never shared it with anyone outside my unit. "There was a woman inside with a little boy."

My breathing is coming fast now, my chest heaving with the effort it takes to relive it, to remember what happened back in the desert that day. It changed me forever.

Her voice is barely a whisper. And it's full of emotion I've never heard from her before. Usually when Sayward speaks, it's matter-of-fact and informative. But this? This is something else.

Something *more*.

"Bennett. I'm so, so sorry. For what happened both times. On your mission...you were doing what you thought was right. You followed orders, and you didn't know that someone you'd built trust with was going to do something like that." Her voice softens, gentles even more. "You couldn't have known about that mother and child, and I understand that you carry a certain amount of guilt for it. But it wasn't your fault."

Warmth, pure and sweet and more welcome than I could have thought possible, spreads through my chest, starting in my heart. My breathing slows, the lump lodged in my throat shrinks.

"And the night you came home? You were betrayed. You were hurting, you were angry, and you had been traumatized. God, Bennett...anyone could have, would have reacted the way you did. You made a mistake...obviously putting your hands on someone is never the answer. But you owned it. You took the punishment. Do you understand how brave that was? How many men wouldn't have?"

I don't even realize I'm shaking until she squeezes me tighter. My whole fucking body quakes, lost in the collision of the memories and the way Sayward makes me feel. I haven't connected emotionally with a woman since my ex-wife, not once.

I thought I wouldn't connect with any other woman ever. My heart was torn out that day, and I swear I thought it'd never beat like this again.

But here I am, with Sayward's arms around me, and she's opening up and coming out of her shell, and damn if I don't *feel* her.

Turning around in her arms, I cup her face in my hands, staring down at her. She looks at me for only a split second before her lids flutter shut. Her bottom lip disappears into her mouth and something carnal inside me growls with need.

"Look at me, beautiful."

She doesn't move but squeezes her eyes shut tighter. Her arms are still wrapped around me, but her body is stiff and unmoving.

"Are you still scared?" I ask, my voice going lower and gruffer, but softer at the same time.

She shakes her head, the action small but determined as hell. Her voice breaks something inside me, but then it puts it back together again. From one breath to the next, this woman's changing me. "No, Bennett. I'm not afraid of you...not in the way that you think."

My thumbs caress her cheekbones, and I breathe her in. Sayward doesn't wear perfume, but she always smells so fucking sweet. It's the fruit in her shampoo, mixed with the addictive scent of her innocence.

"Then what are you scared of?"

She opens her eyes then, and I'm shot through the heart with the stark truth in her pure hazel gaze. "I'm afraid that

I'll fall. And when I fall, I'll break, Bennett. I don't know if I can put myself together again."

That's when I *know* that no matter how hard I've tried to make my life better, how hard I've tried to leave the past mistakes behind and be a better man for them, I'm still a dirty motherfucking bastard.

Because at those words, I should turn the fuck around and walk away. I should leave her alone, I should protect her like my job description describes and leave her untouched. Just the way I found her.

But I don't. Instead, I bring her face to mine and I take possession of her lips. I take, and I plunder, and I pillage. I own her mouth the same way I want to own her body. There's a fire raging inside me that I couldn't put out now even if I tried. I'm not sure what it is about this woman that has me so twisted up in goddamn knots, but there's this desperate feeling when I'm with her. I feel like the only way to untangle myself is to dig in deeper.

Farther.

Faster.

She moans against my mouth, and my cock is so fucking hard it hurts. Her hands go up, so tentative and gentle, tangling in my hair as she pulls me closer. She fuses her mouth to mine, and the heat between us threatens to burn us both alive.

But if I'm going down? Fuck...I want to go down in flames with this woman.

I lift her, feeling her legs wrap around me and I'm walking to her room before I can wise up and stop myself. This time, I lay her so fucking gently down on her bed there's no way she can mistake it for violence, and she stares up at me with an expression in her eyes bordering on thankful. Placing a knee on the mattress between her legs, I lean over her and brush my lips with hers.

So fucking gentle. The only thing she deserves, even though I'm nothing that she needs.

"This okay?" I ask against her mouth.

She nods, a small smile touching her lips. Her voice trembles. "Just sex, right?"

My body recoils, but then I hold myself still. Is she fucking kidding me? After everything I just shared with her? How can she think this will be just sex?

At this point, I know it's gonna be so much more.

But then I remember that I'm dealing with Sayward, and she doesn't process social situations the same way I do. Maybe her defense against everything that's happening between us, everything that scares her, is to deny it's even happening.

I nod without saying a word. If she wants to lie to herself, I'm not going to stop her. Not now.

But we both know damn well this isn't just sex.

This is *more.*

"Sayward... is this your first time?" I hold her gaze, needing to hear her confirm what I suspect. No matter how quickly she was willing to suck my dick, everything in me tells me she's never been fucked.

Under me, she pushes to sit up, and I pull back just enough to let her. With fire and determination and just a hint of defiance in her eyes, she confirms my suspicions with a nod, yanks at the hem of my shirt, and I grab the fabric at the back of my neck, helping her to pull it over my head. She lets her eyes travel down my chest, over my arms, around my abs, and the lust there almost glows.

She'll kill me, staring at me like that.

"Then fuck me, Bennett. Fuck me *now*."

Oh, you think it's gonna be that easy, beautiful girl? You think I'm just gonna stick my dick in you and walk away?

It takes less time than it should for me to remove her shirt and shorts, and then I'm staring down at miles of tawny, smooth skin, her hair lying in a thick crown all around her head. Her knees are bent, her hands fisted in the sheets, an incredibly vulnerable expression in her eyes that makes me ache to be worthy of it.

"Oh, I'm gonna do so much more than fuck you," I promise.

I bend down and press my lips to the slender curve of her throat as my fingers trail a gentle caress over her panties. She shudders at the same time she tenses up, and I'm learning that every time I touch her, at least at first, she's going to rebel against it.

"First with my fingers." I rub the wetness, the heat that I can feel through the soft cotton fabric between her legs, and my dick twitches in response as it revolts against my jeans.

Reaching behind her, I unclasp her bra and pull it off her body. Tossing it to the floor, I place my mouth over one tight nipple and suck. When she gasps, I release her only to lick a slow circle around the pebbled skin with my tongue. God, she tastes even sweeter than I thought she would. Teasing her is going to be so much harder than I thought.

But she needs to learn a lesson tonight, and this is the only way to teach her.

This will never be just sex.

At her gasp, I look up at her with a small smirk and lust-filled eyes. "And I'm gonna fuck you with my tongue."

Hooking my fingers into the simple, black cotton, I pull the panties down her legs and throw them aside. I palm one breast while using my tongue on the other, alternating licking and sucking and tasting until she's writhing underneath me with needy little moans floating up from her perfect mouth. I could stay right here for the rest of the night, knowing there's never been another pair of tits as perfect as these. Every kiss, every taste, I'm becoming more addicted to all things Sayward. Every part of her body I touch becomes my new favorite.

Trailing my hand back up her thigh, I drag my fingers through the shining wetness of her folds and can't hold back my own groan.

"So wet for me, baby."

There's a rough need growing more intense inside me by the second, something I never even felt with my wife. I've been turned on, I've had sex, hell I've fucked more than a handful of women since I got out of prison.

But this? Jesus, this feels like it'll kill me if I don't get inside her *right the fuck now.*

It's taking every ounce of control I have not to let this

beast loose, because I've been given an opportunity, a *privilege* here, that I refuse to squander.

But *damn* she makes me want her. Need her.

She bucks when I dip a finger inside her, and then another, before drawing them out and swirling all that heat around her clit.

"Bennett," she moans. "Oh, God..."

The fact that I get to see her like this, knowing that no other man has, it's making me feel like I could fucking fly if I tried.

My voice is thick, ragged. "And I'm going to fuck you with my dick, Sayward. I promise you all three."

Scooting down the bed, I take my first real taste of her and *holy fuck* I suddenly realize what an epic fucking mistake I've made.

I've never been addicted to anything in my life, but Sayward Diaz has just become my goddamn drug.

12

SAYWARD

*O*H, *my God.*

I tremble. I shake. I writhe in what feels like pleasurable agony. Painful ecstasy. Perfect torture. It's his words. It's his hands. It's the way he looks at me, the way it feels when he touches me. Like he knows every deep, dark fantasy I've ever had. Even the ones I never knew I was having.

And right this very second, it's his tongue.

This man could teach a college course on how to use your tongue to drive a woman completely insane.

He strokes me as he pushes two fingers inside and curves them, finding a place inside me that no one has ever touched. I want to jump out of my own body at the same time I'm forcing myself to stay, because it feels too damn good.

Touch has never felt good to me, not *ever*.

And this is touch on steroids.

"Oh, God...yes."

Wait. Yes? *Yes?*

I'm shocking the hell out of myself, but the words rolling out of my mouth aren't even a choice anymore. Just like letting this man in, letting him feel every part of me, allowing him to own a piece of me, isn't a choice anymore either.

My body has taken over, and it's shutting my mind and my good sense down completely. All I want is more of *this*.

He tastes me slowly, leisurely, but with expert dexterity that lets me know he's treating me with kid gloves. I'm like a scared rabbit to him, someone that will bolt at the first chance I get.

I have to change that.

"Bennett," I gasp, using all my energy to push up onto my elbows. My hair falls around my shoulders as I focus on him and he looks up at me with hooded lids while his tongue laps at my dripping folds like a man dying of thirst.

But it's still, oh-so-gentle. He's still holding back.

Maybe you should let him be gentle. Maybe that's what you need right now...someone who cares enough to take their time.

I flop back down on the bed as an orgasm begins to build slowly inside of me, causing my legs to tremble and my heart to shake. "I can't...I'm going to..."

I grab two fistfuls of his hair, and he hums against me. "Yeah, beautiful. Come apart for me. I've got you."

And now my eyes do roll back in my head as I climb so high I can barely breathe, and his unrelenting tongue takes me to a place I thought I'd never reach.

I fall, hoping to God he'll catch me, and the explosion rocks me to my core.

I squeeze my eyes shut, riding the wave of my own pleasure as his lips kiss me over and over again. My clit, my folds.

When I open my eyes again, Bennett is gone, but then I glance to the side and he's standing next to the bed shedding his jeans. He pushes his boxers down with them, and rolls a condom onto his erect cock. I pull in a breath because the size of him is so intimidating.

I eye him warily. But at the same time that my mind riots, my body urges me on. I *want* this, want him.

More than I've ever wanted anything.

His eyes are dark with lust and brimming with something I can't place, and he climbs back over me once the condom is situated. Cautiously, I reach down and take him in my fist.

His long lashes flutter as his jaw tightens. "Jesus, Sayward."

Guiding him toward me, I watch with fascination as his desire plays out across his face. He's so damn beautiful, even in the dark, and my hips reach out to meet him. He presses into me, just the tip, and we both gasp.

"Holy shit," I whisper just as he groans.

He goes completely still, his breathing erratic and thin, his eyelids slamming shut.

"This...is gonna hurt, okay, beautiful? Just for a second... because it's your first time."

Fear prickles the hairs on my arms, raising them. It trickles along my spine and I stare up at Bennett with caution.

He catches my chin. "Trust me?"

Trust. Something that's so hard for me to do. But Bennett just shared the most painful story in his life with me. Something changed between us tonight, and even though I'm not sure exactly what that is, I know it's something big.

I *do* trust him. I nod.

Then he takes my hand, our fingers lacing together, pinning it above my head as he thrusts into me fully for the first time.

I nod, tears stinging my eyes because the burst of pain was unpleasant, but it's already receding. Bennett holds completely still, watching me as I adjust to his fullness inside me. I can feel him stretching me, and my mind protests even as my body accepts it.

With understanding in his gaze, he bends slowly until his lips are pressed against mine. The way he kisses me, like this is so much *more* than fucking, brings a whole new set of emotions slamming to the surface. His mouth, God his *mouth* . . . it's like he's coaxing feelings from me I thought could never possibly exist.

Trying so hard to close myself off, to fight against the hold he's beginning to have over me, I force my hand free of his and grab his ass. "Move, Blacke."

His eyes flash as he pulls back, staring at me, and then he pulls out of me slowly before easing back in. I gasp, the movement feeling better than I ever could have imagined, and glance down at where we're joined. Complete and utter fascination consumes me as I watch him slide in and out of me so painfully slowly. I want to urge him to move faster, but I also want to slow this moment down so that it lasts.

He glances down, too, and his jaw is so tight I'm afraid the pulsing vein there will pop right out. He's restraining himself, and it's difficult for him. So I squeeze the perfect tautness of his ass again and fire an order.

"Fuck me, Bennett. Like you promised."

With a growl, he retreats and slams into me harder. I cry out as his cock brushes against a place inside me that makes me want to cry with the pleasure of it. I reach for that feeling again, lifting my hips to meet his now-steady thrusts, and each time he stretches deep enough to stroke that spot again, I let out a breathy scream. He reaches down, brushing adept fingers against my clit as the darkness in his eyes grows more and more intense. He stares down at me, watching my face as I chase the pleasure that he promised to bring me.

"Oh...God..." I don't even recognize that voice. Is it mine? I sound like someone who's about to break under the touch of a man.

I shouldn't want to break...but I do. God help me, I do.

It comes without warning. It's not a climb, this orgasm, it's a crash into the unforgiving wall of the man pulling my strings. I scream as I fly apart underneath him, his name and a whole bunch of other words I don't even recognize tumbling out of my mouth. Hell, I think I could be praying.

Then Bennett dips his head, burying his face against my breast as he pulls my nipple into his mouth on a groan and sucks. His rhythm grows frantic, erratic, sweat making our skin slippery and wet as our bodies slide against one another. I'm already sore, but I couldn't care less because this night is going to be something I remember for the rest of my life.

With a grunt, Bennett shudders above me, and his release flows from him as he trembles. He releases my breast, resting his forehead against mine as our breaths slow, and I realize I haven't once thought about how unbelievable it is that he's touching me since he first entered me.

With a shocked laugh, I look up at the ceiling and let out a sigh of disbelief.

"You're laughing right now?" His gruff voice is tinged with amusement. "Seriously, beautiful?"

I don't have words, so instead I pull his face to mine and kiss him like I need him to breathe.

All the while praying that I don't.

13

BENNETT

When I slide back into her bedroom from the hallway bath, I'm not surprised to see she's thrown back on her gray tank top. But her shorts are still missing, leaving those sexy, toned legs stretching out on top of the sheets as she lays in her simple black panties.

I pause in the doorway, staring at her as I lean against the doorjamb. "So fucking sexy."

Her cheeks color, that pretty blush that makes my dick go stiff every time I see it. Reaching for my boxers, I pull them on right before climbing onto the bed beside her. Pulling her against me, I drop a kiss onto the top of her head.

"This okay?" I whisper.

But somehow, I know it is. Her body doesn't go rigid and stiff the way it usually does when she's touched.

She rests her head on my shoulder, and her finger traces shapes on my chest. "Yes."

"Good."

She chuckles softly. "That was...I don't even know how to describe that. I thought...is everyone's first time that good?"

I rear back. "You think that was just *good*?"

And there's the color in her cheeks again. "*Good* isn't the right word. It was...stellar."

Rolling my eyes toward the ceiling, I laugh, low and deep. "It *was* fucking stellar, wasn't it? And no, baby. I don't think everyone's first time is stellar."

She follows the lines her finger traces on my skin. "Didn't think so."

We just lie there for a while, quiet. Lost in our own thoughts. Then I wrap my arm around her. Resting my chin on top of her head, I breathe in the sweet scent of her. "How are you doing, Sayward? Dealing with your father's death? I know it hit you hard. I figure it doesn't matter how far away you are from him, your dad was your dad."

She shrugs, staying silent. Pulling away from her slightly, I tip her chin up so I can read the expression on her face. She keeps it shuttered, but her breathing hitches, and I know that her pain is real and very close to the surface.

"Hey," I whisper, staring into her eyes. "You can talk to me."

"It does." She breathes, blinking rapidly. "It does hurt. He was always protecting me, you know? Even when he was an ocean away."

I smooth her hair back and pull her even closer. "Yeah. That's what fathers do. That's what mine did, and he was oceans away a lot of the time when I was growing up. I always knew he loved me and my mom, though."

She nods, nestling into me. "Yes. I always knew my father loved me, too."

My fingers brush against her lower back where I know her tattoo is hidden.

"Tell me about this?"

She rolls onto her stomach, and I reach over to turn on the lamp beside her bed. When the dim light washes over her, illuminating more of her body than the one from the hall-way had, all the breath in my body leaves.

She's so damn gorgeous it hurts. It physically hurts me to look at her. My dick is stiff and aching, there's a sharp pain in my chest, and my throat burns from all the things I want to say and can't. It's too soon to feel like this about her. If I take this any further than I already have tonight, she'll run.

And seeing as how I don't feel like chasing her, I keep my mouth shut.

Instead, I drop my eyes to the ink scrawled out on her hip. It's intricate work, done by a fucking brilliant artist.

Sayward's tattoo is a shield. It carries the emblem of a cross, and the whole thing is surrounded by pale pink flow-ers. There're initials in script across one corner of the shield.

Tracing her skin with my finger the way she'd just done mine, I swallow hard as I take in the sight.

"Brilliant," I whisper, as I bend down to kiss that spot on her hip.

Her head twisting to one side, she glances up at me. "Yeah? Those are my mother's initials."

I nod, because I already knew it without her telling me.

She takes a shaky breath. "The memories from that

night . . . they're kind of hazy, you know? And, like you, I try not to go back there. But when I do, all I can remember is how brave she was. She would have done anything to protect her children that night."

My throat tightens. This woman . . . she's so much braver than she knows. She has no idea how strong she is, how fucking resilient she is. She's overcome so much to become this amazing woman lying beside me, but does she realize how incredible she is?

Somehow, I don't think she has a clue.

Switching the light off again, I stretch out beside her.

"You want me back on the couch tonight, beautiful? Just say the word."

One of her arms snakes around my stomach and tightens.

"No," she whispers. "I want you right here. With me."

Thank fuck.

This is exactly where I want to be.

14

SAYWARD

I drop into my chair across from Marcos the next day, offering my brother a small smile. The lunch crowd at the busy sidewalk café bustles around us, a relaxed atmosphere that hangs on the edge of excitement in the sunny beach community. Even though the tourists don't frequent Wilmington this time of year, you still can't mistake the vacation vibe the city has to offer.

Marcos doesn't return my smile; instead, he scowls. "What's he doing here?"

I glance at Bennett, who's taken up residence in the seat beside me. His steady gaze returns Marcos's head-on. "Nice to see you, too, Marcos. Did you forget what I told you yesterday? My job is to protect your sister. She's not going anywhere without me."

His voice, though, is different than it was yesterday. There's a harder protective edge to it that wasn't there before, a distinct hint of possession that lets anyone in his way know that in order to get to me they'll have to go through him. At the same time the steely blade of his voice disquiets me, it also covers my insides in warmth.

Safety. Protection. Security.

Those are all things I have when Bennett is with me, and other than when I've been with Jacob Owen, I haven't felt that way in so long. My chest aches as I think of the way Bennett was with me last night. He was tender and careful, but there was so much unleashed passion vibrating inside him while his body moved over mine. A hot flush creeps over my skin as I frown at Marcos.

"Marcos. I haven't seen you in years. Please don't waste our time being confrontational. I'm happy you're here."

His gaze flicks toward me, and there's regret there. "I'm sorry, *chica*. How are you today?"

Relief settles in. "I'm fine. Thanks for asking. Did you sleep well?"

Because I sure as hell did. I hadn't told Bennett, but last night was the first time I'd slept beside anyone since my mother died. I'd fallen asleep in his arms, my breathing slowing to match his, and even though it had felt odd and foreign, there had been no mistaking the fact that it'd also felt *good*. Right.

But when I'd opened my eyes this morning, my bed had been empty. Disappointment had settled over me like a heavy blanket, and I was a little sad when I'd found him sitting on the couch with a cup of coffee, his makeshift bed there wrinkled and mussed with the evidence of his sleep location.

He easily read the look on my face with a lifted brow. "I wanted to give you space."

His explanation was simple. He'd done it for me, left my bed and returned to the couch sometime during the night. All because he knew I wasn't exactly comfortable with his closeness.

The funny thing? He was wrong. I was way more comfortable with it than I ever thought I could be.

"The hotel was nice." Marcos's tone is reluctant as he glances back at Bennett. "Thanks."

Bennett dips his chin in a nod. "No problem."

A server appears and we order sandwiches for lunch, but when the waiter's gone an uncomfortable silence settles over the table. I wish I could figure out how to connect with the brother I've been separated from for years, but I can't seem to catch my footing when I'm around him.

This man is my blood, but I don't know him. And he doesn't know me.

Years of no contact with my family has left my brother a mere stranger to me. I know that Jacob updated my father on how I was doing over the years, but both men agreed that it'd be best and safest for me if I stayed away from my family completely. I'm guessing Marcos found me through information Jacob shared with my father.

"So what is your life like in Colombia?" I blurt the question out and then press my lips together, wishing I had a little finesse.

But I've never had that. If there's a thought swimming through my head, a question sitting on the tip of my tongue, it erupts in words I can't pull back. That's how it's always been.

But Marcos doesn't seem offended by my question. Instead he smiles. But it's tinged with a hint of sadness that I don't understand. Maybe that's just the curse that will always follow our family. *Happiness is an inevitable part of life, but for us, will it always come at a price?*

"I have a simple life, but a good one, *hermanita*. I took over our father's little construction company about three years ago, so that he could retire. I have taken the business a little further than he did. And I married the girl I fell in love with when we were in *escuela*." At his last words his face breaks into a true grin.

Joy blooms in my heart, a flower that settles happily among the weeds. "That's amazing."

"And," he continues, drawing the word out. "We have a son. He's three years old."

God... I have a nephew? My heart, already so splintered, cracks just a little bit more. *And I haven't even met him?*

Under the table, sudden pressure on my hand has my eyes skirting toward Bennett. He's staring down at me, understanding and compassion flooding his expression. He squeezes my hand that he's now holding in his lap, and I'm confronted with the fact that his presence grounds me even when my heart rocks with turmoil.

How did this happen so fast? How did I allow it?

I shoot him a grateful smile before looking back at my brother. "That's...wow, Marcos. I'm happy for you."

Even though I don't think it's something I'll ever get to

experience, not with all the ways I'm different, I recognize the importance of it. Family... the unit that could complete a person, make them feel like nothing else could ever be missing. I see that happiness in Marcos, value its worth.

But then something in his eyes darkens, shifts, and the happiness that was just reflecting out at me is tarnished. *He looks... what? Distraught? That's the best word for it... but I can't understand why.*

"Yeah," he whispers. "I can't wait until you meet them."

My throat clogs and my chest hurts. "Me neither, Marcos."

My brother's expression softens, and I'm aware of how much it hurts, how much I've missed my family. Those kinds of emotions are usually hidden underneath all the ways I'm different from other people, but I can feel them now, bubbling to the surface and making me weaker than I've ever been.

I've always felt so isolated, being apart from the rest of my family. Being sent away immediately after my mother's death, even though I knew it was for my own safety. Those feelings of solitude never really went away. It didn't matter that it's my nature to separate myself. It still hurt, a deep aching pain in my heart that was always there.

Hearing that I have more family, and that I've been missing out on everything that has to do with them, cuts me so deeply that it's hard to take a breath.

Is this what feeling like this does to people? Takes away their strength? If that's true, I don't want any of it. Not the feelings, not the emotions... none of it.

I release Bennett's hand like I've been touching something hot. Like I've been burned.

My head whips to the side as something whizzes past me. The air around me, which previously felt so open and warm, now chills me to the bone with impending danger. I don't know where the feeling comes from...maybe my instincts telling me. But I'm already moving when Bennett's yell rips through the air.

"Sayward! *Get down!*"

A funny, heart-stopping *whoosh*ing sound affects the air around my ears, and I gasp as I slide from my seat, Bennett's hand pushing me down as I drop to the ground.

15

BENNETT

I can *feel* it when the air shifts, rips, around us.

The sound of the bullet wouldn't sound like a gunshot to most people. But I know what a gun fitted with a silencer sounds like, and cold dread mixes with precision, experienced training as my body shoots into action.

When the first bullet whizzes by, millimeters away from Sayward's head, my muscles move without me telling them to. I shove her down, too hard, but I need her safe. Somewhere in the back of my mind, I know it's a damn miracle that she wasn't hit by the first bullet.

As soon as she's flat on her stomach under the table I yell for Marcos to get down and then pull my gun from its sheath at my hip. The tables filled with lunch patrons around us buzz with confusion, and I glance at one of them.

"Shots fired," I snap. "Call the police!"

There are startled cries and screams as the other patrons scatter, but I note one man yanking out his phone as he disappears inside the restaurant, and I know that the WPD will be on their way.

My head swivels as my eyes scan every inch of the sidewalk in both directions, searching for the shooter. Then they rise, looking for a point high enough for someone to aim down to the sidewalk where we're sitting. Sirens lift into the air in the distance.

"Dammit!" Not finding any source of a shooter with my gaze, all I want to do is use my legs, searching every inch of the street until I find him.

He shot at her. Red-tinged haze fills my vision and I want to roar from the feel of it exploding inside my chest. What the hell? We weren't expecting to run into trouble, if any, until we arrived in Colombia next week. Who the fuck is shooting at Sayward on a sidewalk in North Carolina?

I make one last sweep with my gaze before dropping down to a knee on the sidewalk. Sayward glances up at me, her eyes filled with fear.

And *goddamn*, the sight of her terrified face tugs at my chest, rips into my heart in a way I haven't felt in so long it's almost foreign.

A police SUV pulls up to the curb just as I pull Sayward into my arms. Two uniformed officers climb out. Glancing at one of them, I gesture toward Sayward.

"She's the intended target. Help me surround her so I can get her inside."

Together with the officers and Marcos, we use our bodies to shield Sayward until she's sitting at a table inside the restaurant, her skin paler than normal and her eyes wide with shock.

I kneel beside her chair. "Baby, can you sit right here with Marcos for a minute, so I can tell the officers what just happened outside?"

She blinks down at me, and then a fierce determination almost pushes the fear entirely out of her eyes.

So damn brave.

She nods, and I brush my thumb across her cheekbone before rising to my feet and striding toward the officers standing close to the front of the restaurant. I check over my shoulder to make sure I can still see Sayward. Having her out of my sight right now isn't an option.

A surge of protectiveness flares up inside me. It's tied to Sayward, and a flashing light goes off in my head. Warning me. Threatening me.

Reminding me that feelings like this don't lead to anything good. Not for me. The last time I cared about a woman? That shit almost broke me. Blinded me. Drove me to a place where rage ran free, and I never want to go back there.

Never again.

But when Sayward's big, gorgeous eyes lift to meet mine, I know there's no way in hell I'm walking away from her.

Quickly, I relay the events of the past few minutes to the officers, one of whom whips out a pen and a pad and jots down notes as I talk. When Jacob walks in the door, basically carrying a thundercloud above his head, his expression more than pissed, I prepare myself for him to unleash.

"What the hell happened? Friend at the department let me know there was a situation and that one of my men was involved. Why didn't you call me?" His words are ground between gritted teeth, his eyes scanning the restaurant until he finds Sayward sitting with Marcos.

I put my hands on my hips and drop my head, taking a breath before I meet his gaze head-on. "We were eating lunch outside. Shots fired, I got Sayward on the ground. She's not hit. I haven't had a chance to call you, boss. This just happened in the last fifteen minutes. I had to get Sayward inside and situated, and I've just been explaining the events to the cops."

His expression loses a little of its venom. "Dammit! Was anyone outside hurt when shots were fired?"

Shaking my head, I glance around us. "Don't think so."

Jacob sighs, running a hand over his hair. "Thought she'd be safe, at least until we got to South America."

Nodding, I glance at Sayward, who's watching us talk. "Yeah, I thought so, too. Looks like trouble found her here."

He curses again, and then gets on his cell. He barks out an order to whoever is on the other end of the line. I'm guessing it's Abbott. "I'll be back in the office with Sayward and Bennett in ten. Make sure you're all ready to meet us in the conference room."

When he ends the call, he looks at me with a grim expression. "We need to figure out how to keep her safe until next week. If I had my way, I'd make damn sure she doesn't go anywhere until whoever just tried to kill her is caught. But it's not up to me. If she needs to pay her respects to her father, I won't stop her."

"If I'd seen the shooter, I would have taken him out. And if I'd known those shots were coming, I would have thrown myself in front of her. You get that, right? But a fucking sniper? I wasn't expecting that. What the hell's going on?"

Jacob shakes his head, cool determination gleaming in his dark blue eyes. "That's what we're going to find out."

"I'm still going."

Sayward's tone is adamant, her expression stubborn as she glares around at every member of the team sitting at the table. "No one is going to stop me from going to the service for my father."

A vein pulses at Jacob's temple, and I can feel my own blood pressure rising. Neither one of us wants her anywhere near fucking Colombia. But no one at the office knows how personal my stake is in it now.

Jacob grits out: "I told you I wouldn't stop you, Sayward. But these people are dangerous. You understand that, right? The cartel wants you dead."

She spreads her arms wide as her eyes narrow. "Then let them try. I have all of you looking out for me. And they're *here.* Apparently it doesn't matter if I go to Colombia or not. They've already found me."

After seeing Marcos into a car headed back to his hotel, Sayward and I had a quiet ride over to the NES building in my truck. She'd stared out the window, her teeth digging into her bottom lip while I drove. I knew there wasn't anything I could say that would get through to her then, but I sure as hell wasn't going to sit here silently now.

"Yeah, how do we think that happened? She's been hidden here for *years*, right?" Sayward's gaze snaps to mine.

I soften my tone, knowing this isn't going to be easy for her to hear. "What's changed in the past few days?"

The room goes silent, the air thick and heavy with the implication I just laid out there. But knowing the guys on this team, I'm not the only one who's thought of it.

Finally, Jacob speaks. He keeps his gaze leveled at Sayward as he does. "Marcos."

Her chair scraping on the polished concrete floor, Sayward stands. Her palms slam down on the table, and her hazel eyes flash with barely restrained anger. This side of Sayward? I've never seen it. Usually her emotions are in check; she's reserved and focused on whatever she's working on.

But right now, her voice rises as her anger swirls around her. Around all of us. My chest clenches tight with her pain.

"You think Marcos brought them here? He's my *brother*!"

She slaps her hands down once more for emphasis and levels her glare straight at me.

My phone buzzes in my pocket, but I ignore it.

I face her, because it doesn't matter if she's pissed. I'll take her pissed and raise her a "madder than hell." I place my palms on the table and lean forward as I stand. Matching her on every level. My emotions roil and churn, and I swallow hard before I speak.

"Marcos is your brother, yes. But you haven't seen him in years, right? Sayward . . . you have no idea what he's been doing in that time. Hell, he could be a member of the cartel by now!"

She sucks in a breath, her chest rising and falling as she flinches, like I've slapped her. We stare one another down, the tension in the room pulling taut between us like a rope about to snap into pieces. Finally, Conners clears his throat.

"You know what? If Marcos has had a hand in this, that's something we can figure out. What we need to do right now is find out how we're going to keep Sayward safe until all this shit is handled."

I stiffen, my eyes cutting toward Conners. "I *will* keep her safe. That's not a question."

The ex-Ranger's brows lift as he stares me down. "Like you did today?"

A growl rumbles inside my chest, deep and sharp and dangerous. Because I'll be *damned* if he's gonna question my desire or my ability to keep Sayward secure.

Abbott places a hand on Dare's chest, giving him a warning glance before turning my way. "She can't go back to her apartment. They probably know exactly where she lives."

I remember what it felt like when I stepped onto Sayward's back patio yesterday. I knew there were eyes out there. I should have listened to my instincts, shouldn't have let it go.

"She can come home with me." The words are out of my mouth before I can stop them, and when I register what I said, I don't even care.

Whatever it takes. As long as Sayward is out of the line of fire I know I'll do whatever it takes to keep her safe.

Jeremy grins, a knowing expression turning his mouth up while Conners frowns and Abbott studies me. Ronin's eyes are on me, too. And I can feel Jacob's stare, just as sure as if it were burning a hole into my shirt.

"You sure about that?" asks Ronin, his lip twitching at the corner. "*I've* never even seen your place."

That's because it's a shoe-box-size, one-bedroom beach bungalow. It's all I could afford after I moved here and started working at the bar. The rent is cheap because if there's a job to be done around the house I do it myself, and it's way too small for guests. Up until this very minute I never had any intention of having someone over.

"I'm sure."

When I look at Sayward, her eyes blaze with something I can't read. But I recognize it because I saw the exact same look in her eyes last night while I hovered above her.

"You don't have to do that." The words fall off her lips like something broken. And it has my spine straightening, my jaw tightening.

"I *will* keep you safe. You're coming home with me. And that's where you'll stay until we go to Colombia."

And I realize I mean every fucking word.

Which means I'm in more danger than the drug cartel could possibly bring into my own backyard. This is a matter of the heart, and that's so much more deadly where I'm concerned.

16

SAYWARD

The entire team agreed it wouldn't be smart to go back to my place at all. So Bennett drives me to Target when we leave NES and I prepare myself to engage in the one activity I hate more than anything else in the entire world.

Shopping.

We walk in the doors and Bennett veers toward a shopping cart. "Guessing you'll need one of these."

I just stop, frozen in the bright, shining front lobby. Because I'm watching Bennett Blacke, tattoos and scruff and oozing sex appeal pull a red plastic shopping cart from the queue.

When he catches me staring, I force my mouth closed and make a beeline for the women's clothing section.

Without a word, and definitely without trying anything on, I grab two hoodies, two V-neck T-shirts, and two pairs of jeans. Tossing them in the cart, I turn toward Bennett.

"I'm ready to grab pajamas and toiletries."

He leans onto the front of the cart, his face creasing into lines of pure amusement. Leaning on his elbows, he doesn't budge.

"Hey, Sayward?"

"What?" I frown, glancing around because maybe I forgot something.

"I'm gonna call the Guinness book people." He pulls out his phone and proceeds to look something up.

Confusion pulls me closer to him. And a prickle of irritation deepens my frown. "What?"

He doesn't look up, his thick finger scrolling along his screen. "You know...because I think you just set the record for 'fastest female shopper.'"

Realization that he's teasing me dawns, my mouth pulling into a smile before I can stop it. Then I slap his arm.

Hard.

He laughs, but rubs the spot like he's trying to humor me.

Asshole.

"Asshole!"

His full, full lips stretch over straight white teeth as he smirks. Then he pulls me into his side.

Dipping his head toward my ear, his whisper drags a shiver down my back. "You like it."

Shopping has never been fun, but it's almost enjoyable when I'm with Bennett. It's not lost on me, though, alert as he is, that he's also hypervigilant. His eyes miss nothing as they scan the aisles, his body is taut and coiled. Ready to spring. He moves like he's full of pent-up energy that he'd be only too happy to use if necessary.

Thanks to my shopping skills, or lack thereof, I'm done in under twenty minutes, and as Bennett walks me to his truck, he keeps one hand on the shopping cart while the other arm rests on my shoulders.

And I don't realize until afterward that I never once wished he wasn't touching me.

I don't know what I expected. I never really thought about where Bennett rests his head at night. Every time I think of him, I think of him at The Oakes. Like he permanently resides behind a bar. Seeing him all up in my space at NES definitely messed with my head, but now? This? Seeing him in his own space, with his own things?

It's blowing my mind, sending me into a tailspin of wonderings.

Bennett lives in a one-bedroom bungalow across the street from the ocean. I know that it not being backed up to sand, not to mention it size, make it more affordable. Looking around, I can see the place isn't completely updated, either. The style could be considered rustic, with worn furnishings and older fixtures. But the first thing that shoots through me when I walk in the door is a sense of peace. A feeling of contentment.

A sense of *home.*

Pausing just inside the threshold, I try to remember the last time I felt this way. My legs tremble, my mind spinning and whirling as I try to catch up to the emotion slamming into me. A sigh escapes as I try to gain control over my feelings, find my footing in unfamiliar waters.

Noticing my hesitation, Bennett turns back to face me, one eyebrow lifted. "You good?"

Sucking in a deep lungful of air, I move forward, away from the door at my back. Bennett stretches to close it behind me, his warmth trickling over me as he stands close.

Suddenly, I'm crawling with nerves. I try to slam my mind shut against them, try to keep them out and hold them back but it's no use. I remember all the ways Bennett and I were close last night, all the ways he touched me, how he made me *feel*, and I can't beat back the fluttery wings of the butterflies inhabiting my stomach if I tried.

Arms laden with my bags, he places them down on the couch and cocks his head to the side as he studies me. "So, this is it. Casa de Blacke."

My lips quirk upward at his fake Spanish accent, my heart forgetting for just a second how out of place I feel, before I turn curious eyes on his home. My heart takes flight, beating faster in my chest because... *this place.*

White bead board walls cover three sides, while the last wall, the one facing the ocean, is nothing but windows. And one large sliding glass door. Glancing up, I note the natural wood ceiling, vaulted in the center, the thick beams stretching from one end of the little house to the other. The same natural wood color covers the floor, wide planks shining faintly up at me all around the room. There's a navy-blue couch with two small metal tables in front of it and a ladder leading up. When I stand at the bottom, I can peer up and see a tiny loft space above.

When the big sliders are open, I can only imagine the

ocean breeze that'll sweep right through the entire area. I can see straight through to the kitchen, all open shelving and one long stainless peninsula lined with two barstools.

This place.

"It's...it's perfect, Bennett." When I glance at him, his eyebrows pull together and his lips pull into a pleased grin.

"Yeah? You like it?"

Shaking my head with vehemence, I disagree. "No. I love it."

It's only the truth, but Bennett chuckles. His eyes flare with warmth as he glances around. "Thanks. It was a rundown dump when I bought it. That's the only reason I could afford it. Had to put most of the work in myself, but Mickey helped out some."

I gesture around the space, disbelief coloring my tone. "You did this? Yourself?"

He shrugs. "My father was good with his hands, and we used to do projects together around the house when he wasn't deployed."

I frown. "But your best subject in school must have been chemistry. The way you work with explosives...it's innate and intuitive. You're a natural when it comes to things like that, too."

He studies me from across the room, the same way I'm studying him. Suddenly, I'm hyperaware of how all-encompassing he is. The way he stands, like he commands everything around him, even when he's completely relaxed. The way his eyes focus so intently, like he sees more than most people in any situation. The way his lips tug into a charming smirk at will, like he knows exactly how to make a person sell their soul.

I have no doubt about the last one, and the thought leaves me breathless.

Weariness and wariness start to creep into my bones. The entire day's events start to play back like a movie, and I squeeze my eyes shut to fight against the images. The thoughts. The fears.

They don't know my brother. Family, blood, is a bond that can never be broken. There's no way Marcos had anything to do with the cartel's attempt on my life.

If Marcos is guilty of anything at all, it's leading the cartel to my doorstep. But that's something he did without knowing it.

I press my hands to my head, trying to keep the chaos at bay. My hands tremble against my skin.

Then Bennett is there, his strong, hard body pressing against mine as his big hands wrap around my wrists to pull them away from my face.

"Shhh, beautiful...it's okay. It's okay. I've got you." His voice is soft but rough, soothing but stimulating, existing in the space between what makes sense and what doesn't.

I heave a deep, calming breath. But it's like the air doesn't ever reach my lungs. It's not enough. I try again, and it seems like I'm taking in less air than the last breath. "I can't..."

Panic engulfs me like a field of flames, licking at my senses and crippling my limbs.

Bennett's arms circle around me, dragging me against

him as he pulls me onto the couch. He forms a solid place for me to land, cradling me to his chest and stroking my hair. One hand lands on my cheek, forcing me to look up into the endless depth of his eyes.

"Look at me, baby. You need to focus on breathing, okay? One breath at a time. Ready?"

I nod, eyes wide, still gasping in shallow breaths.

"Here we go, Sayward. In..." Bennett's tone is commanding, firm. I have no choice but to follow his directions.

I breathe in, and just the tiniest bit of air travels into my lungs. But it feels like the first sip of water after a trip across the desert.

"Good girl. Now let it out. Now breathe in again."

His voice, soft and safe, leading me away from the dark and into the light. I've had a panic attacks before, but I'll never get used to the ache in my chest that comes with them. Bennett rests his forehead against mine, his breaths mixing with my own.

"That happen often?" He strokes my hair.

Shaking my head, I just focus on the scent of him. Leather, ocean, and musk. It comforts me in a way nothing ever has.

"No... it's just been a very unsettling day, Bennett."

One side of his mouth lifts in a humorless smile. "Yeah. I'd have to agree with you there. You scared?"

My answer is just a whisper. But it's the truth. "Yes."

"I'm not gonna lie to you, beautiful. You should be. This is the cartel we're talking about, and they tried to kill you today." His voice wavers the tiniest bit on those words. "You should be wary. But you should also know that I'll die before I let anything happen to you. You get that?"

Shock rolls through my belly, freeing a horde of butterflies and making me swallow against the lump rising to my throat. "Why? Why would you do that for me?"

I'm nobody. That's how I've always liked it.

Bennett doesn't even hesitate. "It's my job. But even if it wasn't . . . you're worth it."

We stay like that, our skin touching, his arms wrapped around me, my hands pressed against his chest. I don't doubt him. But it doesn't stop me from wondering how this happened. How does a man who looks like Bennett end up here with a woman like me?

Slowly, turning my head slightly, I press my lips to the hot skin of his neck. I kiss him softly before shifting to another spot and dropping another kiss. Inhaling, I slide my mouth up to his ear and pull the lobe into my mouth, sucking softly. He tastes so good, like everything I've ever wanted but have never been brave enough to take.

Bennett goes still under me, his voice a rough scrape of words as he speaks. *"Sayward."*

It's a warning, a caution to go slow, to stop even, but I ignore it completely. I run my tongue along the shell of his ear, feeling the evidence of his arousal rising under my hip, pressing against my flesh, as his fingers dig into me. My hands find their way under his shirt, pressing against rock-hard muscle that jerks beneath my touch.

"Fucking hell, baby. What are you doing to me?"

Bennett's growl is cut off abruptly as he grips the back

of my neck and captures my mouth in his. His lips form to mine, his tongue licking at the seam of my mouth. I open eagerly for him, moaning at the feel of his tongue stroking against mine. He explores my mouth with a purpose I've never experienced.

He tilts his head to the side, deepening the kiss, and I shift so that I'm straddling his lap and pressing my chest flush against his. I can't get close enough. It's like now that I've let him in, let him peek past my walls, all I can do is hold on and pray I'm not making the biggest mistake of my life. All of my old aversions are there, my fear is real, but with Bennett I'm able to fight past all of it. I want to cling to that safety line he's thrown, reel myself in until I'm home for good.

All my life I've had trouble understanding other people. I'm fluent in two languages, but I've always felt like a foreigner. I don't comprehend the subtle nuances that come with social and cultural interactions, and it's hindered me in one way or another for as long as I can remember. But being with Bennett is like transcending all the languages. All the barriers are down, and it's like breathing for the very first time.

I don't want it to end.

My fingers play in the soft hair at the back of his neck, while his hands run up my back, taking my shirt with them. He tosses it away, making quick work of my bra until both of his hands are cupping my breasts. I drop my head back and let out a strangled cry.

"Your body...fuck, Sayward. You're amazing. Do you

know how goddamn lucky I feel to be the only one who gets to see you?"

He dips his head and takes one pert nipple into his mouth, sucking hard. My hips grind against his cock straining against his jeans and a low rumble of approval sounds in his throat.

A volcano of desire erupts inside me as my body remembers the release it experienced last night. My hips rock against his as the ache between my thighs becomes almost unbearable, and Bennett switches from one breast to the other. I'm spilling out of his hands, my curves being something I've never been bold enough to explore and appreciate. I'm the first girl to throw on jeans and a hoodie, because I've never even considered showing off the toned, shapely body I know is underneath.

But with Bennett? Every fear, every instinct I've ever had to hide turns into pride and a sense of profound sexiness I never even knew was possible.

With one hand, he reaches down and flicks the button on my jeans just as I grip the hem of his shirt and yank it up. He rips the garment over his head and I slide from his lap and onto my knees on the floor in front of him.

His hands stroking my bare shoulders, he watches me with heavy-lidded eyes as I undo the button on his jeans and slide down his zipper.

"Are you going to stop me this time?" I'm dead serious, but he smiles as he looks down at me.

"Not on your life."

He lifts his hips so I can help him out of his jeans and

boxer-briefs, and I lose my breath at the sight of his thick erection standing at attention before me. Licking my lips, because *this* is something I know I can do and do well, I slide my hands up rock-hard thighs and hear his intake of breath as I take just the tip of him into my mouth.

Fisting him in both hands, I stroke upward as I lick his head, and a muttered curse rolls from his mouth as his hips lift almost in sync with my slow strokes. I find the bulging vein that runs along the side of his shaft and trace it with my tongue, loving the way his hands fist in my hair and tug.

Sucking Bennett off isn't methodical or analytical for me. It's not just something that has to be done. I'm getting something out of this, too; my body is practically humming with the waves of desire rolling from me. Every time Bennett groans or grunts, every time his hands tighten in my hair I'm sent into another tailspin of rocketing need and want.

I glance up into his eyes, my mouth full of him, and the expression there sends my heart into a frenzy inside my chest. He's darkness and light in one, and I'm helplessly, hopelessly drawn to him, a doomed moth to the flickering flame.

"Come here," he grinds out, his eyes flashing with lust and something else entirely. "I need to be inside you when I come."

He pulls me onto the couch and is across the room grabbing his wallet off the counter before I can take a breath.

When he's back, a condom covering him, his eyes meet mine and his tone gentles. "I want to take you from the back, Sayward. I want to see that perfect ass in the air while I drive into you. That okay?"

There's a rough edge to his question, but I know it's from desire, not from violence. The words send a dark shiver running through me, and I catch a breath. "Yes."

He bends, kissing me deep while his hands rove over the ass he seems to like so much, before he pulls back and turns me to face the end of the couch. He presses down on my back, urging me to bend over. I do, my forearms sinking into the soft blue cushion. Then I feel him bending over me, his entire torso warming the skin of my back and the darkest corners of my heart. He's so much bigger than me, his body swallows me whole and I should feel afraid.

But I don't. Not anymore. Not now that I know him.

His whisper in my ear is low, rough, but the stroke of his hands on my skin is tender.

"Still can't believe you don't know how gorgeous you are. The sight of you like this?" The hard tip of his cock nudges my ass just before he drags it through my dripping wet folds. My moan is almost lost in the cushions as I push back eagerly against him. *God, I want this. I want* him.

"You're fucking perfect."

Then Bennett takes my hips in his firm grasp and yanks me back against him as he buries himself deep inside me.

This man is going to ruin me.

17

BENNETT

She feels more than perfect. She feels like fucking *heaven* when I'm inside her. Like I'm sliding *home*.

Her long dark hair, streaked with brilliant red, is piled up on top of her head in a messy bun. But fuck that shit. Reaching up, I pull out the band and it all comes tumbling down around her shoulders. She gasps as I slide out of her and rock right back in, feeling her wet heat tighten and clench around me. My eyes almost roll back in my head.

"Damn, girl. You...Jesus Christ." The words are nothing but nonsense, I know that, and I can't do shit about it.

I knew Sayward was closed off when I met her. I could see it in her eyes, tell from her body language that there was something going on there no one would be able to penetrate. But when I started spending time with her...something shifted. I could see glimpses of who she was beneath the walls, and behind the screen of the autism. Her mind is brilliant, but her soul? It's even brighter.

Maybe I'm a bastard for letting her open up to me, for forcing down those walls that she took so long to build. Especially when I know I'm not the man who deserves her. Especially when she's grieving. I'm not the man who can give her the happily-ever-after every woman wants. I thought I had that once, and it slipped through my fingers. I don't know if I'll ever be able to get back to that place. There was a time, not long before this, that I thought it'd be impossible.

But being here with Sayward like this right now...she's reaching someplace deep inside me I thought I had shut down years ago. My chest tightens as I continue to fuck her, my cock finding that spot deep inside her that will make her come apart in my hands.

Bending my knees with each thrust, I start a rhythm that's going to be the fucking end of me and her. My palms find her breasts and I roll the puckered nipples between my fingers, biting down hard on my bottom lip just to keep from asking her to fucking marry me.

Because that would be ridiculous, but the thought of being allowed to sink inside her every single day for the rest of my life sounds really fucking good right now.

"Oh, God...*please*, Bennett." Her words are strangled, and I bend over her to speak in her ear.

"Please...what? What do you need from me, baby?" I'm toying with her, testing her to see how she reacts. *Is she gonna be able to play? Or will she revert to throwing those walls back up?*

Her answer is quick and in such a matter-of-fact, Sayward Diaz kind of tone, it makes me freeze midstroke. "I want you to fuck me harder, and touch me until I come." The only thing that lets me know she's close to falling apart is the breathiness of her tone.

Fucking. Hell.

This woman.

Gripping her hips with one hand, sinking my fingers into her heated flesh, I snake the other around until my fingers are playing in her folds. She gasps, pushing back against me as she glances over her shoulder. Her hair is all over the place, her eyes are so fucking bright I swear there are stars swimming in them. She steals my goddamned breath, and there's no way I'm ready for any of what this woman brings to my life.

She lifts a brow, urging me on, and I growl. Pulling out for just a second, I slam home. She cries out, her eyes squeezing shut and heavy pants of pleasure escaping her parted lips.

"Bennett!" she screams.

My thumb presses down hard on her clit, and she flies to pieces. Right here in my arms. All I can do as I watch her is think about what a lucky motherfucker I am. And then I follow her over the edge, groaning my own release into the side of her neck right before she collapses onto the couch.

I stay flattened against her for too long, probably giving her too much of my weight. But it feels so *damn good* being pressed up against her. Her tight body touching as much of mine as possible. Feeling the heat of her skin sinking all the way down to my soul.

Eventually, I retreat to take care of the condom in the bathroom off the living room before returning and scooping her into my arms. Settling back onto the couch with

Sayward against my chest, here in my house, I can't remember the last time shit felt so right in my life.

Maybe this is temporary, but I'm sure as hell gonna enjoy the ride while it lasts.

Neither one of us speaks. It's like we don't need the words to describe what just happened. I listen to her breaths and I know she can hear my heart pumping in my chest as I struggle to calm down. To get my shit together. To separate my thrashing spirit from her calm one.

She traces an absentminded circle on my chest, and I try so damn hard to hide the shiver that rockets through me at her touch. *What the hell is this? What's she doing to me?*

"You hungry?" I tilt my head down so I can look her in the eye.

She meets mine with only a little hesitation, and the thought makes me happy. It wasn't long ago that she never met my gaze.

She nods. "Yes. But I'm also worried."

I stroke her hair. "You don't need to be worried right now, beautiful. I got you."

She shakes her head. "No, it's not worry for myself. I'm worried about Marcos. Bennett, I know he would never intentionally hurt me. He was on that sidewalk today, too. What if he's not safe?"

I swallow a sigh. She's worried about a man I know in my gut is keeping something from her. From all of us. There's something he's not saying, and I'm gonna make damn sure I find out. The Colombian drug cartel hanging out in my city, shooting up these streets, targeting *this* woman?

It's not okay with me.

"He *is* safe. Jacob sent an NES man to keep watch outside his hotel room door tonight, remember?"

Her troubled gaze searches my face before she sits up. I watch as she stands, allowing my eyes to rove the miles of bronzed skin just begging to be touched again, and try not to groan with disappointment as she puts on her clothes.

"I need to talk to him, Bennett. Tonight. We can grab dinner on the way to his hotel."

There's no talking her out of this. I can tell by the stubborn set of her jaw, the determined gleam in her eye. I want to give her the solace she's looking for. If that's going to come in the form of a conversation with her brother, I'll take her. But there's no way I'll let her out of my sight. Not once.

"Yeah...okay." I reach for my jeans and my phone. "We can go."

But before I pull on my clothes, I remember the text I ignored earlier and read the message.

Bennett...you can't ignore me forever. One way or another, we will talk about things. I miss you, baby.

Fucking Valarie.

Why now? Why is my ex-wife choosing this moment in my life to show her face again? *We need to talk.*

No, we really don't. I said everything I needed to the night I lost my shit and landed myself in prison. When I had the divorce papers delivered to Valarie from prison, she didn't contest it. I figured she'd moved on, and I never once wanted to look back.

So why's she doing this now?

I know I can't ignore her forever, but I sure as hell won't take any time away from my job protecting Sayward and give it to Valarie. Her closure can wait until Sayward is safe.

Sayward appears in front of me, dressed and ready to leave. "Hey, you spaced out there. Something important on your phone?"

I shake my head, pulling on my jeans and shoving the phone into my pocket. "Nothing at all. Let's go."

When we pull up to the hotel where Marcos is staying, I order Sayward to stay in the car while I sweep the street. I expect her to argue, because arguing is something she's really good at, but aside from her jaw going tense, she stays put. Slamming my car door shut behind me, I take a casual stance against the car and allow my gaze to swing from left to right, taking in everything around me with practiced calculation.

When I decide the street looks clear, I turn my gaze upward, looking in earnest for anything out of the ordinary in the windows and on the rooftops above us. Not only do I see nothing unusual, I don't feel the familiar prickle of being watched.

I walk around to the passenger side of the truck and open the door for Sayward. She steps out as I reach into the backseat and grab the small backpack I keep stashed in my car. Sayward checks out the street herself with skeptical eyes.

"We're good, baby," I murmur, closing the truck door

behind her and pulling her into my side. "Let's go see your brother."

The lobby isn't crowded, giving me the chance to take stock of everyone inside. I nod at the man standing behind the front desk as we pass and head for the elevator. It's a quiet ride up to the fifth floor, stress and anxiety flowing off of Sayward in excess.

"What's making you so nervous?"

She glances at me, tucking a strand of her thick hair behind her ear as she shifts her weight from foot to foot. Everything about her body language says that she'd rather be anywhere else, doing anything else. But she needs this, because she needs to believe her family isn't fucking her over.

I can only hope that she's right.

"I just hate being on high alert like this. I mean...the cartel in Wilmington? I thought I was safe here." Her words trail away to almost nothing at the end, and I step into her space as the elevator doors open.

Pulling her out behind me, I scan the empty hallway first before dropping my bag and swinging her around until her back is against the wall and I'm cupping her chin in one hand while the other braces on the wall above her head.

"Listen to me, Sayward. The shithead cartel is no match for the men you have protecting you. You hear me? We will get you through this. *I* will get you through this."

What is it about this woman that has promises rolling off my tongue like they're nothing?

She blinks up at me, slowly, her long black eyelashes briefly brushing the tops of her cheekbones before she looks up to study my expression. I don't move, and neither does she. It's like she's trying to read me, trying to measure my sincerity. I give her a full minute to figure out that I mean every damn word I say.

Every. Damn. Word.

Slowly, her eyes rake over every feature on my face. I can't read anything in them until they meet mine again, and she reaches tentative fingers up to touch my face. And then I don't need to read her, because I can *feel* her. I *know* her, regardless of the minuscule amount of time I've spent with her.

"You mean that, don't you?" she whispers.

Something in my chest, something I shoved way down deep a long time ago, breaks free and crawls up into my throat. I swallow around the lump forming there.

This woman.

All I can do is nod, because words won't come. Then I reach down and do something I thought I'd never do again. Something so simple that most people don't think anything of it. But to me? It means something. And judging by the way Sayward's fingers tremble in mine, it means something to her, too.

I take her hand.

Marcos answers his hotel room door after one knock. I nod to the NES team member, a guy named Thorn, stationed outside his door just before Sayward's brother lets us inside.

I let Sayward's hand go as Marcos pulls her into a tight, stiff hug. I give the room a quick check, because even though there's security stationed outside the door I won't take any chances with Sayward's life. The room is clear, and I turn back to where Marcos is now holding Sayward at arm's length and staring into her face.

Her gaze is downcast.

"Are you okay?" He shakes her shoulders, not hard, but still my teeth clench together.

"I'm fine. Are *you* okay? I was worried, Marcos. You were on that street this afternoon, too."

He sighs, dropping his arms from her shoulders and running one hand through his black hair. "I'm fine, *hermanita*. I don't need a guard outside my door."

Sayward's voice turns firm. "Bullshit, Marcos. You'll have a guard until we know you're safe. I have one."

She smiles over at me, and I want to pull her back into my arms. Instead, I turn to Marcos.

"Did anything happen right before you left Colombia?"

His eyes narrow. "Yeah, *mi padre* died."

The words carry plenty of bite, but I don't back down. "Other than that. Anything out of the ordinary? Did you receive any threats from the cartel?"

Marcos lets loose a deep, humorless chuckle before glancing at Sayward. "The other men already asked me this question."

Sayward looks from her brother to me. "Why are you asking him this?"

"Because I want to know why the cartel is here spraying bullets around our town."

Marcos raises his voice. "You spoiled Americans don't know shit, do you? What it's like living in the shadow of the cartel every single day? Yeah, I received threats. Because they threaten every single person who lives in our city *every single day.* This is nothing new to us."

I flex my fingers as my jaw clenches tight. He knows nothing about me. I'm about as far from a spoiled American as you can get, but that's not something he needs to hear right now. It won't do any of us any good.

I'm here for her. I'm here for her. I keep up the mantra in my head, reminding myself that this isn't about Marcos. It definitely isn't about me.

Keeping my yes trained on him, my voice is cool. "You didn't answer the question. Is there any specific threat you can think of that might explain how the hell the cartel was able to follow you right into your sister's backyard?"

Marcos's nearly black eyes flash with rage, his nostrils flaring. Then his tone softens as he turns away from me and toward his sister. "I'm sorry, *chica*. If they followed me here...I don't know, I wasn't thinking. I only knew I needed to tell you about our father."

"Ever hear of a burner phone?" My words cut the air, bitter and harsh.

Maybe I'm being an asshole, but I can't care about that right now. He brought danger to her door, and that's something I'm not willing to overlook.

He tosses a glare over his shoulder. "The death of a family member is news delivered in person. What, no one you loved has ever died? Do you even have a family?"

Has no one I loved ever died? Try getting word from Saudi Arabia that your father has gone down behind enemy lines when you're only a kid. A kid who still needs his dad. Try serving with men you call your brothers, only to watch them die beside you.

His words slam into me like a punch. I rear back, as the memories from receiving news about the death of my father and watching men fall to the ground around me in the desert bombard me. And then Mickey's face joins in the fray, reminding me that even though he wasn't actually my family, we shared a father-son type of bond, and now that's gone, too.

The shock of the words and the memories both sink deep, before I glance at Sayward. Her eyes are sympathetic, and I reject that shit immediately. Turning away from them both, I walk toward the wide window and draw back one corner of the curtain to survey the city below.

Fuck this shit. It's the last thing I need. This is why I don't do this kind of attachment. It's messy. It puts you in the line of fire, makes you a slave to your goddamn emotions.

Behind me, Sayward's voice is low, but she's clearly pissed. "You didn't have to do that, Marcos."

He blows out a frustrated breath. "He started it."

My phone buzzes in my pocket, and I pull it out and place it to my ear. "Blacke."

"We have company."

It's the NES man, Thorn, stationed outside the door. "I'm calling Lawson Snyder now. He's outside doing surveillance. We're gonna need backup."

His voice is low, clipped, and I know we don't have much time. My heart picks up an erratic rhythm in my chest. *Sayward. Goddammit!* "How many?"

"Three of them just stepped off the elevator."

Three of them, three of us plus Marcos. I like those odds.

But then Thorn mutters a curse on the other end of the line. "Fuck. Two more just entered from the stairwell." His voice is strained.

Fuck! I want to tell him to move, to get out of the line of fire, but his job is to defend that door with his life if that's what it comes to. "I'll call the front desk to send the cops." Then I end the call.

Making the call to the desk, I bark into the phone. "There are intruders breaking into my room, five-twenty-seven. Call the police."

Both Sayward and Marcos whirl around to face me.

"What did you just say?" she asks, her voice sharp but her face draining of color.

Moving fast, I grab Sayward and toss her toward the bathroom. "Get in there, Sayward. Lock the door behind you."

She hesitates. Her eyes search my face. I want to reassure her, but there's *no time.*

I raise my voice. "*Now,* Sayward! Get your ass in that bathroom and don't come out until you hear my voice telling you to."

Her eyes widen in fear, and her hair whips out around her as she turns for the bathroom.

Hell.

Grabbing her wrist, I pull her back to me. Slamming my lips down to hers in a crushing kiss, I make it count because I know this could be the last time I kiss these lips.

When I pull back she puts her fingers to her mouth. Then I shove her away again.

"*Go.*"

I send up a quick prayer that I can keep her safe.

18

BENNETT

Dropping down to crouch beside my bag, I glance up at Marcos. He's standing there, staring at the door, legs tensed and fingers flexing.

"You packing heat?" I ask him around the extra clip of bullets I've shoved into my mouth.

He shakes his head. "Not here. I couldn't carry a gun with me from Colombia."

I toss him my Glock, knowing I have an extra pistol fitted in my ankle holster. "You take this. My hands are gonna be busy for the next minute or so, anyway."

"Doing what?" His tone sounds like he's close to losing his shit, but I don't have time for that right now.

I can't babysit him and keep his sister alive. My voice goes sharp and there's the edge of command in it I know makes people listen. "Eyes on the door, Marcos."

As he turns toward the door, I toss the clip between his feet and unzip the duffle bag I brought just in case. Rifling through the contents, random objects and sealed containers of liquid no regular person would ever put together, my fingers close around a small lead pipe. The sound of a shout from the hallway, Thorn's voice, doesn't stop me or even make me pause in my intentions.

My fingers are steady as I work, pulling match heads off the sticks and dumping them inside the pipe and capping one end. The fact that this is going down in a hotel full of people registers somewhere in the back of my mind, and I take that fact into account while I work. But Sayward's face, scared and alone in the hotel bathroom, also flashes through my brain, and I force myself to take a deep breath before standing.

Pulling my extra pistol with one hand and holding the now-sealed pipe with the other, I stand and face the hotel door. From just outside the room, the sound of gunshots rips the air.

Let it be Thorn's and Lawson's guns. Let it be Thorn's and Lawson's guns.

Knowing my colleagues are out there, possibly being shot to hell, dying, I have to act. Dipping my head toward Marcos, I indicate that he should step the fuck back. He complies, holding his weapon at the ready. His eyes are locked on the hotel room door, where a commotion is clearly going down in the hall.

Moving fast toward the door, I crouch and place the pipe beside the thin crack letting in light from the hall. Then, striking a match, I place the tiny stick topped with flame inside the pipe. Then I retreat. The purpose of this bomb, by both size and type, is to create a distraction so that I can get Sayward out of this hotel room. My own guys are in that hallway, too, and I don't intend for anyone to get hurt in the small explosion that's about to take place.

For me, this is tame. I've manufactured explosions ten times this size, and there's almost always been a plan in place detailing exactly what will happen before and after the explosion. So even though a pipe bomb is like goddamn child's play, the ill preparation sends a jolt of trepidation jamming into my gut.

"Get down!" I toss the words at Marcos as we both hit the ground.

My lips moving quietly, I utter a quick prayer just as the hotel room door explodes.

BOOM.

"Move to the outside of the bathroom door. Cover Sayward no matter what!" I toss the instruction back at Marcos as I storm the hallway.

Out in the hall, it's pretty evident that the explosion shocked the hell out of not only the three cartel assholes, but also Lawson and Thorn.

"Move!" I shout as I land a roundhouse kick to one of the cartel members. My priority? Disarm him so that we can cart his ass back to NES. I want him interrogated before he's arrested.

I need to know what the cartel's plans are for Sayward. And I need to know it before the next attack.

The kick sends his weapon flying, and as he recovers, I hurtle toward him. Landing a jab with my left fist into his jaw, his head snaps back. He grunts as he retaliates, swinging way too wide to connect. I catch his arm, wrenching it behind his back until I hear a snap and kicking his legs out from underneath him. Shoving him toward Thorn, I jerk my head toward the stairwell at the end of the hall. Opposite direction of the lobby elevator and stairs.

"Get him out of here. Back to NES."

With a nod of understanding, Thorn plants his fist into the side of the fading cartel member's head and the dude's legs give out totally. Thorn drags him down the hall.

I turn just in time to catch another cartel member aiming his weapon. Ducking as he fires, I move in so fast he can't keep up. Getting in front of him, under his weapon, I jab a knee into his balls, using every ounce of motherfucking strength I have. He goes down, and I plant one of my boots into the side of his face for good measure. When he's sprawled out, I turn to Lawson. But he's all good, taking his adversary down just like I did mine.

Pivoting, I rush back into the hotel room. "Stand down," I snap to Marcos.

He reluctantly lowers my pistol.

Heading straight for the bathroom, I turn the knob and find Sayward backed all the way up against the shower stall. She's leaning against the glass doors, both hands tucked under her chin. Her eyes are wide, staring without blinking, and her bottom lip is clutched between her teeth so fucking hard I'm scared she might've drawn blood.

"Hey," I say low and gentle, closing the distance between us. "Baby, you're safe. *You're okay.*"

She blinks, and I grab her shoulders. Watching as her eyes try to focus on me, I grasp her chin in between two fingers. "You hear me? We got them. No one's gonna hurt you."

I stare into her eyes, willing her to believe me. To see me. Seeing her like this, this scared? This dazed and confused?

It guts me.

My hands travel down her delicate shoulders to her upper arms, where I hold on a little too tight. "Come on, beautiful. Take a breath for me."

She finally comes back to life, sucking in a deep breath as her clear hazel eyes focus on me. She blinks.

"I...I heard gunshots," she whispers. "And the explosion. I thought...I thought you and Marcos were..."

Shaking my head firmly, I cup her face in my hands. "Not gonna happen, Sayward. I'm right here, and they couldn't drag me away from you. I'm going to keep you safe. Got that?"

She nods.

"Good girl."

Jacob Owen steps up to the bathroom door. His voice booms around the small room. "Is she hurt?"

Keeping my eyes trained on Sayward's face, I shake my head. "No."

"Do you realize you just set off a bomb inside a hotel?" The irritation in Jacob's tone is clear. I just made a big-ass mess for him to clean up.

Turning to face him but keeping Sayward's hand in mine, I look him straight in the eye. "It was the *Colombian cartel*. I used a bomb to distract them long enough for Lawson and Thorn to get the situation under control, or they would have been coming into this hotel room guns blazing. I didn't want Sayward at risk. It's my job to protect her, right?"

Jacob's jaw ticks as he evaluates me. "Go. Get her out of here, because the cops will be all over this room in about thirty seconds. I'll handle the cleanup."

His eyes tell me we aren't done discussing this, but I don't have regrets. I did what I had to do, and Sayward is walking out of this place alive. To me, it's a win.

"Copy." Grabbing Sayward by the hand, I tow her out of the hotel room, making sure to grab my duffle as we pass. I lead her down the hallway toward the back stairs and out of the building.

She's silent as we head for my truck and as I open her door and tuck her into the front seat. She doesn't say a word as the engine turns over and we set out toward NES. Reaching for her hand, I lace my fingers through hers and count it as a win when she doesn't pull back. Her hand is stiff in mine, though, and I bring her fingers to my mouth. Turning on to a quiet back road that'll lead us to NES, I glance at Sayward.

"Talk to me, beautiful."

Still staring out the truck window as the dark city rushes by, Sayward draws a breath. "Everyone around me dies because of the cartel. It's been that way my whole life. I don't want to drag you into this any further than I already have, Bennett."

Understanding mixes with sympathy in the pit of my stomach, swirling around with unease. Her voice is so sad it borders on desperate, and I can tell it's taking everything she has to stay with me. Her mind wants to shut down, withdraw, protect her from the fear and the anxiety warring inside her.

I know fear and anxiety well. I served in the army. I'm ex-Special Forces. I've entered war zones. I saw shit no living soul should ever have to see, made choices no human being should ever have to endure.

And then I went to prison.

Anxiety and fear? They're where I lived for a long fucking time.

I squeeze her hand as I glance at her. "I get that, baby. You're scared. But everyone who's working with you on this? They're doing it because they want to. You don't have to protect anyone. We can all protect ourselves, and you."

"But Bennett...don't you realize that I'd never be able to live with myself if anything happened to one of the NES team members? Or to either Jacob or Marcos? Or...to you?" Her voice catches on the last word, and my chest clenches tight, so tight it hurts.

I open my mouth to console her, but she speaks again before I can. And the words that come out of her mouth are the last thing I expect to hear. They stop my heart.

She turns those big eyes on me, wide with fear and wet with unshed tears. "I...I think I have to run."

19

SAYWARD

The truck swerves as Bennett yanks the wheel hard to the right, pulling us over to the side of the deserted road. He doesn't glance at me as he jerks open his door and climbs down, slamming it behind him. He stalks around the hood before wrenching my door open. Grabbing hold of my legs, he turns me toward him just before cupping my face in his big hands.

"Listen to me, beautiful," he grits out through clenched teeth. His tone is full of fury, but his eyes show the depth of the emotion he's feeling right now. They hold my stare captive. "You want to run? Go ahead. But know that you won't be going alone. There's no way in hell I'd let you go off by yourself right now. The second you landed in my bed, you belonged to me. This isn't just about protection detail for me. Not anymore. I want more with you, and if you leave we can't have that. I'm not letting you go *anywhere without me*. Got that?"

Stunned, I'm silent as I stare at him. I don't even have time to consider his words for more than a second before his lips are crashing down on mine.

Bennett devours me with his kiss. His lips demand that I respond, even as I try to close myself off against it. There's no point, because my body and maybe even my soul react to him instinctively no matter how hard I try to fight against it. I open my mouth to him on a gasp. He takes advantage, tightening his grip on my face as his tongue delves into my mouth, sweeping left to right.

Suddenly, I'm clinging to him, needing to get as close as possible. My fingers grip the short hair on the back of his head and he groans, sliding his hands down my back until he's gripping my waist and sliding me toward the edge of the seat. His body hums with his natural predatory energy; I can almost feel the possession pouring from him as his hands make their way up under my shirt.

Possessed? Yep, that's about right. It's how he's making me feel—like I belong to him in a way I've never belonged to anyone.

The scary part? *I like it.*

Pulling down the fabric of my bra, his fingers roll my nipple and it immediately pebbles as pleasurable pain rockets through me.

"*Bennett,*" I whimper. But I don't even know what I'm asking for.

I just *want.*

Both hands now full of my breasts, Bennett leans back, his gaze intent on me as he watches my reaction. He pinches both nipples, and I bite my lip against my moan. My head drops back against my shoulder blades, and his voice is gravelly rough when he speaks.

"Fucking hell, woman...you're so goddamned gorgeous. Where'd you *come* from?" The awe in his voice steals my breath.

"I've been right here all along." I cry out as he pushes my shirt up farther, tucks my bra down, and sucks one of my nipples into his mouth. He hums against my skin, the sound of pure approval causing the ache starting between my legs to grow and spread at an alarming rate.

I push my hips against him, seeking relief from the intensity of this moment. There's a fire burning deep in my belly, and Bennett's the only thing that's going to put it out.

"Please." Gripping his shoulders, I bury my head in the crook of his neck. Inhaling, I melt against him because his scent calls out to me: a mixture of spicy soap and sweat with the faintest hint of smoke.

Bennett slips a hand inside my stretchy pants, stroking me over my underwear.

"Baby, you're soaking wet," he groans as he slowly rubs my clit through the material. "I can feel you through the fabric...*Jesus*."

I rock my hips against his hand, and his answering chuckle is only a little bit strained. "I got you, beautiful."

Moving my panties to one side, he thrusts one thick finger inside me. I close my eyes, my nails digging into his shoulders as I wiggle against his hand.

"Tight as fuck," he growls, pushing another finger inside

me as his thumb strokes slow and steady circles around my clit.

My legs start to tremble.

It's a combination of his hands, his dirty mouth, and the freedom I feel in his touch. Never in a million years could I have imagined being free in someone else's hands. And I know that this doesn't apply to anyone but Bennett. I still shy away from physical contact where any other human is concerned.

Bennett makes me feel things I've never before experienced, and it's not just physical. My connection to him goes beyond that. So much deeper. Like I was stranded on an island before, all alone. And this man? He built a bridge and stormed across it to save me.

My impending orgasm rides on top of the wave of emotion threatening to drown me, and I hold on tight to the life raft that is Bennett Blacke. Pleasure washes over me.

"Bennett!" I don't recognize the cry, but I know it'll always belong to him.

He claims my mouth while I soar, kissing me deeper than I've ever been kissed. He murmurs words against my mouth, but I don't understand a single one of them. I'm lost to sensation, to the moment, to the feeling of being in his arms and knowing I'm safe here.

When I come back to reality, Bennett stares at me, his eyes searching every inch of my face.

"You're so fucking beautiful." He brushes my hair off my forehead, his touch so tender where just a moment ago it made me want to climb the walls.

I've never believed it before, but his words make me feel like it's true. Like I really am beautiful.

I cup his face and kiss his lips softly. His eyes close as he pulls my bottom lip into his mouth and sucks. He groans when he pulls away, carefully tucking my clothes back into place.

"We have to go. Damn...that's not what I intended to happen when I stopped the truck." Shaking his head like he can't believe himself, he glances around at the quiet road. "But I'm not sorry I did."

I'm still smiling ten minutes later when we pull into the NES parking lot.

But then my smile falters, because everything that just happened back at the hotel comes rushing back. I could have lost all of those men. Men who were only there protecting *me.* They're all caught in the middle now. I know better than anyone that it's their job to protect people, but it's a whole different story when I'm the one putting their lives at risk. It's something I didn't foresee happening.

I *work* at Night Eagle Security with the Rescue Ops team. I never intended to become a client.

Bennett sees the change in my demeanor immediately as he cuts the engine. Lifting my chin with a finger so I can meet his gaze, he looks into my eyes.

"We've got this."

Sucking in a deep breath, I close off the rioting force of emotions funneling into my stomach and nod. We exit the truck and Bennett takes my hand as he swipes us into the building.

Thorn is standing at the desk, waiting for us as we arrive, with Ronin and Grisham.

Bennett glances around. "Conners here?"

I belatedly glance around and see that Dare and Jeremy are missing. I'm alternating between replaying the hotel cartel attack and the much more personal attack on my heart and my body by Bennett in the truck on the way here.

Ronin steps forward. "He's with the suspect. He's detained in the chamber."

I shudder. The chamber is where we keep suspects that we need a little time with before we release them to law enforcement. It's really Ronin's house of worship, where he does all the dirty work it takes to make someone talk. I've never been in the room, but I know it's detached from the NES building, out back, and that it's a place where I probably never want to go.

Ronin bends so he can inspect my face. He doesn't touch me, though, for which I'm thankful. "Hey, sweetheart."

Bennett stiffens next to me. Ronin glances over at him and smirks before giving me his attention again. "You okay?"

He's never called me sweetheart before. None of the guys have. They've always seen me as part of the team, not some damsel to be rescued. And I'll be damned if that's going to change now. Straightening, I square my shoulders and look him straight in the eye.

"I'm absolutely fine. All I need is to get behind my computer so I can figure out how to put these bastards away before they kill someone."

Ronin shoots me a grim smile. "Atta girl, Viper." He turns to Bennett. "I need anything you can give me on this dude, something I can arm myself with before I head into that room with him. I'm not coming out of there until he tells us something useful, something we can use to take this goddamn faction out."

"I'm going in there with you. I need to see it for myself." His gaze slants toward me, something flashing in his eyes. "This is personal for me now."

Ronin glances between the two of us, and a slow, knowing smile dawns across his face. These guys know me well enough to know that if Bennett broke through, he earned that right. Thorn glances between all of us like he's a little lost, which I can only imagine he is. He runs a hand over his closely shaved blond hair. Just as big, rough, and ruggedly handsome as the rest of the guys, Thorn Ryder is an ex-navy SEAL with tons of pent-up energy.

His caramel-colored eyes lock on me. "I'm glad they didn't get to you, Viper."

I give him a nod and a small smile. "Thanks for protecting me, Thorn."

Ronin studies Bennett. I know the two are close, having met at The Oakes when Bennett arrived in town and began bartending there. They bonded over their Special Forces history and discovered that they have more than a few friends and experiences in common. Their brotherhood runs deep, even though they haven't known each other longer than a year. Understanding passes between them.

Ronin jerks his chin in the direction of the hallway

leading toward the back of the building. "Let's go, then."

Bennett immediately turns to me. Taking my chin between his index finger and thumb, his blue eyes bore into mine. "Be back soon, beautiful. Do your thing and find us something we can work with, all right?" He leans in, dropping his voice to a whisper. "And no more thoughts about leaving me. Yeah?"

I nod, and his lips land on my forehead in a whisper of a kiss. He drops my chin and glances at Grisham. "Keep eyes on her, Ghost."

Grisham looks amused and slightly annoyed. "Don't have to tell me that, Blaze."

Bennett freezes. I glance at Grisham, an eyebrow lifted in question.

Ronin chuckles without turning. "Once you earn your spot on this team, we give you a nickname. You earned yours the day you saved my woman. But it took the guys here a little longer to figure it out."

I can see the pleased expression in Bennett's eyes as he nods, and with one last look at me, he disappears down the hallway with Ronin.

I head straight for my office, knowing Grisham and Thorn will shadow me. Sinking down into my desk chair I turn on my laptop. It flares to life, and my muscles immediately relax. Flexing my fingers, I start typing.

20

BENNETT

We exit the NES building through a back door just as secure as the front. Solid metal, requiring a badge for entrance or exit. I saw the back lot when Ronin showed me around my first day at work here, but we didn't go inside "The Chamber" then. It's a smaller brick building, much like its bigger counterpart, where the main headquarters is located.

Dare is standing outside the door. He's at the ready, alert with his hands clasped together in front of him. When we step up in front of him he gives me a once-over that would normally piss me off. But right now, my mind is on a million things other than Dare Conners's approval.

He stares me down. "You set off a bomb inside a fucking hotel?"

Stopping short, I return the stare that's supposed to intimidate me. "Had to. My job is to protect Sayward no matter what."

For a few seconds, no one speaks. Ronin just watches us both with amused interest.

Finally, Dare lifts his chin once.

What the fuck? Respect? *Did hell just freeze over?*

"Nice one, Blaze." His lips twitch and I almost fall over.

Ronin pulls his identification card from the small chain on his belt loop and throws over his shoulder: "We done with this love-fest, ladies? I have a suspect to interrogate." He swipes it at the door. His tone changes to complete and total seriousness. "Let's go."

Dare follows us inside The Chamber. The place isn't what I expected.

What I expected to see was an actual interrogation room. Two-way mirrors, lots of shiny steel and polished concrete like the main building, a big table where the suspect sits on one side and the interrogator sits on the other. Classic. Vanilla. On the up-and-up.

That's not even close to what The Chamber really is.

It's like a motherfucking cave.

No windows. One big, open room with a dirty concrete floor. Fluorescent bulbs being the only lighting, shadows dip and hide throughout the space. A chain-link fence separates one half of the room from the other, and waiting on the other side, his back against the cinder block wall, is the cartel member Thorn dragged out of the hotel.

He looks worse for wear as he watches us with wary eyes, one eye blackened and a giant bruised lump marring one side of his forehead. Knowing he's been disarmed, I head straight for the gate in the middle of the fence.

Ronin steps in front of me. His look tells me to slow the fuck down and follow his lead. Knowing that this is his area of expertise, I nod once. My heartbeat drums against my rib cage, and my breaths are coming shallow and quick. I didn't know just how much I wanted to hurt this bastard, the representative of the entity threatening Sayward, until this moment.

Ronin, without tossing a glance at the waiting perp, crosses to a cabinet pushed against one wall on our side of the fence. It's red and stainless steel, the kind of cabinet you'd see in a mechanic's garage. Pulling open the largest drawer, he removes what looks like a slim black briefcase.

It doesn't take me more than a second to figure out what's in that briefcase.

After unlocking the old-school padlock on the gate with a key, he eyes me and lifts his chin in the direction of the cell. I follow him inside, and Dare locks the gate behind us.

Ronin places the suitcase down on the floor near the gate, and then he glances at me. He lifts his voice. "He look like he has anything to say?"

I glance at the cartel man. He looks between us with defiance in his eyes. I shake my head, keeping my gaze locked on him. He relaxes against the wall and smirks. Then he spits on the floor.

Shaking my head, I look back at Ronin. "Nope."

Ronin strides over to the man and without even taking a pause, punches him hard in the jaw. The man stumbles back, has nowhere to go, and sits down on the long wooden bench behind him. The man spits again, this time a mouthful of blood.

He says something in Spanish and Ronin hits him again. Turning away, Ronin walks over to grab the briefcase while the man coughs and splutters.

I step over and drop down in front of the man whose face is now bloody. "He's just getting started. Why don't you answer one question for me, and we'll go from there. How many cartel members are in Wilmington?"

He stares at me, resisting.

Ronin pulls a needle from the briefcase. He eyes the man while testing the liquid inside the syringe. "Oh, did you expect something more lethal-looking, like a knife? A gun? Torch, maybe? Don't worry...I have those, too. But do you want to know what this is?"

He gazes down at the man, who sullenly stares back. No answer.

"You don't?" Ronin gently places the syringe down on top of the briefcase and then lunges for the man, grabbing his throat. The asshole struggles, fingers clawing at Ronin's hand squeezing his neck. He wheezes, gasping, but still Ronin doesn't let go. I watch, sickly fascinated and not feeling even a little bit sorry for the bastard.

When the man's face starts to turn purple, Ronin throws him backward, and he clutches at his throat as he presses his back against the wall. "Yes! What is in the needle?"

He speaks in thickly accented English.

Ronin nods. "That's better. When we ask you a question, it's your only job to answer it. I'm not going to kill you.

That'd be too easy. But I am going to hurt you, and I promise you that's going to be so much worse."

Finally, a flicker of fear shows in the man's eyes. It's not from the pain Ronin promises to inflict. This man is a member of the Colombian drug cartel. It's the indifferent, matter-of-fact tone Ronin uses when delivering his threats. It's fucking chilling.

That's why they call him Swagger.

There's no hint of hesitation or deliberation in his words. Just pure, cold, truth.

"There are six of us." His voice is hoarse. "We have been staying in a corporate apartment in a building owned by a shell corporation tied to the cartel."

Ronin's face doesn't change. I lean in closer. "Where? And why does Suarez want her dead?"

The man's mouth clamps shut.

Ronin picks up the needle. "This is an illegally potent neurotoxin. It takes thirty seconds before it hits your nerves. The pain? It'll be unlike anything you've ever felt. It'll only last three minutes, but those three minutes will feel like a fucking eternity. After that three minutes is over, you'll return to your conscious state and we'll ask you again. Hopefully this time you'll be smart enough to answer."

When the man still doesn't answer, Ronin, moving like a cobra, injects the drug into the man's neck.

Thirty seconds later, the perp starts to scream.

21

SAYWARD

After thirty minutes, I now have all of the information the U.S. government has on Pablo Suarez, as well as some that they don't. My skills as a hacker are unmatched, and, not for the first time, I'm thankful for them. I sit back, staring at the photo of the man on the screen in front of me.

The son of the man who killed my mother.

I'll never forget the elder Suarez's face, and that of his son is similar enough that it sends chills skating along my spine. I shut my eyes against the rush of memories threatening to bombard me.

I can't succumb to them now.

"Tell us what you got, Viper." Grisham stands over my shoulder, peering at the picture.

"Pablo Suarez has several shell corporations hiding cartel money in several countries around the world. One of them is right here in Wilmington, and it was only purchased three days ago, right after my father's death."

Grisham sucks in a breath. "Which could indicate that that's when he located you."

I stare at the screen. "But we don't know why." My index finger taps against the computer screen as I stare at the information I've scoured the Web to find. Finally, I shake my head. "I'm going to print all of this out. Jacob likes an old-school file to study."

Grisham snorts. "Old man runs an office that's modern as hell, but he still needs to hold real manila folders full of papers when he's reading up on an adversary. Never fails."

I smile as I hit PRINT. "That's just Jacob."

My office being down the hall from the front lobby, we all hear it when the front door buzzes with the sound of a security badge before it clicks open. I stiffen, fear gripping me before I can stop it, but Grisham glances at Thorn. From his position by my office door, Thorn pokes his head out into the hallway.

"It's Boss Man," he informs us.

I sigh, relief flowing through me like a river. That's what this situation has done to me: It's turned me into someone who jumps at every sound, someone who turns tense at the first sign of anything amiss.

Jacob's boots thud down the polished concrete floors as he strides down the hallway. When he appears in my office door, his usual stoic expression is set firmly in place, but his eyes soften when they land on me. Worry and fear and concern live there in his gaze.

"Sayward. Are you okay?"

I glance down at myself. *Why does everyone keep asking me that?* "I'm not hurt."

He nods, his lips twitching. "I know that, Sayward. I wasn't referring to your physical condition."

I stand, walking toward the printer. "I've created a file on Pablo Suarez."

I can feel Jacob's eyes on me as I place the papers neatly into a manila folder, just the way he likes.

"And we have information on the location of the cartel." Bennett's voice rumbles from the doorway, and I turn to face him.

My stomach floods with warmth, pulling me toward him like tide meets sand. He pulls me in like the need to touch me is more than he can take, and his lips land on top of my head as he inhales. "Hey."

I tilt my face and look up at him, unaware that there's anyone else in the room. "Hey."

He holds my gaze for a moment saying a million things that only I can understand, before lifting his gaze to Jacob over my head. "Ronin's good at what he does."

Ronin chuckles darkly from the doorway. "Thanks. You ready for information, Boss Man?"

Jacob nods. "You get much more than location?"

Ronin shakes his head. "He doesn't know much. Seems Suarez doesn't freely show all his cards to the lower rungs on the ladder. But yeah, he knows where they're staying. Best we get there before they move. Also, he knows that Suarez wants Sayward, they were instructed not to kill her on sight. The men who first shot at her on the sidewalk and then came for her in the hotel? They weren't going for a kill shot."

I stiffen and try to pull back from Bennett, but his arm tightens around me.

Ronin glances around the room before his green eyes land on me. Finally he dips his chin in a solemn nod. "Viper. He wants you dead. But he wants to make a production out of it. Make an example of you. Wants to bring you back to Colombia and..."

My heart thuds against its cage, a panicked bird trying frantically to fly far, far away. I almost feel the target on my back, and it burns like nothing I've ever felt before.

My story has never been a secret; I've always known about the cartel. But I've felt safe, living in an obscure town like Wilmington, North Carolina. Hacking came naturally to me, and I used it as a defensive weapon, a way to make sure I'm not found by anyone who might be looking. I've erased any trace of my whereabouts online, keeping my digital footprint nonexistent for my own protection. I use cash, not credit, and I was fortunate enough to find a landlord who doesn't ask questions about things like that. With a protector like Jacob watching over me, and my shell built up around me, the fear that settled into me after that night seeped away.

Until now.

Now, terror slithers all over me, into my veins like a virus, spreading and growing until I can hardly contain it inside me.

"What if they get to me?" My voice is hoarse. I clear my throat and try again. "What if they *hurt all of you* to find me?" My breath comes fast, too fast. The room starts to spin as darkness encroaches at the sides of my vision. Just the thought of that happening to any of these men who've done nothing but support me is enough to bring on another panic attack.

The cartel takes lives. I don't want to be responsible for any more death. I *can't* be.

Oh, God. I'll lose it if I have to bury any one of these men.

And then I think about Bennett being the one to take a bullet for me. He signed up for it, put himself on the line *voluntarily*, but it doesn't matter.

I don't want to lose any of them, but I especially can't bear the thought of losing him.

Bennett turns me in his arms, strong hands landing on my shoulders. He dips his head so that he can look directly into my eyes. "Don't go there, beautiful. That's not gonna happen. You hear me?"

But I can't hear him. I'm too busy losing little pieces of myself to the paralyzing fear. In the back of my mind, I realize he thinks I'm scared for *myself*.

"Blacke." Jacob's voice is a commanding bark no one ever dares ignore. Bennett's eyes flick toward him. "Get her out of here. Your job is to keep her safe, and she doesn't need to be here for this. I'll keep you updated, but it's past midnight and she needs to rest. We'll be moving in on them within the hour."

Nodding, Bennett doesn't hesitate before he's moving with me, out of the office and placing me into his truck. I take deep gulps of the salty, damp night air and don't register the fact that we've left until Bennett turns over his big truck's engine.

"We're leaving?" My voice, usually so controlled, is startled. "Why?"

He takes my hand, his words nothing but a gentle caress.

"They don't need us for this, baby. I want to get you home."

I rest my head against the back of my seat. *Home.* I test the word in my head, trying it on to see if it fits. To me, my tiny little apartment is home. I'm at home in front of my computer. I'm at home when I'm with Jacob. And that's about it. But when Bennett says it, home isn't just a feeling or a place. It's a living, breathing thing with a *soul.* It sounds so right, but I hesitate.

Can I trust it? Whatever Bennett is offering me, all I want to do is reach out and grab it. Hold on tight and never let go.

But a small part of me is terrified that if I do, my carefully guarded heart, free for the first time in my life, will never recover.

No. You can trust Bennett. The tiny voice inside me reminds me that I didn't give my body to this man lightly. He's protected me, he's made me feel things I never thought were possible.

He's earned my trust.

By the time he pulls into the small parking pad in front of his house, I'm done debating. Whatever Bennett Blacke is offering, I'm going to take it. I place my hand in his, and he squeezes gently, reminding me that beside him is exactly where I need to be. Maybe it's crazy to feel this way after such a short time, but it doesn't change the fact that I *do.*

"Bennett."

The clear, melodic voice seems to be floating from a dream. I glance around in confusion, searching for it. Beside me Bennett is as still as a statue frozen, his hand turning to ice in mine. Dropping my fingers from his grasp, his steps stutter to a stop as his voice scrapes up from his throat.

"Valarie?"

The woman steps into the circle of light from the rustic-looking lantern over his front door. For the first time maybe ever, my attention is immediately drawn to her beauty. Familiarity tugs in my brain, but I can't place where I've seen her before, or heard her name. Long, silver-blond hair, lifting delicately in the breeze rolling in off the ocean. Lithe, willowy limbs on a tall, thin model's frame. Whoever she is, I'm immediately comparing myself to her, and we're as different as two people can be. She's all light where I'm all dark, all tall where I'm not, long and lean where I'm curved and soft. And she's definitely not dressed in jeans and a hoodie—her long legs go on for miles under a short, chic dress.

She steps forward, her eyes running over me from head to toe before she focuses her total attention on Bennett. He shoves his hands in his pockets, and I drop my gaze, finding it impossible to make eye contact with this stranger. It's even more impossible to keep my eyes on Bennett. Every single awkward moment I've ever had in my life, every single one of them out of my control, suddenly feel insignificant compared to this.

"What the hell are you doing here?" he grinds out through clenched teeth.

But he takes a step toward her. Like he's drawn, even though he doesn't want to be.

The blood running through my veins, pumping oxygen to my heart and rational thoughts to my brain...it stops functioning altogether.

She smiles, tilting her head to one side the way I've seen women do so many times before. "You might be ex-Special Forces, babe, but you're not the only one with resources. It took me awhile to find you, but I never would have stopped trying."

She glances at me again, her smile faltering just a tiny bit, before tucking a strand of her perfect hair behind her ear. "Plus, I'm your wife. Where else should I be?"

His wife.

When I researched Bennett for the team at NES, I came across her name and her photo in my search. It's why she looks familiar.

My stomach heaves, a sickening roll of my belly that has me reaching for Bennett's keys. Plucking them from his hand, I flee. Brushing past the woman standing on the front walkway, I unlock the door and let myself into the house.

All before the first tear rolls down my cheek.

As soon as I'm inside, I pull out my phone. I don't know where I'm going to go, but I know I have to get the hell out of here.

I text Marcos.

I need to see you. Can you meet me?

The three little dots that indicate he's typing back appear immediately.

Yes. I'm staying at a different hotel. Meet me here. There's a bar downstairs.

My fingers fly across the keys even as everything inside me goes numb.

I'll meet you there.

Pulling up my car service app, I note that there's a car just a couple of minutes away. I arrange to meet it about a block away. I know I'll be safe with Marcos. He's my brother and he'll protect me. And I know that the NES team will take the cartel down soon, anyway. I need to be as far away from Bennett and his *wife* as possible right now.

Shouldn't be too hard to sneak away from him, now that he's distracted, right?

My stomach rolls again as I slip my phone back into my pocket. Brushing away the tears, I bark out a laugh. There's no way I'm going to wait around for him to ask me to leave. Guilt tugs at me, knowing he wouldn't do that. But I don't want to wait for him to close himself into a room with *her* so they can talk it out, either. I'll never put myself through that kind of humiliation.

Bennett Blacke held your heart in his hands, and look what he did with it. All it took was for her to walk back into his life.

Determination overwhelms me, even as tears threaten to crush me completely. I swallow down the lump climbing up my throat and wrap my arms around my stomach to hold myself together.

I can do this. I'll just have to be stronger than my first heartbreak.

22

BENNETT

My head spins, but I snap right back to the here and now and what's most important as soon as Sayward disappears into the house.

Fuck. Fuck!

Raking an agitated hand through my hair, I shoot a stony stare at Valarie. "*Ex*-wife. I don't know what the fuck kind of game you're running right now, Valarie. But I have zero time for this shit."

My movements feel stiff as I walk past her, but she reaches out and grabs my arm to stop me. "You never let me explain, Bennett. We still have things to say to each other. I'd like us to give our marriage another try."

Her voice, sweet and soft, used to hit me someplace deep inside. It would stop me from doing anything, at any time. And yeah, maybe even a month ago that still would have happened. Maybe I still would have been willing to hear her out. Even after everything that happened, and after all this time.

But that was before Sayward happened. Before she rolled into my life like a feisty little hurricane. Before she completely fucked me up in the head and wore me out in the bed.

Now? Valarie's voice does nothing for me. Nothing *to* me. I can't even look at her, because when I do all I see is my past.

This woman won't even have a single minute of my future.

I pull my arm out of her grasp.

"No, Val. Go home." I keep walking, straight through my front door, and close it behind me.

I never look back at Valarie... not once.

Searching my small living room for Sayward, I don't see her and my eyes close momentarily. She's not waiting for me here. I can't imagine what the hell she must be thinking. I'd dropped her hand when I'd seen Val, but that was because I was *shocked as all fuck.* Nothing about Valarie could have dragged me away from Sayward. Not now.

So the first thing you need to do is tell her that.

Heading for the one and only bedroom in my house, I open my mouth in preparation of seeing her, ready to explain.

She isn't here.

The room's empty.

Dread sinks into my gut, spreading like an oil spill. I spin around, checking the limited space like I'm expecting her to jump out of the closet or from under the bed.

No, no, no. Please... no.

Thinking—no, *hoping*—that she'd just gone out back for

some air, I head over to the slider that takes up half the back wall and step outside. The nearby crashing of waves against sand mocks me, calling attention to the fact that she's. Not. Here.

Knowing that my Rescue Ops team is busy preparing to bring down Suarez and his crew is minimally comforting. At least they'll get to him before he gets to her.

Where the fuck would she go?

Guilt gnaws at me, reminding me that it's my fault she's not with me right now. I should have known...I should have told her exactly what she meant to me so that when fucking Valarie showed up she wouldn't have questioned it. But instead...she'd taken the fact that I'd been too god-damned shocked to react at first to mean I didn't want her.

Fuck.

She's run away. *From me.*

Turning, I stalk back into the house, grab my keys off their hook, and slam the door behind me. Climbing into my truck, I pull out my cell phone. There's a text from Jacob. He details the time and a sketch of the war plan. They'll send the team out to the corporate housing complex in the next twenty minutes. They have a plan for entry and extraction, and a strategy for making sure the citizens in the complex remain safe. Teague will be on the coms during the op, the place Sayward would normally be. But his nickname, "Brains," isn't bullshit. He knows what the fuck he's doing.

I type out a quick text to Jacob. The last thing I want to do is distract the team from the op they're about to run. I can handle this. I can get Sayward back.

Where did you relocate Marcos?

He answers after only a minute with the name of the new hotel. I start the truck's engine and head out. As the truck bears down on the Wilmington roads, dark and wide open at this time of night, I send up a prayer.

Let me find her, fast. And let me have the right words to explain my fuckup. I want her back in my arms.

I walk into the hotel lobby. When the woman behind the counter opens her mouth to greet me, I silence her with a photograph. "Have you seen this woman here tonight?"

She closes her mouth and peers closely at the photo of Sayward. It's one I snapped of her on my phone. She was lying in my bed, her face turned toward me, the most peaceful look on her face I'd ever seen. Her head rested on her elbow, and there was something in her eyes I hadn't been willing to see there before.

I see it now.

She's looking at the camera—no, at *me*—with adoration in her gaze. Maybe even...love.

The woman taps a finger on her lip. "Yes...she stopped by the desk when she came in. I noticed her 'cuz she's so pretty. She headed to the bar over there." She gestures toward the neon blue sign with the bar's name scrawled out in script over the entrance.

I put my phone away. "Thanks."

When I enter the small hotel bar, I scan it once without seeing Sayward anywhere. My heart sinks like a damn stone, but I head over to the bartender anyway. Flashing him Sayward's photo, I ask him the same question I'd asked the woman in the lobby.

He lifts his chin. "You a cop?" His tone is casual, and he continues pouring amber liquid into a highball glass.

I aim my gaze at the glass. "You didn't put enough Fernet-Branca in that highball glass. If you're making a Hanky Panky, you need more or it's gonna turn out sour as fuck."

When the bartender's brows shoot up and he eyes the glass with sudden doubt in his skills, I lift a shoulder. "I'm a bartender, not a cop. And trust me on the drink."

Eyeing me, he pulls out the rare whiskey and pours in another finger before sliding the glass to a lonely, obviously rich, old lady at the end. When he returns, he folds his arms and leans forward. "Your girl was here."

I sit up straighter, my body going tense. "Where is she now?"

He looks toward the entrance of the bar before his gaze strays back to mine. "The man she was with? I overheard them talking. He wanted her to leave with him. She seemed reluctant, but she ended up going. Heard him speak into his phone when she went to the bathroom. Said they were headed to Jefferson Airport."

Every piece of information the bartender hands over hits me like a fucking bullet. It's all important, but it's not what I expected. When I got here, I thought Sayward would still be here. The fact that she'd run straight to Marcos wasn't hard to figure out. With Jacob out of commission, and with her no longer needing to run, thanks to the fact that the Rescue Ops team was preparing to take down Suarez's team, she had nowhere else to go. But why the *fuck* would Marcos want her to leave Wilmington with him now? When the service for her father isn't until next week?

And why would Sayward agree to go with him?

The answer to the last question's easy. *Because she trusts him.* He's her brother.

And, yeah, maybe she thinks she can put her faith in him. But my feelings about the dude have been wary as fuck since I'd met him.

I don't trust him. Not in the fucking slightest. Tossing a folded bill on the bar for the bartender's trouble, I don't waste any time hauling ass back to the truck.

23

SAYWARD

When I'd joined Marcos at the bar, he'd taken one look at my face and asked the bartender to make me something strong. Sipping my double Jack and Coke, the story spilled out. How I feel about Bennett, how scared I've been. How good he's been at protecting me, but how wrong I was about how he felt.

"The second she stepped back into his life, he forgot all about me." I'd hated the way my voice sounded. Weak. Sad. *Broken, broken, broken.*

Marcos had listened without interrupting. "Where is he now?"

I'd shrugged and told him I assumed he was having a heart-to-heart with *Valarie.* "But the NES team should be on their way to take out Suarez."

Marcos's brow had furrowed. "They know where he is?"

I'd nodded.

Then I'd swallowed down the rest of my drink and excused

myself to go to the restroom. When I'd returned, Marcos leaned toward me, his expression earnest and pleading.

"*Chica*, I'm planning on leaving for Colombia tonight. After everything that has happened here, I don't want to stay. I was going to call you to say good-bye but you beat me to it." He sends me an apologetic smile. "Please...come with me. Now that your friends are apprehending Pablo Suarez, you have nothing to fear in Colombia. Come meet your nephew. Help me remember our father. Come home."

Marcos's words flipped over and over in my mind, a tumult of thoughts whirling into a tornado of emotion inside me. As shocked as I was, it made total sense that Marcos would want to leave. Nothing good had come from his visit here. But was he right? Could I go home? I did need to clear my mind, rebuild the walls around my heart. And I wanted so badly to say good-bye to my *papi.*

There was a tugging in my chest, a tight pull that let me know I'm anchored here now, whether I like it or not. But a surge of determination rises within me, because I know that anchor is attached firmly to Bennett. But I can't be tethered to him, not when he can't give himself to me completely. The memory of the way he tensed up and dropped my hand at the sight of Valarie sliced through me, causing real, physical pain. I winced against it, hugging myself tight.

My answer had flown from my lips before I could stop it, and then only part of me wanted to. "Yes. I'll come with you."

Marcos had nodded in encouragement. "We leave tonight."

And that's how I ended up getting out of a car at a private airfield. The deep darkness is pierced by bright white overhead lamps where the car drops us off, and I can see the blinking red lights of the runway beyond the tall, chain-link fence. There's a man waiting for us at the gate, dressed in a pilot's uniform.

"Mr. Diaz." He nods, tipping his hat. "We're ready for takeoff, sir."

Marcos leans toward me as I stare at the pilot. "My friend back in Colombia...a businessman I built a complex for, has offered me the use of his plane to return home."

Unease spikes, lancing through me as I stare through the fence at the waiting jet. It's glossy, black engines whirring as it waits to take me home.

Home.

It's the second time tonight I've thought of that word, and it felt more real when I thought it earlier than it does now. Confusion simmers, making me blink several times as the plane blurs out of focus. I sigh, shifting my feet.

Marcos places a hand on my back. "Let's go, Sayward."

I let him lead me toward the plane. I can't figure out what's making me feel so tense. *Nervous.* Is it the fact that I'm returning to Colombia for the first time since I fled for my life? Is it because I'm putting my faith in a brother I barely know?

No. Marcos is my blood. If there's anyone I can put my trust in, it's him.

My feet take me up the plane's flight of steps and into the cabin.

Where the smiling, triumphant face of Pablo Suarez waits for me.

24

BENNETT

Why the fuck don't I drive a goddamn sports car?

The truck's big engine rumbles as I hurtle down the streets, headed for the airport on the outskirts of town. I've always loved my truck, but damn if tonight I don't wish I had something with some speed.

I need to be at that airfield. I need to be there now, because if I don't get there in time, Sayward and Marcos will be in the air.

Just the thought of losing her like this sends a shot of heart-shredding pain straight through my chest, and it's hard to fucking breathe. I'm not gonna lose her.

I can't.

My foot stomps down harder on the gas, adrenaline making me take risks I wouldn't normally take.

When I pull up at the airfield, gravel flying around my tires, I slam to a stop and jump down from the cab. Sprinting through the gate in the chain-link fence, I look around frantically. In the distance, the sound of a jet's engines rise to a roar, and then I spot the small, black plane hurtling down the runway.

No. Please don't let her be on that plane.

I'm fucking helpless as I watch the jet lift off into the air, the wheels lifting up into the belly of the beast, and my hands lift to the back of my head. Tugging on my hair, I don't even notice that my lips are moving while I beg, silent and desperate.

"Help you?"

A man rolls toward me on a cart. He quirks a brow, and I can see the curiosity in his expression under the white circle of light from the security lamps. I can only guess what the hell I must look like, and I'm standing inside the gate of a private airfield after midnight.

"That plane...was there a woman on it? Long, dark hair?" I want to grab the guy, shake him until he answers, but I fist my hands at my side to keep them in line.

Now his expression turns suspicious. "Why do you want to know?"

I take a step toward him and let my voice drop. All the authority I have inside me, some of it learned and some of it instinctual, bleeds through.

"I want to know, because it's my job to protect her, and I need to know whether or not she was on that goddamned plane. Her name is Sayward Diaz, and she could have been in the company of someone who wants to hurt her. Do you fucking understand me?" The man's eyes are wide by this time, suspicion gone and straight-up worry sitting on his face instead. "If you want to keep breathing, tell me whether or not she was *on that plane.*"

The man holds his hands out in front of him. "Look, man. She was on the plane, okay? All I did was get them ready for takeoff."

I size him up as rage boils in my blood, mixing with cold, black fear. "I need to know who else was on that plane and where it was going."

He licks his lips, nerves getting the best of him as he glances from side to side. "Yeah. Okay. Let's go into the office and I'll pull the manifest."

I don't know why the fuck we're still standing here. "Do it."

When he pulls out the manifest, he checks the names. "What's her name again?"

Grabbing it from his hands, I scan the document. Sayward's name is on it, as well as Marcos's. My phone begins to ring in my pocket just as I read three names that I don't know. The fourth name, I know way too well.

My phone stops ringing, and then starts right the fuck back up again. And I know why.

I slam the manifest back down on the counter and don't even remember walking out of the airfield office. I'm running for my truck as I pull my phone out of my pocket. Jacob's voice shouts from the other end before I can even take a breath.

"Suarez is ghost. Do you hear me? He's in the wind, Bennett. We didn't get him, or any of his guys. I want you to bring Sayward—"

"I don't have her." The words sound like a foreign fucking language to my own ears. I can't believe I'm saying this to my boss.

I can't believe I lost her.

Climbing into the truck, I switch to hands-free when I start the ignition and slap my palms against the wheel. There's enough energy racing through my veins that I could run a marathon, box in a full-length match, go to fucking war.

"Jacob..." I swallow hard around the blockage in my throat. "She's in the air. I'm at Jefferson Airfield. Marcos brought her here... *goddammit*!" Losing it for just a second, I slam my hands down again, this time making them sting.

"What do you mean, you fucking *lost* her? Where *is* she?"

I squeeze my eyes closed and press a hand to the side of my head. "She's on a private jet headed to Bogotá. Marcos is on board... and so is Suarez."

Silence stretches across the line as Jacob comprehends what I've just told him.

Finally, he growls out a response. "Stay your ass at the airfield. By the time the rest of the team gets there, a jet will be waiting for us."

Hope rises inside me, just a small bud, but it's definitely there. "We're going to get her?"

I was going to get her regardless. It's my fault she's gone, I was headed for the airport to book a flight out. I should have known I wouldn't have to do it alone.

"You're damn right. We're going to Colombia."

25

SAYWARD

I sit in a plush leather seat, my gaze aimed just to the left of Marcos's shoulder where he sits across from me. Suarez sits across the aisle from us, his ankle resting on his opposite knee. There's been a Cheshire-cat smile on his face for the past thirty minutes.

Because he's won.

Every time I glance at Marcos, there's real pain in his eyes. He pleads with me silently, asking me to understand this.

But I'll never understand.

"You set me up." Rising from my seat, I take the half step into Marcos's space and slap him across the face.

His head snaps to the left, but he doesn't make a sound. When he looks at me, I don't avoid his stare.

This is not my life. I was safe, hidden behind my computer. And then Bennett came along and stole my heart. And then Marcos came into town and tore me apart. Everything I thought I had feels so far away right now.

I'm completely and utterly lost.

Suarez finally lets out a heavy sigh. He flicks an invisible piece of dust from his gray slacks. His outfit confuses me. It makes me think that maybe he doesn't even know he's a low-level criminal drug dealer. Yes, he has money. But he carries himself like he's a legitimate business mogul. When all he is, is a snake.

As I sit back down my gaze snaps toward him. "Why don't you just kill me already?"

I really do want to know. Why am I on a plane to Colombia? *Is he really going to string me up in the town square for all to see?*

He ignores my question, focusing on my face. I immediately avert my eyes. "It's not Marcos's fault, you know. I kidnapped his family."

I suck in a breath, my entire body tensing up like I'm gearing up for battle. "You *what?*"

Marcos speaks up then, his tone full of disgust and heartbreaking remorse. It's too bad I don't have a heart left to shatter. Mine's already in smithereens. "He took them, *chica.* My wife and my son? Stole them right out from under me. He killed our father, and then made me come here to tell you in person."

"Why now?" My eyes flicker toward Suarez, and I look him in the eye for the first time. Discomfort crawls through my insides like rats, but I press through it. This I have to know.

Suarez shrugs. "I looked for a Sayward for years. Your name was the only tie I had to who *really* killed my father. You did a good job leaving the country, hiding out. I probably wouldn't have found you if it wasn't for coincidence. I overheard your father in the village speaking to his grandson—saying he wished the boy could meet his aunt Sayward. I figured it out pretty quickly after that. Killed your father—an eye for an eye. And then had Marcos lead me right to your doorstep."

Marcos's voice rises. "You want to carry on your piece-of-shit *padre*'s memory like this? You're nothing but shit under our feet." He spits the words, the anger running through him so potent he's trembling.

Suarez lifts a brow, anger flaring in his dark eyes. "You want your child's throat cut? Keep insulting my family." The words are said through a hiss, his teeth pressing hard together as he glares at Marcos.

Marcos's throat works as he swallows. Tearing his gaze away from Suarez and focusing on me again, I can almost feel the cabin of the plane squeezing in on me. The air feels cloying, too tight, and all I want to do is jump out of this airplane. Anything to get me away from these two men.

In the back of my head, a little voice tells me that I never should have walked away from Bennett. If I hadn't, I wouldn't be sitting on this plane right now with a gangster and a traitor. I manage to glare at Marcos without blinking.

"He'd found out where you were, and he was coming for you, *chica*. I was just his insurance policy. With me here, he knew I would be able to get you to come back to Colombia with me. And Sayward...he *has my family.* My whole world! What was I supposed to do?"

He's begging, pleading with me now for forgiveness. It's

in the hunched posture, the downtrodden tone in his voice. He's been truly broken, and maybe I can't blame him for what he did. He threw me under the bus, but not because he wanted to.

I turn away from all of them and stare out the window. There's nothing but blackness beyond, but that's fine by me. It matches the way I feel on the inside.

Black and empty.

When the plane lands, I'm not sure how long we've been flying. Somewhere over the Atlantic, I zoned out and tried really hard to forget who I am and what I'm doing. But now, the jet's wheels touching down on a foreign runway jar me back to myself, and I realize that I can't hide from this. I can't turn away and pretend it's not happening. There's no laptop for me to use as an excuse.

I have to face this, and I'm alone.

But then, a flicker of hope flares inside me. I've worked with the Rescue Ops team, and I know how good they are at their jobs. There's a good chance that by now, they know where I am and who I'm with. The only question?

Whether or not they'll get to me in time.

"I hear you're highly intelligent, Ms. Diaz. I hope that means you're wise enough not to try to run when we step off this plane. My security team will meet us outside."

I aim my gaze a little to the left of his nose. "And what do you plan to do with me once we leave this plane?"

His mouth curls into a smug smile. "I intend to let everyone know what happens when you fuck with a Suarez."

26

BENNETT

I stretch my legs out in front of me and lift my arms in the air, grateful that Jacob was able to charter a jet for the five-hour flight to Bogotá, Colombia. My muscles are coiled, tight. I'm ready to fucking spring, and all that nervous energy is eating me up inside.

Ronin, Conners, Teague, Jacob, and Abbott all hold similar positions in the bucket leather seats around me. A couple of the guys stare out the window, seeing nothing, while the others sit with their elbows resting on their knees.

All I can think about, over and over again in my fucked-up head, is that I disappointed her, she left me, and then I lost her.

Fucking Valarie.

But it's not Valarie's fault. I led Sayward to believe that I was ready for everything when it came to her. I know she didn't go to bed with me lightly, and in my heart I was making a promise when I slipped inside her for the first time.

Maybe I didn't say it out loud, but at some point during the time that I'd started guarding her and the first time we fucked, I'd fallen for this woman. I should have told her. I should have showed her by pulling her closer when Valarie showed up on my doorstep. Instead, I let her walk away.

And now I'm suffering for it, because shit got real the second she was out of my sight. I roll my eyes toward the ceiling, wanting to laugh at the irony. But laughing is the last thing I want to do right now. The fact that I have to sit still on this plane when I really want to jump out of my skin makes my soul riot. It feels so wrong.

I explained what happened to the guys and the boss the second the plane had taken off, having to go into detail about Valarie's reappearance and the status of my relationship with Sayward. Not that I'd been going out of my way to hide it.

Jacob's mouth had drawn into a thin line, but he hadn't snapped or lost his shit. He'd just listened, and the rest of the guys? Whatever this was between Sayward and me, they got it. Because they'd all been through it themselves. Not even Conners gave me shit. Protecting a woman they'd fallen for...It's like a twisted Rescue Ops tradition, one I had no idea I was gonna follow when I agreed to take this job.

But here I am. Sitting in their shoes, going after the woman I *fell for*, and losing isn't an option.

We've spent the last two hours strategizing. Teague had pulled up maps of the area, and each member of the team had taken turns studying them. He'd pointed out some of the physical and city data features of Bogotá, and we'd all committed them to memory. Then Abbott, Jacob, and Conners had begun kicking around ideas about how we'd mount a rescue mission.

First, we needed to know where Suarez would be holding Sayward. And just the thought of him touching her, keeping her against her will, maybe even hurting her for the fucking fun of it, sends me into a silent rage. My blood bubbles as I contemplate it, and my fists automatically clench.

She'd better be okay when I find her. It was going to be hard enough keeping myself from killing Suarez. The son of a bitch deserved nothing less than a slow, painful death. If it came to it, I'd be the one to give it to him.

"I've been connected, through a CIA acquaintance, to a contact in Bogotá. He'll meet us when we land, and he'll have information on where Suarez went when he arrived in the city overnight. The guy is too high profile in his city to be able to move without eyes on him. We'll have a location on him ASAP, and then we'll know that Sayward isn't far." Jacob's remained calm throughout this flight, even though a vein pulses in his jaw, flexing and tensing more often than I've ever seen.

The man cares about Sayward like she's his own daughter. I've seen them interact together, and even though he didn't raise Sayward with his own three daughters, he thought of her like his own. And he's suffering right now, same as me.

We need to get to her.

Jacob stares around the plane, holding each of our gazes for a beat, holding mine for a second longer. "We're going to have to play this one by ear, figure out exactly how to work it when we get there. There's not going to be an elaborate war plan like we'd normally use for a rescue. But Sayward is one of our own, and I'm guessing you're all okay with that."

Each of us nods once. No question. We'll do whatever it takes. As long as the end result is having Sayward on this plane with us when we leave Colombia.

The next couple of hours pass without anyone saying much. The other guys drift in and out of sleep, but I can't make myself rest. It'd be good for me to catch a couple hours shut-eye, but short of knocking myself out, there's no way in hell I can sleep. Not while every time I close my eyes all I can see is the hurt, stricken look on Sayward's face when she ran into my house last night.

I should have grabbed her then, should have held her back and told Valarie to get the hell out right then and there. Those few seconds of hesitation cost me Sayward, and I'm always going to remember that.

I get up to take a piss, and when I walk out of the bathroom Jacob is there, leaning against the wall. He stares me down, and I pause, waiting for it.

"You good?" he finally asks. "I need your head in the game for this. She's too important for your guilt trip right now. I need you focused. You're gonna have a job to do once we land in Bogotá."

I reel back like he's slapped me. "The only thing I'm focused on right now is her."

He nods, his blue eyes narrowing. "We all make mistakes. Especially where our women are concerned. You care about her?"

I blow out a breath and stand up straighter. "It's more than that."

Jacob nods, like he's not even a little surprised. "It's written all over you. When we get her back, make sure you tell her." He turns, prepared to return to his seat.

That's it? He's not gonna lay into me about how royally I fucked up?

"You're not pissed? Not gonna fire me?" Because let's face it, I had *one job*.

Jacob doesn't look back. "We'll talk after this mission is over."

When I settle back in my seat, the intercom comes alive with the copilot's voice. "Gentlemen, we have about thirty minutes before we begin our descent into Bogotá. Weather is nineteen degrees Celsius, clear skies. Should be a smooth landing."

I walk out of the bathroom in the hotel Jacob's contact booked for us, knowing we'd need a place to shower, change, and regroup once we arrived. He'd left us in the lobby, telling us he'd be back within two hours with information on Suarez's location and whether or not he was keeping Sayward with him.

Toweling my hair off, I sink onto the bed and discard the towel, dropping my face into my hands and taking a deep breath. Hours. It would only be a matter of hours until I had Sayward in my arms again, and only a matter of hours until that fucker who took her from me would either be behind bars or dead.

I don't really care which.

The bed across from me squeaks, and when I glance up it's to see Ronin staring at me. There's concern and sympathy written out all over his face, and I frown because I don't want either. I don't deserve anyone's sympathy.

"She'll be okay," he says with authority in his voice. "The woman is strong, stronger than most. There's something about her, man...Sayward's a survivor."

I nod. "Yeah. I know that. She's coming back to me, and then I can make this shit right."

A shadow crosses Ronin's face. "I know you're blaming yourself for all of this. But it doesn't all fall in your lap. It was a perfect storm of shit going wrong all at once. I saw the way she looked at you, man. Tell her and you'll both be okay."

All I can do is nod.

He glances at the smart watch strapped to his wrist. "Got about twenty minutes before we meet everyone downstairs. Jacob wants to get a quick plan set in place after we hear back from the informant."

Nodding, I reach for the clothes I'd picked up from a store down the street. I didn't pack shit before boarding that plane from Wilmington. All I'd been thinking about was getting here. I knew everything else could wait.

"Jacob also wants you to make a list of any supplies you might need. He's gonna send it to the contact, make sure he brings us everything we might use."

I lift a brow. "Supplies?"

Ronin's expression doesn't change. "We'll all be armed well...but you? You're probably gonna need to blow some shit up."

Understanding dawns on me, and I nod. "Yeah, okay." I pull out my phone to text Jacob a list.

I finish getting dressed, and ten minutes later finds us sitting down around a solid oak table in a room off the hotel lobby. The manager took a folded-up bill from Jacob to look the other way while we used the room as Jacob laid out a vague-as-fuck war plan while his contact stood off his shoulder.

"Listen, boys. Lockman here's been living in Bogotá for the past twelve years, and if anyone can get us close enough to Suarez to snatch Sayward, it's him. His intel tells us that Suarez went straight to his estate after leaving the airport last night. The thirteen-thousand-square-foot mansion sits on sixteen acres of land."

"That's it?" Teague glances up, one side of his mouth kicking up into his signature cocky-ass grin.

It's similar to the one I used to wear, before I went and fell in love with a woman who got herself kidnapped and taken to a foreign country. My grin is nowhere to be found right now.

Jacob nods. "It's not the largest piece of property, but that's a big chunk of real estate for this city. It's not going to be a cakewalk, Brains. Suarez is a dangerous man, and he has a lot of enemies. His estate is something like a fortress, and it's going to be work to get in and get Sayward out."

Fuck. I was hoping this shit would be easy. Not because I'm afraid to do the work and get my hands dirty, but because I want Sayward in my arms *now*. I don't want her to have to spend one second longer than necessary in the hands of her captor.

"Weak spots on the perimeter?" Conners speaks up. He's laser-focused, like Abbott and Ronin.

Lockman tugs the backpack from his shoulders and pulls out a hand-sketched map. "This is a drawing of the estate. Here you'll see the fortress-like wall that stretches around the house. The property line runs out much farther than the wall, and there's a chain-link fence running the route around the sixteen acres. However, there's a stream that runs through the back edge of the property, and the land there is wild. We should be able to breach the fence, but we'll need to take out the security cameras aimed toward each part of the land just before we encounter them."

Teague opens his laptop. "Damn. Hacking into security systems is Sayward's thing, but I'm on it."

"Once we've breached the perimeter fence, we can make our way up to the estate wall."

Abbott nods. "Up and over?"

Lockman frowns. "During broad daylight, with a manned security system and guards on patrol? I don't think so."

Frustration bleeds into Abbott's tone. "Then what the hell do you suggest?"

Grisham's nickname is Ghost because he built up a reputation for being able to get into enemy territory without that enemy ever knowing he was coming. He's a planner, a strategist, and walking into the situation blind is wearing him down. He's fucking pissed that he hasn't had the opportunity to study the map of the Suarez compound before now. It's scrawled out all over his expression.

Lockman aims a cool stare in Abbott's direction. "Isn't that what you're supposed to figure out?"

Grisham stands, his chair scraping back as irritation turns to outright pissed-offedness on his face. Jacob stands, too, a hand on Abbott's chest.

"All right, settle down." Jacob's voice is forceful without being loud. "Take the map. You have twenty minutes with it, and when you come back I want you to tell us how we're getting over that goddamned wall."

Fuck that shit. I respect Abbott and his skills, but I can't sit through this. I stand, too. "We don't have twenty minutes. If we can't go over the fucking wall, then we're going through."

Everyone's eyes move to me, Ronin's mouth tipping up in a "hell yeah" grin.

Jacob lifts a brow. "If we blow a hole in the wall, we lose the element of surprise."

Abbott starts to grin, a slow smile that lets me know he's on to something. "Not necessarily. Not if they think the explosion is mechanical." He scans the map again, and this time, his face lights up. "See, right here. There's an above-ground propane tank here. Probably used to heat the entire estate. We blow it up, Suarez's people think *it's just the tank blowing.* It's a diversion. It gets us inside."

I nod, knowing I can rig a propane tank to explode in my sleep. Glancing around at my team, I feel the nervous energy animating me, pushing me to move.

"Let's do this. Let's get my girl the fuck out."

27

SAYWARD

The car travels up a long, winding driveway. When we stop outside a tall, stucco wall my mouth falls open. Who does this man think he is? A king?

The entire time I've been forced to be with Suarez, he's given off an air of importance. Like nothing can touch him. He's nothing more than a criminal, but he carries himself like a prince. He's prideful, and he treats the people around him like lowly staff members. Does he have a single friend? Anyone he loves, trusts, cherishes?

Marcos hasn't spoken since he explained to me what happened to his family a few hours ago. But he speaks now from his place beside me. "Is my family here?" His voice is flat. He stares out his window, and I can't see his face in order to read his expression.

I bet if I could, his face would be as flat as his tone. Marcos isn't a monster. He sold me out to save his family; it was an impossible choice. Logic has always been more understandable to me than emotion. But this isn't some situation I'm judging from the outside. This is *my* brother, *my family.* Betrayal threatens to overwhelm me; my chest aches and I keep rubbing at the spot, hoping to alleviate some of the pain. But who's really to blame? Marcos? Me, for trusting him?

Or Pablo Suarez?

Of course, the answer is the Colombian cartel's leader.

Suarez glances back at Marcos from his place in the front seat. "We had a deal, Mr. Diaz. And you lived up to your end. Your family is waiting for you inside the estate. Once we arrive, you'll all be free to go. Well, not *all* of you." He glances at me and smiles.

I hate his smile. It sends nausea swishing through my belly, and I can feel my skin growing pale under his cool stare.

Marcos looks at me then, really looks at me. Before I turn away, I see pure pain and regret flash in his eyes. He wishes he could save me, and I wish there was some way I could absolve him. I wish I could tell him it's okay, that he'll have his family and that's all he needs to worry about.

But I can't find the words, so I say nothing.

The car pauses outside a gate in the wall, where the driver scans an identification card. The monitor at the gate beeps, and then the iron railing swings open. The car continues its slow progression up the winding driveway. We roll to a stop in front of the most massive home I've ever seen. It's more like a castle, with stucco walls and a red-tile roof. Manicured lawns surround the estate, palm trees the most prominent feature on the grounds. Everything here is like a tropical paradise, a mecca of peacefulness and civility, which I know is a complete farce.

Maybe this is where Pablo Suarez comes to relax, where he finds solace from the horrible, gruesome acts he performs every day. But to me? This is just another form of hell.

The passenger door opens, and one of the members of Suarez's security team pulls me out by my arm. His grip is too tight, and I wince, but I don't bother to try to jerk my arm away. There would be no point.

I'm immediately towed toward the house, and I hear Marcos's voice behind me shouting with panic.

"Wait! Let me say good-bye to her!"

No on answers him. Marcos's voice rises. "Where's my family?"

Suarez chuckles. "Family?"

I jerk my body to a stop, righting against the man dragging me along. "Wait. Stop! You promised him his family!"

Wrenching my body around to find Suarez's evil smile fixed on me, I shiver.

"We'll see how well you behave," he say, his voice full of darkness. "Maybe your brother can have his family back eventually. But for now? You all come inside."

Marcos's bellow of fury echoes behind me as I'm jerked around and forced to walk again.

Inside me, cold fear settles heavily in my limbs. I thought that me being his prisoner, and eventually his example, would be enough. That it would mean my nephew would live.

But what if all of this was for nothing?

I'm led inside through two enormous double doors into a white-tiled foyer. The entry hall of the mansion is grand, just like the exterior. I don't have much time to evaluate the bright, airy atmosphere or the colorful art pieces on the wide expanses of walls because I'm corralled straight up one side of a double staircase and thrust into a cavernous room. The shiny wooden door slams behind me, and when I glance back I see two men dressed all in black, members of Suarez's security team, taking up their post inside the closed door.

Turning back to the room, I glance around me with tightness in my stomach. So many emotions are swirling around inside, I don't know which one to focus on first. I'm terrified, because I know that at some point in the very near future Suarez plans to end my life. I'm sad, because even after betraying me, my brother still doesn't have his family back. But hope manages to spread, strange and unexpected, though my heart because despite the bleakness of my situation, I know the Rescue Ops better than anyone else. I know that if anyone has a chance to survive this, I do. Because of them.

But there's a very real and present danger lurking somewhere in this big, beautiful mansion. And his name is Pablo Suarez.

I drop into a big, comfortable leather chair. This room appears to be some kind of office or study, because there are shelves lined with books and comfortable seating, but there's also a massive L-shaped desk and a laptop computer. My eyes linger on the laptop, my fingers twitching with the desire to run to it and pull it open.

What would I find on Suarez's computer?

Staring around at all the books, I'm almost tickled into laughter. *What kind of books does the head of a drug cartel like to read?* It's such an absurd thought. Everything about this monster is juxtaposed. It's like he thinks he was born into royalty, someone whose blood makes them better than everyone else. But really, all he is, is a thug.

I'm sure Suarez wouldn't appreciate the thought.

The two men beside the door stare straight ahead, and the silence in the room grows heavy, oppressive.

"How long?" I ask them. "Until he hangs me in the town square?"

One man snorts. "You won't hang unless you disobey. You're Suarez's property now. He owns you. Like a pretty, shiny trophy. Your brother and his family, on the other hand?" He curls his fingers into a cruel good-bye wave.

My stomach rolls as I turn away from his sickening face.

As a protective instinct, my mind wanders: away from this room, across an ocean, to a town that I call home. To a little, perfect house beside the waves, where a man I never saw coming lives.

Bennett.

The thought of him, the picture of his beautiful face as it flickers through my mind, is almost enough to make me crumble.

I miss him.

I shouldn't have left him. What happened when he talked

to Valarie? Does she want another chance with him? I can't imagine that she wouldn't, now that I've spent time with him. The way Bennett Blacke made me feel, both between the sheets and out of bed, was enough to change my life. I can't imagine being with another man, not ever. He changed me in ways I never could have expected. He made me see myself as someone who could be beautiful. Desired.

Loved.

And now I may never get the chance to thank him for that. How far away is my team? Could Jeremy find the information they would have needed to locate me?

God...the hope. I almost don't want it to take flight inside my chest, because the crushing effect of disappointment will kill me faster than Suarez ever could.

Again, I glance at the laptop on the desk, before darting a look toward the men by the door. They seem bored.

I lean my head back against the leather of my chair and close my eyes.

28

BENNETT

Hold tight for just a sec...there. Video feed to that portion of the perimeter fence is down. You have thirty seconds."

Teague's voice travels clearly through the coms, the tiny earpiece he outfitted me is working perfectly despite the wooded environment. Around us, wildlife continues about their business without caution. Five men with Special Forces training creeping through the woods with almost silent precision isn't a disturbance that alarms them. It's like we aren't even here. Glancing around at the other members of the team, I take less than a second to think about the fact that I'm doing this again.

I'm dressed in camouflage cargo pants and a brown T-shirt, blending in with my surroundings, outfitted with protective gear and highly specialized weapons, carrying a duffle on my back filled with bomb-making supplies.

This. I'm doing *this* again, and adrenaline rushes through my system like a goddamn wildfire.

At the other end of this mission, Sayward Diaz is waiting for me. There's no way I'll fucking fail.

Abbott produces a small torch from his backpack, and sliding a pair of safety glasses into place from the top of his head, he gets to work cutting a hole in the fence large enough for us to slip through. It takes seconds, and as soon as he's done we slide through the fence one by one. Once we're on the other side, we follow Teague's instructions on which direction to take.

"Ghost, proceed with a hard cut east-northeast. That'll put you in the vicinity of the propane tank buried outside the wall in approximately seven minutes."

Abbott nods. "Copy."

Instead of walking in a straight line, we stagger and set off in the direction Teague instructed. Each outfitted with a smart watch that lets us know how far we've traveled and the direction we're moving, we don't need Abbott to keep us on the correct course or to lead us in the right direction. But the foliage grows less and less dense as we move, and soon sweat beads on my forehead and the back of my neck. Not because of the heat; it's only about sixty-seven degrees Fahrenheit. But we're out in the open in broad daylight, and I don't like that shit one bit.

Teague works ahead of us from his position outside the perimeter with our contact, Lockman. We're hiding in plain sight in the crime boss's security system. Apparently, he feels like if he has cameras aimed at the perimeter fence and the wall, that's enough. The entire sixteen acres of property in between is unwatched, and he's one dumb motherfucker for letting that happen.

Conners has similar thoughts. "He should have hired NES to install his security system. No way would we have let this area go unmanned."

Teague's chuckle comes through my earpiece. "Damn straight. Guess he figures he'll catch anyone stupid enough to intrude at the gate or the wall, huh, Wheels?"

"Then he doesn't know the Rescue Ops team," I mutter darkly to myself, but the answering laughter from the other guys tells me they heard.

My lips twitch into a smirk, and I'm suddenly lifted to a place where I'm hopeful. Where I come out at the end of this with Sayward in my arms and the respect of a team I never asked to be a part of.

"Everybody. Stop. Moving." Jacob Owen might as well have shouted his order, for the way we all instantly obeyed it. Our footsteps all came to an abrupt halt, and my heart starts to hammer against my rib cage like a wild animal trapped inside my chest.

"Drop." At the Boss Man's one-word order, I fall to my stomach like the other four men, the side of my face slamming into the hard ground. My ear, the one facing the sky, pricks as a dull buzzing sound rises from somewhere above us.

"Talk to me…oh, *shit*." Teague's curse lifts the hairs on my arms.

"What the fuck does that mean, Brains?" Jacob grinds the

question out through what sounds like gritted teeth. I can't see the members of my team from my position frozen on the ground, but the buzzing grows louder and dread fills me up.

"Drone," Teague grinds out. "Dammit! Viper would have caught this. They have a drone patrolling the no-man's-land between the fence and the wall. Looked too easy, because it fucking was!"

"Don't move." Jacob's voice is low, even. He's not panicked, he's in command of the situation, and he knows it. "Stay still and you'll blend into the landscape."

My muscles rigid, my nerves buzzing with anticipation and nervous energy, I do as I'm told. I'm frozen, becoming a part of the land around me. The drone's buzzing gets louder with every passing second until it sounds like it's right above our heads.

And then the air I was holding inside my lungs is expelled all at once, because the sound fades as the drone flies away.

"Fucking hell," mutters Abbott as we all stand.

"You need to *move*." Teague's voice is laced with urgency. "Don't know if the drone saw you or not, and if it did they'll be on you. Get to the high point, *now*."

Our pace increases to a jog and we reach the point highest on the grounds. It's far enough away from the wall for our purpose, and we get there within three minutes. Spreading out along the hill, Conners, Abbott, Jacob, and Ronin take up positions with weapons at the ready. I crouch low, pulling off my pack. I study the large, one-hundred-gallon tank through a rifle scope. When I think I've got it figured out, I take what I need out of my pack and jog down toward the propane tank. I squat beside it and reach around to the back side. I locate the relief valve and pull out the plug I brought with me. Stuffing it inside the valve, I focus on the materials Lockman secured. Then I focus on the tank. I zero in, seeing nothing but what's in front of me. I trust my team to cover my six, because I have one job during the next few minutes and one job only. I try to momentarily block out Sayward's face in my mind. It's just me, this goddamn tank, and the explosion I'm about to create.

My chemical knowledge tells me exactly what to do as I carefully mix three ingredients that will cause the propane to heat way too fast. Without the use of the relief valve, which I've made sure is useless, it won't take long until the whole thing goes *kaboom*. Retreating to the rise where the team waits, I attach the mixture to the ammunition and hand it over to Conners.

He takes it from me, loads it onto the rocket launcher Teague procured, and sets his sights on the scope.

"Aim." He says in a low tone. "Fire."

He squeezes the trigger.

As a Ranger, Dare wasn't a sniper. But his aim is damn good, and my bomb lands directly under the target, just like it should. We all watch, and everything in the air around me seems that much louder as I catch my breath and wait.

Whoosh.

The propane tank is ignited as the chemical mix I rigged engulfs it in flames. Without the relief valve meant to save the tank during situations just like this, it only takes seconds before the entire tank explodes. The blast radius doesn't reach the mansion beyond, but the wall crumbles, just like we wanted it to.

We can hear Jeremy's celebratory whoop on the coms, but we're all silent as we spread out into our planned positions and *move*.

Sayward's face is back at the forefront of my mind. It's a beacon guiding me through that goddamn crumbled wall, and I'm not gonna stop until every single fucker standing between us is annihilated and the woman I love is back in my arms.

29

SAYWARD

I jerk upright as what feels like a sonic boom ricochets through my body, and my eyes snap wide open. My back teeth clamp together and my heart skips two beats before stuttering to a stop and then taking off like a racehorse's galloping hooves.

An explosion.

The words come to mind almost instantly, and my heart lifts, soars. That was the sound of an explosion, and that can't be coincidence.

NES is here.

Bennett is here.

Both men standing beside the door jump, turning toward each other with confusion before one of them opens the door and peers out into the hall. They speak to each other in rapid-fire Spanish, asking what the hell that noise was and wondering what they should do.

Then, something happens that's better than anything I

could have asked for. They both disappear out the door, leaving me alone and locking it behind them.

I'm up and out of my seat in a second, running to the desk and lifting that laptop lid open. A password screen pops up and I roll my eyes before typing in a few keys at warp speed and bypassing it completely. I don't even know what I'm looking for, all I know is that I want to make sure Pablo Suarez never sees the light of day again. I don't waste precious seconds logging into the NES network to communicate my location, I trust my team to find me. But if I make it out of this mansion alive, I need to know this time that the man who brought me here is in prison. For good.

My fingers fly across the keys as I open folder after folder of documents. From Pablo Suarez's demeanor, it doesn't surprise me. The man is smooth and put together, and I'm not even a little bit shocked that he's brought his father's cartel into the twenty-first century with digital recordkeeping.

Each time I scan a folder's title and open it, I then send the file to the NES cloud. I'm getting everything, and I'll sort through the information later. Or I'll let the FBI do it.

Then the cursor rolls across a phrase that makes me pause, and I read it again.

MOBILE PROPERTY HOLDINGS

Glancing at the door, knowing I'm almost out of time, I click on the folder.

And almost swallow my tongue.

Names. Name after name after name, in columns and rows for pages.

All female.

And if I were a betting woman, I'd bet money that these are the names of women who've been considered "property" of the cartel for years. Sold to the highest bidder. Or held as slaves.

I send the information along to the cloud with the rest, knowing I've just found the nail that will keep Pablo Suarez's coffin closed forever.

In the next minute, voices rise on the other side of the door, shouts and the sound of thudding footsteps. Urging myself to hurry, I download the last file that I can find. I'm closing the lid to the laptop just as the door is flung open. I step out as far from the desk as I possibly can.

Suarez strides in with one of the security guards previously stationed as my gatekeeper trailing behind him. The man's gun is at the ready, but Suarez opens both arms wide, almost in apology, before clasping them behind his back.

"It seems we've had an unfortunate accident. The propane tank on my property just exploded. We are lucky the entire estate didn't go up in flames."

Satisfaction swims inside me, a rising tide of hope and jubilation I hide under the mask of a blank expression.

"Oh?" *Idiot. Doesn't he know the chances of a propane tank explosion happening on its own are slim to none?*

Suarez gestures for me to step forward. "Yes. We are leaving now. It is not safe for us here, not with the fire. Let's go."

Nervous agitation makes my palms sweat. I don't move. "Where are we going?"

I can't leave this place with him. Not now, not when I know that my team is close. They're here, I just need to give them time to get to me. Suarez's men must be crawling all over this place like worker bees in a hive. It's going to take them a few minutes to get to me.

"*Now*," snaps Suarez. "Come."

He reaches forward, grabs my arm, and shoves me in front of him. He pushes me past his man, the pressure of his hand gripping my arm never lessening, and the man takes up his place walking behind us as Suarez hurries me out the door. Once we're in the hallway, I glance both ways and see that the place is surprisingly empty.

We're hurrying along the landing, the security guard advising Suarez in Spanish that the staff has been evacuated, but that a team is waiting downstairs to escort him.

My heart sinks. *Was I wrong?* Maybe the propane tank really had just coincidentally exploded. Maybe thinking that the Rescue Ops team was in full-blown mission mode to save *me* was just that: wishful thinking.

But then the sound of gunfire erupting downstairs causes all three of us to falter. The security guard lifts the weapon he's been carrying by his side, a semiautomatic rifle. The sight of it makes my heart pump too much blood into my veins, inciting my fight-or-flight reflex. My muscles twitch and jerk, urging me to turn and flee from this man and his weapon.

But Suarez grips me tighter as he reaches down under

his slacks to an ankle holster. He pulls up a pistol, holding it expertly in one hand while he turns this way and that, searching for any sign of an intruder on this level.

"Go," he murmurs to his security professional, and the man shoulders his weapon and edges toward one side of the dual staircase.

Still keeping me in front of him, Suarez, the fucking coward, jerks me back against his chest and hauls me backward. His steps are quick and sure, and panic bubbles up inside me as I open my mouth and scream.

White, blinding light explodes behind my eyelids. Pain blossoms in my head, and I realize that all Suarezes fight the same: dirty. Pablo took a page out of his dead father's handbook and slammed the butt of his gun against my head.

My knees buckle and I lose the ability to hold myself up as my head lolls to one side. Suarez drags me, half-conscious, into a room off the hallway and kicks the door closed.

"Stupid bitch," he hisses, all hints of his sophisticated facade now long gone. "Shut your fucking mouth."

His breath is hot against my neck, and I can't respond to anything he says. My mouth doesn't seem to be working, and my brain is only half-registering what's happening right now. The pain in my head is so intense all I want to do is close my eyes, but something, probably my own will to live, forces me to keep them open.

A beautifully rugged face with warm cerulean eyes and dark blond hair works its way into my mind, and I focus on him.

Bennett.

"Are you responsible for the commotion?" Suarez's voice is nothing but a pissed-off grunt. He's dropped his other personality completely, no longer acting the suave and educated prince. Instead, he's reverted back to the place he belongs and is truly comfortable.

The gutter.

He spits on the floor beside us as he pushes the muzzle of the gun hard into the tender spot on my head. Something wet and hot—my own blood?—drips down the side of my face. I moan in pain as my stomach revolts, nausea rising.

"Your people are stupid enough to come to *mi casa*, blow up *my* shit? All to what...rescue you?" He says the words like they're truly disgusting to him. Like the idea of someone risking themselves to save me is the most impractical move a man could make.

I try to move my lips, but my mouth fails me. I blink rapidly as the scene in front of me swims in and out of focus, hazy darkness creeping in on the edge of my vision.

"I'll show you what—"

But Suarez doesn't get to finish his sentence before two sharp thuds on the door stop him. Then the entire thing flies off its hinges and that face—the one I thought I'd only see in my imagination again—materializes on the other side.

Dressed in camouflage, his chiseled face scuffed with dirt and hair dusted with leaves and twigs, he carries an assault rifle as he steps across the threshold looking like an avenging angel.

30

BENNETT

The explosion worked better than we could have hoped for. All we had to do was step aside and stay out of the way while the mansion's staff fled the place. The heat from the blast lingered, raging flames rising up into the sky on the heels of a black cloud of smoke, and fire puts the fear of God in people. No one really noticed us as they ran until we entered the foyer and encountered members of the cartel. Armed and ready to escort Suarez off the premises, they got a nasty surprise when we entered, fast and hot.

Gunshots ensued, and some of the men were taken out before they realized we were the real deal, and the rest of the fucking cowards ran like the pussies they are.

Jacob told Ronin to sweep the downstairs portion of the mansion, sending Conners and I upstairs. Through our coms, Jeremy instructs us that we have less than ten minutes until Bogotá law enforcement arrives.

"Copy. We need to be out before that happens, men."

Jacob's voice is gruff across my earpiece. "With Sayward in hand."

Conners is right behind me as we clear the stairs fast. At the top, I poke my head around the corner and see one man, armed to the hilt, coming in hot. Ducking back behind the corner and down one step, I wait until just the right moment and reach out, grabbing him. He shouts, firing off a round into the air before I fling him down the stairs behind me. Conners flattens himself to the wall until the man tumbles past, and then we're both in the hallway. Opening doors one at a time and clearing rooms in record speed, the adrenaline in my system seems to spike with each second I spend inside this goddamned house.

Sayward's face keeps flashing in my mind, the only thing driving me forward. Anything that comes between me and her is susceptible to being taken the fuck out.

My blood pressure skyrockets. The last time I've felt like this? This intense, this close to the edge? When I beat the shit out of the man I caught fucking my wife.

But this is totally different. I realize that now. This man, the fucking *animal* who hits first and asks questions later, is what's going to bring Sayward home alive. Because I won't stop until she's in my arms again. Period.

The very thing that scared me about returning to this life where I use my training, my skills, to hunt and defend, is the very thing that's going to save her life.

"Clear!" Conners shouts from the room beside the closed door I'm standing in front of.

One booted foot comes up and I kick twice before the

wood splinters and the locked door flies open. And the only thing I've wanted to see since she left me is right in front of me.

Sayward.

I take one second to feel the relief and motherfucking joy before it all turns to red, blinding *rage.*

The breath catches in my throat. My vision laser-focuses on the man standing behind her, crushing her to his chest as the coward uses her as a fucking shield. The muzzle of his gun presses to her head, and bright red blood trickles down the side of her face.

From where I'm standing, fifteen feet away from her, I can see the way her eyes swim in and out of focus. She's barely standing on her own, held up by the motherfucking *monster* standing behind her.

My heart explodes.

Pain.

And fury like I've never felt in my entire life. All swirling, mixing, turning into a potent chemical inside me.

I feel rather than hear Conners come up on my six. I don't know how I know it's him, but sometime between starting this mission to go after Sayward and now, we've started working in sync.

"Settle, brother," he mutters.

That's all he says, but it's all I need to inhale. I need to fucking breathe in and breathe out before I fuck this up for Sayward.

"Viper." Conners' voice lifts so that Sayward can hear him. "Status."

My eyes don't leave her, but I assess the situation around her. We're in a bedroom. There's a queen bed pushed against the wall at my right, and a closed closet or bathroom door to the left. Suarez has Sayward backed up as far as he can go, his back to a large window.

Window. That's not good.

I need them to move away from the fucking window.

Sayward frowns, little wrinkles forming in her forehead as she tries to focus on Dare and me. "Fine...head hurts. Dizzy."

Fuck! He definitely hit her...her words are slurred and it sounds like her tongue is thick. She's only minutes from passing out. I don't know how she's still conscious now.

She works her mouth a couple of times and tries again. "Bennett?"

"I'm right here, beautiful." My words are low, calm.

Steady. That's what she needs right now. Steady.

Then Suarez opens his mouth, and I'm right back to the rage. Burning through me like napalm, threatening to take me over completely.

"Shut up, bitch." He presses the muzzle tighter against her head and then looks at me. "You want me to use this on her? I don't want to, but I'll kill her, just like my father killed her cunt *mama.* Sayward Diaz hid from me for years. But my father told me, all those years ago...he told me she was mine. And I've come to collect. The Diaz family owes me. This bitch belongs to *me.*"

A small cry of fury escapes Sayward, and I see red. "Let her walk. You want to talk about how you're gonna save your own ass right now? We can do that. But let go of the girl."

His face twists even further into an ugly sneer. "You walked into my house uninvited. Bet your government doesn't know you're here, do they? You're on my turf, cowboy. I'm not letting go of shit."

He tugs Sayward even closer to his chest. Her eyes roll back in her head.

"Time's up." Teague's voice travels through our coms just as the wail of sirens rises outside. "Get her out, now."

Beside me, I feel Dare tense and know what's coming. I open my mouth, barking an order for Sayward.

"Hey, beautiful." Her eyes drift open, focusing on me for one clear second. "Drop."

Her eyes immediately comprehending, her entire body goes limp in Suarez's arms. He doesn't have time to clutch her tighter and he loses his grip. In the half second it takes for him to glance down to see what's happened, Dare squeezes his trigger.

The window behind them bursts out, and I see Sayward staggering backward from the force of the gunshot that hits Suarez in the shoulder.

I surge forward, everything around me fading to black as my whole world shifts, tilts.

This is fear.

Fear like I've never known it before.

31

SAYWARD

I'm dropping toward the ground when Suarez's body knocks me off course. He's been hit by Dare's shot, and he's flying backward toward the blown-out window.

Then I'm hurtling backward right along with him.

For one strange moment that seems like it's frozen in time, my eyes lock with Bennett's. God, if this is the last thing I get to see before I go crashing through that window...it's a wonderful last sight.

"Sayward!" He shouts my name as he hurtles forward, his arm outstretched. I can feel his fingertips graze mine as my back touches open air, but then his hand is gripping my fingers and pulling me sharply against him.

The pain in my head ignites; feeling like my brain is on fire. My eyes flutter closed, and all I see is blackness.

Beep. Beep. Beep.

The steady noise breaks into my consciousness before I'm

really awake, and I want to frown in annoyance. I want to keep sleeping.

But my eyes peel open against their will. There's a harsh, bright light above me, and I wince against it. Closing my eyes again, I moan softly.

Pressure lands against my hand, and then Bennett's voice pulls my eyes open again. His face, so achingly handsome, looks down at me. There are dark circles beneath his eyes; they look like bruises. But his lips curve into a smile, a real, genuine smile.

"There you are, beautiful."

I blink, refusing to glance away from his tawny eyes to look around me. "Where am I?"

"Hospital." He brings my fingers to his lips and kisses them. "Do you remember what happened?"

Closing my eyes again, I think back. I remember everything that happened, every single horrible detail. "Suarez." My voice is scratchy.

Bennett nods. "Dead."

Then my body begins to tremble, and my eyes widen as I look to Bennett to confirm my worst fears. "Marcos? Suarez didn't—is Marcos and his family—" I can't finish the question, can't make myself say the words.

Bennett's words soothe me like nothing else could. His hand brushes against my forehead. "Shhh. They're safe, beautiful."

My tongue darts out to lick my dry lips as relief floods me, and Bennett reaches for the call button. When a nurse answers, he doesn't take his eyes from me as he speaks.

"She's awake. Can you bring some water, please?"

Bennett holds my small hand in both of his large ones now, rubbing softly. It's like he's afraid to let go of me. When the nurse bustles in, he doesn't move an inch and he doesn't glance at her.

He has eyes only for me, and that thought sends butterflies swarming around in my belly.

It's not the first time I've ever experienced butterflies around Bennett. I kind of like the feeling.

"Ice chips," says the nurse brightly. "You're on some pretty strong painkillers, so we want to see how those affect your stomach before you can have anything else. Would you like me to help you eat these?"

I shake my head at the same time Bennett says, "I got it."

The nurse gives a knowing smile. "Okay. I'm going to send your doctor in shortly. He can explain your condition."

She leaves, and I take a bite of the ice Bennett holds out with a spoon. Swallowing it, I eye him with curiosity. "Do you know my condition?"

H clears his throat, his expression looking pained. "You were hit...with the gun. The fucker almost hit you hard enough to crack your skull, but as it is you have a severe concussion. It's been scary, baby. You might...not have woken up." He swallows, the sound audible among the beeping. "We've been waiting for you to wake up so we could ask you if he...hurt you in any other way."

Real pain shadows his eyes. Squeezing his hand, I shake my head quickly. Too quickly.

It hurts.

"No." The word is forceful. I can't imagine how he's been handling sitting here thinking about all the things Suarez could have done to me. "He didn't touch me, Bennett."

All the air leaves him on a heavy sigh, and he sags a little in his chair. "Thank fuck for that. God, baby... I'm so goddamned sorry."

My eyes leave his face for the first time, glancing down at the blanket covering my legs. "Bennett—"

My hospital room door opens, and Jacob walks in. He doesn't bother to knock, just strides in like he owns the place. Bennett's eyes close for a second too long, but I smile over at Jacob.

"Hi."

Jacob's voice is more gruff than usual, and his eyes are actually shining. I'm so taken aback, I can't even say anything else. "You're a sight for this old man, Sayward. Jesus... you scared the shit out of all of us."

I glance behind him, but the door stays closed.

Rolling my eyes at the "old man" comment, because Jacob is only fifty, I lean back against my mound of pillows.

Jacob's lips twitch. "They're all here, sweetheart. Waiting until they can see you. But I gotta tell you... coffee in Colombian hospitals? Really excellent."

I burst into laughter. Bennett doesn't take his eyes off me, but he grins, and I know that everything will be okay.

"Tell me more about Marcos," I say softly, pleading with Jacob and Bennett both.

Bennett growls, and Jacob drops a hand onto his shoulder.

"We sent Abbott and Conners to question Marcos. Did Suarez really have his wife and kid?"

I nod.

"Jesus," mutters Bennett. "It doesn't fucking matter to me, Boss. The fucker is her *blood.* He brought the cartel to Wilmington. He allowed them near her. He threw her under the bus. *We can't let it go.*" His voice is full of venom and fire.

I reach for Bennett's hand again, pulling his attention back to me. Tugging him closer, I place my palm on his cheek. "He's my brother. He loves me, but he had an impossible choice."

Bennett's eyes soften as he stares into mine, but then his gaze flicks toward what must be a pretty sizable bandage on my head, and the fury in his eyes glows bright. He shoves back from the bed and paces away, his hands raking agitatedly through his hair.

"I can't forgive him for this." His words are broken, empty.

I look at Jacob. "His family needs him. I want to let it go, Jacob."

Jacob seems torn. He glances at Bennett, and the expression on his face says he's inclined to agree with his feelings. But when he looks at me, I know he's going to do as I ask.

"I want to see him," I whisper.

Bennett turns toward me, disbelief and anger scrawled across his face. "You're serious right now?"

I'm suddenly so filled with anger and exhaustion, it all comes tumbling out through my mouth.

My eyes defiant, my head throbbing, I snap, "Where's Valarie right now?"

I want to take the words back as soon as I say them. Hurt, pure and unhidden, flashes in Bennett's eyes. He holds my gaze for only a moment before he strides out of my room without looking back.

Jacob sighs and drops into the chair beside my bed. Big, fat tears roll down my cheeks, and I marvel at how different I am since this whole roller-coaster ride began. I've never cried in front of Jacob before.

With a sad smile, he reaches out and wipes away a tear with his thumb. I suck in a breath, trying not to sob.

"You fell in love with him." It's not a question. "What happened?"

The story tumbles out, about arriving back to Bennett's house that night to see Valarie waiting for him. I recall the way it felt, seeing her there, and thinking that there was a possibility of everything I'd just begun building with Bennett.

"You were jealous when you saw her." Jacob's eyes are kind, but his expression doesn't give an inch. "But did he give you reason to be?"

I open my mouth and then close it again. *Jealousy?* Now that he'd put a name on the sickening emotion I felt that night, and every time I've thought of it since, it makes me feel petty and small. "He let go of me."

Jacob nods. "So he'd just been ambushed by his ex, the woman whose cheating was the very thing that sent him over the edge and straight into prison after he returned from deployment. Do you really think he'd want to be with her again?"

Jacob's voice is kind and patient, not accusatory, but I'm still filled with shame.

Silence stretches around us, and I drop my eyes to study the white blanket once again.

"You need to consider the answer to that, sweetheart. I saw the way he looked at you, acted around you, protected you with everything in him. Hell, every man at NES saw it. His feelings for you weren't hidden. Not at all."

My stomach bottoms out. "I never should have run from him that night. I know that, Jacob. I realized it during that plane ride with Suarez. I should have stayed, talked it out. Maybe if I had, none of this would have happened. Marcos never could have made the trade. But then...would my nephew be alive?"

It's a rabbit hole I could get lost in if I go too far.

Jacob nods. "I'm going to do what you asked and get Marcos here. But I have a feeling there's someone you want with you when that happens."

I nod, feeling exhaustion seeping into my bones. "Can you find him for me?"

But the door opens and Bennett is already there, darkening the doorway with his hulking frame, his arms folded across his chest.

Jacob leans down and kisses my forehead. I don't even flinch.

"Talk to him. And then get some rest. Marcos will be here when you wake up."

I nod, offering him a grateful smile. Before he leaves the room, he glances back.

"You know Suarez is dead. The bullet that Dare shot killed him before he hit the ground. But I want you to know that every single cartel member in that house is in Colombian police custody, and our government has their hands in it to make sure justice is served.

"We saw those computer files you sent from Suarez's computer. Not only will they put every member of the cartel away but they're also going to save hundreds of lives. The CIA is already looking into finding and rescuing those women. You're a hero Sayward." He smiles at me before he leaves the room and I'm left alone with Bennett.

My eyes remain trained on the door that Jacob just closed, mulling over the fact that he just declared me a *hero*. Me, Sayward Diaz. The hacker with no family and no social skills.

A hero?

When I finally glance toward Bennett, he stands there, staring at me, waves of emotion rolling off of him. I don't look away, because at this point no matter how much I want to crawl out of my skin I need him to know that I'm not running away.

Not this time.

"I'm sorry." He finally says, voice rough and laced with remorse. "I shouldn't have walked out. Marcos is your family, I have no right to tell you not to see him."

I'm already shaking my head before he finishes his sentence. "I understand your concern, Bennett. Of course I do.

It's just . . . I have a nephew. All Marcos wanted to do was save his wife and child . . . the same way you saved me. " My voice breaks. "I want my family back."

He nods, and with just two long strides, he eats up the distance between us and drops into the chair. Folding his hands on top of my blanket, he rests his chin on them, eyes holding mine.

"You have to know that I don't want Valarie. I want you." His words are simple; his eyes are sincere.

Everything about Bennett is honest. It always has been. I have no reason to doubt him. And now that I know the emotion fueling my behavior that night was jealousy, my cheeks heat with flame.

"I'm so sorry, Bennett. I never should have left you. I should have trusted that what we had was real."

He lifts a brow, his mouth pulling into a taut line. He takes my hand. "You need to trust that what we *have is* real. I'm not going anywhere. Not now . . . not ever."

My eyelids droop. I try to force them to stay open, but it's a battle I'm just not strong enough to fight. Bennett's warm, probing eyes are the last thing I see before mine close.

"Promise?" I whisper.

"I promise. Sleep, beautiful. I'll be here when you wake up."

32

BENNETT

The last six hours have been hell.

The worst hours of my fucking life, and I've been to war.

When Sayward collapsed in my arms at the mansion, I found out what pure desperation feels like. All I wanted was for her to open her big, beautiful hazels and tell me she was okay. I'd scooped her into my arms and carried her out, head cradled gently against my chest. Jacob and Abbott had cleared the house, but Conners walked behind us, covering our every move as a precaution.

The entire time Sayward was in my arms she was limp and lifeless, and the fear inside me grew into a panic like I've never known. Teague and Lockman pulled up out front with a van, and we loaded Sayward in and got the hell out of there before law enforcement showed. Taking her to a secure hospital in Bogotá was the first priority, and once she was checked in I didn't leave her side unless they took her out for tests.

The first time she opened her eyes and spoke to me, all the fear, anxiety, and dread that'd been sitting inside me since she collapsed grew into one huge lump in my throat and I thought I'd fucking come apart at the seams.

Now, I keep her hand held captive in my vise grip as I watch her sleep. The steady rhythm of beeping machines keeps me company and the vision of her beautiful face keeps me sane.

She belongs to me. Sayward is mine.

After the conversation we just had, I know I'm going to spend every day making sure she knows it, never doubts it. There's no other woman I want, no other person in the entire world I'd rather have by my side day in and day out. We've been together for no time at all in the grand scheme of things, but in my world? I've learned that time is irrelevant, and that I need to grab opportunities by the balls when they swing my way.

I'm not letting Sayward go.

That means letting her make her own decisions, even when they threaten to drive me insane. Letting her see Marcos is one of those decisions.

Right on fucking cue, the hospital room door opens and Jacob pokes his head in. He takes one look at the sleeping form of my girl and inclines his head to one side. He wants me to come out into the hallway, and I know why.

Standing, I drop a kiss onto Sayward's forehead. She doesn't even stir, and I glance over my shoulder at her before I exit the room.

Pacing the hallway, his arms clasped behind his head as

his nervous steps eat up the white tile floors, is Marcos Diaz.

I blow out a deep breath even as fury builds inside me. It's a fucking steam train, barreling down the tracks and there might not be any stopping the blowup about to happen. Trying to combat it with reason and thoughts of Sayward, I grind out my most important question through gritted teeth.

"Why should I let you anywhere near her?"

Marcos stops pacing, whirling to face me. He looks like shit. Like a man being hunted down by his own demons, and I can relate. But no sympathy finds its way into my heart for him.

The man who took Sayward, the one who hurt her and kept her from me, taking her away from her home and the people who fucking love her, might be dead. And there's a huge sense of satisfaction that comes with knowing that. But this man?

He should have protected her, not thrown her to the motherfucking devil himself.

The dark circles under his eyes prove that Marcos doesn't feel much better about himself than I do.

I stalk toward him, not stopping until I'm right in his face. My breaths come sharp and fast as my hands ball into fists at my sides. Restraining, holding myself back.

But barely.

"Blacke," warns Jacob. "Easy."

Marcos doesn't break my stare. "I don't deserve easy. I know that. What was I supposed to do?"

I throw out a hand toward Jacob, and then jab a finger to

my own chest. "You should have asked for *fucking help.* You knew we were on your sister's side, that we care about her. You should have known we'd do whatever it took to protect her."

Marcos's eyes finally fall. The fight goes out of him, his body sagging against the wall. "Yes, but what about my family? My wife, my child? They had no one here to protect *them.*"

I don't know if we'll ever come to terms with this. I don't know if we'll ever arrive at an answer that both of us can live with. He feels like he did what he had to. I feel like he made the wrong fucking decision. There had to have been a way that all innocent lives involved could have been protected.

But we'll never know for sure.

I take a step back, hand running through my hair as I eye him with disgust. "She wants to see you. I think a big part of that is how fucking pure her heart is. But she also wants to meet her nephew."

He nods, eyes lifting. There's hope there, and I can't stand to look at it.

"She's sleeping now. Be here for her when she wakes up. Don't fuck this up again. If you do, I swear to God I'll take you out of the equation myself."

He holds my gaze for just a few seconds, understanding written all over his expression. Then he pulls out his cell phone and turns away. I'm guessing he's calling his wife.

When I turn toward Jacob, he's standing against the wall with his arms folded across his chest. He gives me one solemn nod, and there's approval in his eyes I've never seen there before.

"Do I still have a place with the team when we get home?" It's the first time I've thought about it since this all went down. But it's clear, from the way my heartbeat picks up, that the answer to this question matters.

I want a spot on this team.

Jacob's expression doesn't change. "Your spot on the team was never in question, Blaze."

I smile.

It's only been a day, but Sayward sitting up in bed when I walk into her hospital room is like the sun rising over the horizon after a long darkness. Her face breaks into a nervous smile when she sees it's me.

"I wasn't sure where you were," she admits, fiddling with the blanket situated over her lap.

Pulling up the chair beside her bed, I drop into it and can't resist the immediate need to touch her. I reach out and brush the hair back from her forehead, liking how her eyelids flutter at my touch. Seeing her looking healthy, except for the bandage marring her gorgeous head, does something to me. I want to take her home, to my house. I want to make it *our house*. I want to show her in a million different ways how important she is to me.

I want to make all kinds of commitments I never thought I'd want to make again.

"Sorry, beautiful. I just went to the hotel to shower and grab my stuff. They're letting you go today. We're headed back home."

She sighs out a huge puff of relief. "Thank God."

Then she's quiet for a moment. "I want to make a stop on the way to the airport. I want to pay my last respects to my father at his home."

So strong. I nod.

The hospital room door opens tentatively, and we both turn to look.

Marcos stands there, holding a little boy in his arms. As he steps into the room, the boy peers curiously at Sayward. His deep, dark eyes study her and the room, all while his thumb stays securely put in his mouth.

Marcos visited Sayward yesterday after she woke. It was a longer visit than I would have liked, but I said nothing. She allowed me to stay with her in the room the entire time, and I got to see how important rebuilding their relationship is to her.

She needs her brother and his family in her life. And I need her in mine. It's something I'm going to have to learn to live with.

Eventually, I'm going to have to learn how to forgive him. Even though at this point, I don't see how.

"Sayward, meet your nephew, James Ricardo Diaz."

Sayward sits up straighter, her eyes shining in a way I've never seen before. I can feel my own chest filling up with some kind of unspoken emotion, something that's showing me pictures of a life where Sayward looks at another baby boy like that. One running around with her hazel eyes and bronze skin, and my blond hair. The vision stops me cold, steals every ounce of breath from my lungs as I stare at her.

Jesus. Waves of awareness slam into me, because *I want this.* I want it all, and I want it with her.

I watch, like I'm in a trance, as Marcos puts the little boy down beside the bed.

"You named him after *Papi?*" She breathes, staring at her nephew with a smile that wrecks me.

Marcos nods, and nudges the little boy. "This is your auntie, *niñito.* Go and greet her."

"Hi, James." She grabs a small container off the tray beside her. "You want to share my Jell-O?"

The little boy's eyes light up and he scrambles onto the bed as Sayward makes room. They sit side by side, spooning heaps of Jell-O into their mouths.

She's incredible. And she's mine.

I can't wait to get her home.

33

SAYWARD

One Week Later

The bar door behind me opens and closes, and a cool draft brushes the back of my neck where I sit on my stool.

Fall will slide into winter anytime now, and the temperature drops a little bit more every passing day.

Bennett doesn't make it to the bar every day after work, but he's checked in three times this week. I think he feels like he needs to make up his sudden absence to Kandie, but every time he mentions it she rolls her eyes and waves a manicured hand.

She nods her head toward the door now as I run my straw along the rim of my glass of sweet tea.

"Your people are here," she muses as she tosses one long braid behind her shoulder.

Whirling, I grin as all my favorite people—minus one—stride into The Oakes.

Dare's wife, Berkeley, has an arm linked with her best friend and fiancée of Grisham, Greta. Their significant others walk behind them, laughing about something Jeremy said. He throws his head back and laughs from just behind them, sliding out a high-backed bar table chair for his wife, Rayne. She pats the seat next to her for her sister, Olive. Ronin slides up behind Olive, wrapping an arm around her shoulders from behind and placing a kiss on her neck. She leans back to look at him.

Hopping down from my stool, I walk over to them and set my tea down on the table. "What are you guys doing here?"

Dare swoops in and kisses my cheek before he leans right back out again, and I manage not to go all stiff and antisocial no matter how hard I want to.

"It's Friday night, and we could all use some time to chill out after the past few weeks." Grisham leans back against the back of his chair and pulls Greta in just a little bit closer.

This dynamic would have made me uncomfortable just a few weeks earlier. It would have been obvious just how much I didn't fit in, and I probably would have declined an invitation to hang out with all the guys and their significant others.

But now? Now I have Bennett.

It's amazing how much can change in the matter of a few weeks.

Rayne dips her head toward me. "Where is that man of yours, anyway?" She gives me a knowing smirk, letting me know she'd just read my mind.

"He just went to grab something from the stockroom. He should be back any—" I'm cut off when Bennett's voice lifts over the din of the bar.

"I work with all you fuckers. Do I have to see you after hours, too?"

And then I can *feel* him, without even turning. He slips up behind me, his presence heavy but not oppressive. It feels like the air around me has been lit with an electrical charge, like everything inside me is attuned to him. I lean back just as his chest presses against my back, and his voice rumbles in my ear.

"Shit. I was planning on taking you home. Now we gotta hang out for a few."

I shrug, enjoying the feel of his body heat warming me from the inside out. "No, we don't."

His chuckle, dark and rich, sends a shiver skating across my skin. "Bad girl."

My response is prompt and serious. "Only for you."

He groans, just as the bar door opens again. Jacob strides in, a beautiful, dark-haired woman on his arm. Her hair, thick and long, is streaked with a few strands of gray, but her eyes are sparkling with vibrancy. Otherwise, she looks just like her daughter, Greta.

I can feel Bennett straighten, and I turn to look at him. I almost laugh at the shocked expression on his face.

"Who the fuck is *that*?"

"That," I answer with a smile as I glance at Greta, "is Jacob's wife, Laura. This is their second time around. Aren't they cute?"

It's a rare event, Jacob joining us out for drinks. It seems like since we all returned from Colombia, he's reluctant to let me out of his sight. I offer him a warm smile as he pulls out a chair at the table for Laura, and she reaches over and pats my hand.

"It's good to see you, Sayward."

I return her smile. "Thanks, Laura. You, too."

Dare pipes up. "Know how we have that rule, about the newest member of the team always buying the first round during their first year of employment?"

Jeremy nods, deadpan. "Yep. Guess that's you, Blaze."

Everyone looks at Bennett, who's gone completely still. He glances around at everyone, waiting for the joke to settle.

When no one speaks, and no one smiles, he lets out a curse.

"This is bullshit!" He tosses over his shoulder as he heads for the bar, and that's when the entire group loses their minds with laughter.

"I want to show you something." Bennett's voice is quiet as he pulls me from my barstool an hour later. Curious, I give him a quizzical stare, but he just takes my hand.

I follow him down the back hallway to his office, and he stops in the doorway to face me.

His expression is more serious than I've seen it in awhile, and my heartbeat takes off in my chest. Staring up at him, I try to gauge whether or not I should be nervous.

"What is it?" My voice trembles just slightly.

"Close your eyes." He runs his index finger along my jaw line, but his gaze holds mine.

"Why?"

Smirking, he leans forward and brushes his lips against mine. "Humor me."

With a sigh, my eyes drift closed. Bennett takes both my hands and pulls me a few steps forward into the office. He turns me slightly.

"Open." He stands behind me, his hands rubbing up and down my arms.

When I open my eyes, I find I'm staring at the wall where he told me Mickey used to hang maps and photos from the places he visited. I scan the wall, a small smile on my face.

It seems like so long ago, the first time I was in here. It's only been a few weeks, but everything seems drastically different now.

My eyes scan over a photo I haven't seen before and keep going, but then my heart slams to a stop. Slowly scanning the photo I'd almost missed, my breath catches in my throat and my hand flies to cover my mouth.

"Bennett." I whisper around my fingers.

There's a photo there that I've seen before, somewhere in my distant memories. It's me as a little girl, long pigtails hanging down past my shoulders, wearing a pink sundress. I'm sitting on my *papi's* lap, and we both have smiles on our faces as we look up at my laughing *Mama*. The backs of my eyes sting as I blink back the tears. I stare at the photo of a scene I'd completely forgotten, of a life I've lost but somehow rediscovered.

I turn to face him, my heart squeezing and growing at the same time.

Bennett's thumb grazes my cheek, wiping away a tear I didn't know had fallen. His eyes probe, reach, search mine and I can feel myself opening to him more than I ever have before. I can't stop the tumbling of my heart.

I can only hope he'll reach out to catch hold of it.

"How?" I whisper.

"Marcos." His answer is simple. "I told you that I wanted to add to this wall the first time you were in this office. I wanted to add a piece of you. I made a copy for you to have at home, too."

I throw myself into his arms, the need to get as close to him as possible setting a fire inside me.

He kisses me back, his arms snaking around my waist and hands sliding down to grab my ass. Pulling me against him, he tilts his head to the side and deepens the kiss.

Kissing Bennett is something that I'm definitely used to, but something I'll never get tired of. His lips draw out the raw emotions hiding inside me, and when he pulls back it's always too soon.

He stares down at me, bringing his hands up to cup my face. "I love you, Sayward."

My stomach flips. There's nothing but honesty shining out of his eyes, pure and good and *right*.

"If I tell you I love you, too, will you get me out of here?" A little breathless, I lean into him.

His lips curve, his eyes going dark. "What do you want me to do when I get you out of here?"

"I want you to take me home and fuck me until I can't remember my name."

Blunt honesty, no finesse. *That's me.*

A growl rips from him and his strong arms tighten as he lifts me. My legs wrapping around his waist, I laugh softly and run my nose along the coarse, trim hair of his scruff.

My fingers play in his hair, and he strides out of his office.

"I'm taking you home." His voice is sandpaper thin and rough and oh, so Bennett.

Exactly the way I like it.

"I love you."

34

BENNETT

Kicking my front door shut behind me, I edge Sayward toward the bathroom. "Let's go wash off the day."

I smirk, because there's an ulterior motive there. Right now, I just want my woman hot and wet. I haven't taken her in the shower yet, and tonight seems as good a time as any to check it off the list.

Since we've been home from Colombia, I've been keeping Sayward close. I took her straight to her apartment and told her to pack her shit. After spending time with her safety being my number one priority, just dropping her off at her place felt so utterly *wrong*.

She'd looked at me, an amused expression on her face. "My shit? How much of it?"

I hadn't even hesitated when I told her to pack all of it. This man I've become since Sayward turned my life upside down? I never thought I'd see him again, much less be glad he's here. But I can't go back... I can only move forward.

And I want to move forward with Sayward.

She glances back at me over her shoulder as she slips off her shoes and places them in a bin under the brand-new bench I bought to sit beside the front door. My lips tug into a smile as I watch her.

But then I freeze. Because usually, my woman would go take off her clothes in the bedroom and put them away neatly in the space I've cleared for her in my dresser.

Not tonight.

Tonight, Sayward pulls her long-sleeved shirt over her head and drops it on the floor as she walks toward the bathroom.

Slowly. Then she peeks at me over her shoulder again, her plump bottom lip pulling between her teeth.

Oh, fuck.

Sayward's trying to seduce me. And judging from the way my dick stirs to life at the sight of her backward glance, it's working. Her lashes are lowered, her lids hooded as she reaches back to unclasp her bra.

It falls to the floor, and she just steps around it. It's like she's dropping a trail of motherfucking bread crumbs straight to heaven.

I'm rooted to the floor as miles of exposed, sienna skin tease me in my living room. Just outside the bathroom door, she pauses again, and her hands go to the button on her jeans. She unfastens it, the sound of a zipper being undone is like a lightning bolt through my own senses, shocking me into action. My jeans are too fucking tight, the material of my shirt irritates my skin. I need to be free of all these clothes, and my shirt is bunched up in my hands before I think about it.

Sayward bends, sliding those skinny jeans down her curved thighs, leaning down to show me the simplicity of the white cotton panties she wears underneath. They might be simple, but they're cut halfway up her ass cheeks, showing off the perfectly round apple of her bottom, and my hands itch to touch her.

She disappears into the bathroom, leaving her jeans on the floor. I stare after her, my hand going to the button on my own fly. A tiny pair of white underwear flies out of the partially open bathroom door and the sound of the shower is music to my fucking ears.

A striptease? If these are the kinds of little surprises Sayward's gonna give me because I do something nice for her, sign me up.

For a lifetime.

She's the kind of woman who, despite the predictability of her behaviors, will keep me guessing every single day. She's never gonna be boring, not for a second. And that's something I can't wait to see day after day.

I shed my clothes while I stride to the bathroom and inhale the steamy air as I step through the door.

Making my way to the shower, Sayward's form calls out to me from behind the frosted glass of the door. Her hands roam over that beautiful body, her hair a thick, heavy curtain around her shoulders.

Stepping inside, I close the door behind me and her voice drifts across the steamy haze.

"Will you wash my back?"

My cock fully standing at attention now, the throbbing almost painful as I'm overwhelmed with everything Sayward. Her scent, amplified by the steam. Her body, accented by the water sliding over her skin.

Her beauty, magnified by ten. She's fucking gorgeous.

I crowd her, stepping up into the space behind her. I hear her gasp as my arms cage her in, bracing on the wall in front of her. Her head falls back against my bare chest, her hair tickling my skin as she peeks up at me.

Dipping my head, I catch hold of her earlobe between my teeth. "No," I murmur. "I want to start with your front."

Turning her around in my arms, my mouth crashes onto hers, and it's like a fucking flip switches in my body.

I've been holding back with her all week, letting her head heal before I made her mine for good. It's been a fucking feat, sleeping beside her every night with that lush body pressed against me. Driving to work with her every day, passing her in the office when she smiles that smile that no one else understands. She belongs to me in every way, except I haven't had her body since before Colombia. Her concussion needed to heal, and so did her emotional state.

So being with her like this now, my body's working itself into a frenzy and I don't know if I'm gonna be able to hold myself back.

Groaning as she opens her mouth to me, our tongues tangle and I yank her body even tighter against mine: no space, not a breath between us.

I can't get enough of this woman.

Her nails rake up my back as I pull away, staring down at her. Both of my palms cover her perfect tits, feeling their heavy weight as I pinch her nipples and roll them between my fingers. They're hard and needy, and I drop my head to pull one into my mouth. Sucking hard, I feel Sayward's deep moan as I use my teeth and my tongue to ramp up her arousal. Making her hotter, wetter, more impatient for me.

She whimpers as I draw a line with my tongue across the valley between her breasts, her hips thrusting forward. My cock strains to get to her, pulling forward with a lust so fucking strong I'm blind to everything but her.

Just Sayward. This moment.

This lifetime.

My hands slide around her back, holding her close, as my eyes meet hers. Those deep hazel irises are dark with desire, and it's taking everything I have not to slam into her right now.

"It's been over a week." My voice drops low as my eyes rake over her goddess-like body. "I need to taste every fucking inch of you."

She sighs as I drop to my knees in front of her, pressing a hot kiss to the inside of her thigh. She shifts her weight, ready, restless.

Waiting.

Holding her firmly in place in front of me, I bury my nose between her legs. Water drenches the thin line of hair leading to her pussy, and I inhale her sweetness. It's like a drug. One I'm never giving up.

"Damn, beautiful...you're the sweetest thing..." My

tongue dips into her folds, lapping up the desire that clings to her swollen skin. "... I've ever tasted."

She shudders in my hold, and when I glance up her head drops back against the wall.

"*Bennett,*" she says, her voice strained.

I pull her clit—so fucking sensitive—into my mouth and suck. Her knees go weak as she moans again, and my hands tighten around her to hold her upright.

Sliding two fingers inside her tight little pussy, I'm just driving myself insane. *She's the hottest thing in the world, and she belongs to me. Jesus.*

She rides my hand as I use my fingers and my tongue to bring her to the edge, and just as I feel her walls start to clench around my hand, I pull back.

"Don't come," I order, my voice like gravel in a blender.

She lets out a frustrated little mew, and I grin as I stand. Jerking her leg up around my hip, my cock settles between the warmth of her legs. Her eyes go wide as she moves her hips, creating a friction that she hopes will satisfy her ache.

Rubbing my finger through her heat, I shake my head slowly. "I want my dick to make you come. I'll make you come again with my tongue after."

Her eyes go all heavy and she licks her lips. I fucking love her like this, lost to the way my body makes her feel.

It gives her a little taste of what she does to me.

"Bennett." She breathes. Her eyes plead with me, and I pause with my head cocked to the side. "Don't be gentle this time."

All the breath leaves me. The last time I wasn't gentle

with her...I scared her. I never want to experience that again.

I swallow, my dick feeling like it could explode if I wait another fucking second. "You don't want that, Sayward." It's a warning, but it's also a prayer. Her asking me to unleash the beast I keep caged inside?

She's not ready for that.

Her fingers go to my face, holding me in place and forcing me to look at her. It's like she can read my goddamned mind. "I'm ready. I want you...the real you. *All of you.*"

I groan, seconds away from losing my shit as I drop my forehead to hers. "No condom. You want me to grab one?"

She shakes her head, slow and deliberate. "No. I trust you."

"I'm clean," I offer.

She smiles. "I know."

And then her smile turns to the sexiest, hottest expression in the world when I slam into her with no other warning. Her lips part, her eyes roll back, and I grip her leg tighter to keep her from falling.

"Fuuuuuuck."

Being inside Sayward with a condom on was a game-changer. But being inside her bare, with hot water running all around us while her slick body is pressed against mine?

It's a fucking *life-changer.*

Glancing down at where our bodies are joined, I pull out and slide back home. This time I grind my hips against hers, pressing against her clit, and her moan is almost feral. Grabbing her wrist with one hand, I slam her arms up above her head and pound into her again.

"God," she cries, her eyes closing with pleasure. *"Harder."*

And that's when I lose my *motherfucking* mind. This woman . . . Jesus fuck, she's gonna kill me slowly.

I empty all of the craving, the devotion, the hunger that I've ever felt for her into that moment. My body meets her relentlessly, again and again until my name is all I hear as it falls repeatedly from her lips. When her voice rises into a wail, I grip her other leg and pick her up completely off the ground.

As I feel her walls clench around me, pulling at my dick like she's starved for it, I see stars. My balls draw up tight, so tight I think it'll fucking kill me, and I roar as my release pours into her in a hot rush.

I drop my head against her neck, panting as my heart pounds like a racehorse in my chest, my hips jerking as every muscle in my body tenses and then releases, draining the strength from me.

I go down, sliding to the shower floor, pulling Sayward safely into my lap as my ass hits tile.

We're both silent, panting, catching our breath as the reality of what the fuck just happened washes over us.

"Are you okay?" I ask, a little frantic as I push the hair away from her face.

She smiles up at me, a sleepy, peaceful expression in her eyes. "I'm perfect. I love the real you."

She blushes, the faint pink tinge turning her skin the most perfect shade of red, and I know for a face that I'm gone for this woman.

Done. They can call the game right the fuck now, because I'm never going back.

She's mine. For as long as she'll have me, and even then I'll fight to make it longer.

I stand with Sayward in my arms, turning off the shower and wrapping a towel around us. Padding to the bedroom, I lay her across my bed and sprawl out beside her.

Gathering her into my arms, I inhale her sweet scent and close my eyes.

"I don't know when this happened," I admit in a whisper. "It was my job to protect you, and I accepted that without question. Hell, it was my idea. And then when you were taken, it wasn't just my job anymore. It became my life's *mission* to save you."

I pause, trying to figure something out. Sex with Sayward shouldn't be as addictive as it is. Her inexperience alone should have meant that one time was enough. But every time I'm inside her, I'm taken to a place I've never been before. Even when I was married, I never experienced anything like it. I just want more of her, and I know I'll never get tired of it.

But it's not the sex that holds me to this woman. It's the very heart of her, the essence that makes her *Sayward.* I want to hold on to her, keep her safe, make her smile every single day. I want to draw laughter out of her, because I know that I might be the only one who gets to hear it.

I want to be the center of this woman's world, because she sure as hell has become the center of mine.

She turns into me, her strong fingers tickling my scruff as she strokes my jaw. It's something she's taken to doing, and I fucking love it.

"I don't know when it happened, either. But I think you started saving me the second you agreed to work at NES. And now? I can't imagine my life without you."

I brush my mouth against hers. "You're staying here, you know that right? With me."

She smiles and lets out a sigh, her sleepy eyes drifting closed as she settles against me. "Don't want to be anywhere else."

It doesn't matter how we got here. Because we're here now, and she's right.

There's nowhere I'd rather be.

Epilogue

BENNETT

Six Months Later

The sun sinks closer to the tops of the palm trees, and I glance out over the waves crashing against the shore under our feet. Then I glance left and right, analyzing the line of men standing in white shirts tucked into light brown slacks beside me.

It still blows me away, being included in this group of men who have become my brothers. At the front of the line, Grisham stands, shifting from his prosthetic foot to the other, looking nervous as hell. But the second the music changes and everyone seated in the white chairs on the sand stands, his expression goes calm.

Greta appears on Jacob's arm at the top of the dune about fifty feet away, and every single man in our line breaks into a huge grin. As Greta travels down the aisle, my eyes travel to Sayward, where she stands holding a bouquet of white flowers. Her yellow dress looks amazing against her bronzed skin, her dark hair hanging down her back in a long, thick braid. I'm caught staring at the way the dress hugs her sexy curves as her eyes lock with mine.

Her lips tug into a knowing smile, and I turn mine up a notch and send it right back. God, I know this is Greta and Grisham's day, but it's gonna be damn hard to keep my eyes off my woman.

The ceremony progresses, hitting all the important points as we watch Grisham and Greta promise to love each other forever, exchange rings, and kiss for the first time as a married couple. As they retreat down the aisle and the rest of the bridal party follows suit, I fall into step beside Sayward.

She takes my arm, and I lose sight of everything but her, the way her small hand grips my bicep, the way the setting sun shines on her glossy black hair.

"You look so damn beautiful tonight," I whisper as my lips brush against her sweet-smelling hair.

She smiles up at me, holding my gaze like a social champion. She still struggles with the same things she always has, but I'm okay with that, because it's a part of her. And she's gaining the confidence to know that the people around her love her no matter what.

After we've taken photos, everyone heads over to the huge white tent set up just down the beach.

Tugging Sayward into my side, I let everyone else walk ahead of us, their excited chatter dying down as they retreat.

"Sayward." I squeeze her hand, making her look at me.

She stops walking, brushing a stray lock of her hair behind her ears as her bare feet pause in the sand.

"We're going to be late." She smiles. But she doesn't sound like she's in a hurry, and I'm sure as hell not.

"I love you." I take both of her hands in mine and look at her, really look at her, to make sure she knows just how deeply I feel those words.

Because I do. I feel them all the way down to my soul, and that's never going away. This woman has marked me for life, and I've been biding my time for the past six months, trying to make sure that she had everything she needed to be okay after the whole ordeal with the cartel.

I finally feel like she's ready.

She nods, her eyes melting into pools of chocolate. "I know, Bennett. And I'm grateful for the way you love me. Every day."

"You changed my life, you know that? Meeting you, convincing me to join the NES team, allowing me into your heart...it was all such an honor. It still is, beautiful. And I'm at the point now where I can't wait another second to do this." My voice trembles on the last words, and I shake my head a little.

Get your shit together, Blacke. This is only the single most important moment of your life. Don't be a pussy.

Her forehead creases, and I can see her trying hard to read between the lines and the frustration that always comes when she knows she's missing something other people might get. "Do what?"

Dropping down to my knee, I release one of her hands in

order to reach into my pocket and pull out the white leather box.

"This." Using one hand, I open the box and with the other hand just squeeze her hand as hard as I can without hurting her.

Her gasp lets me know she finally gets it.

She finally realizes I'm about to ask her to spend the rest of her life with me.

"Sayward Diaz, I want you to be my wife. I need you to know that in the little house that we share together you're an equal partner. I need to know that you belong to me, and I belong to you, and that it's gonna be that way for the rest of our lives." The words tumble out on one breath, and I force myself to slow down and breathe steadily. "Marry me, beautiful."

She glances at the ring, but my eyes never leave hers. Tears well up in them, and my heart squeezes tight just before it expands at her next word.

"Yes."

It's a simple answer, but it's all I need. Standing up, I pull her into my arms and spin her around.

"Yes." I breathe. "The rest of our lives start right now."

A NOTE FROM DIANA GARDIN

Writing about a heroine with autism was something that happened organically. When Sayward first appeared in *Sworn to Protect*, I knew that she was going to be different than any other female character I had ever written, and as her character traits developed, it hit me very suddenly one day: Sayward has autism.

As a teacher, I've taught many children with autism over the years, and they've always had a very special place in my heart. It seemed as if many of them had many things they wanted to say and no viable way to communicate their innermost thoughts and feelings. They were wired differently, but oftentimes their differences made them feel inferior or as if they didn't belong. That's why Sayward is written the way she is. I was drawing on my classroom experiences working with children with autism.

But Sayward isn't a child, and I wanted to make sure I wrote a believable adult character on the autism spectrum. So I hunted down my friend Kennedy Ryan, who has a son with autism. I knew she was plugged into the autism community, and she directed me toward a sweet lady who is the mother of an adult child with autism. This woman, Karen Lowenstein, read the *Mine to Save* manuscript and gave me her honest opinion on Sayward's character and whether or not I did her justice as a brilliant, beautiful, quirky, high-functioning young woman with autism. Without Karen's feedback, I never would have felt comfortable enough to let Sayward out into the world, but as it is, she's become one of my favorite heroines to date. I hope you love her as much as I do!

For research, I read a lot about the autism spectrum and talked to parents of children who live with it every day. For more information about autism, visit www.autismspeaks.org. And consider visiting Kennedy Ryan's organization that unites authors together in the fight against autism at http://lift4autism.com.

Did you miss Jeremy and Rayne's story? Read on for an excerpt of the first book in the Rescue Ops series, *Sworn to Protect*.

Available now!

RAYNE

My heels click on the polished marble floors as I hurry from the inner office back to my desk in the outer suite. The air, chilly in the late evening hour, feels extra frosty as it filters through my silk sleeveless blouse. I throw a glance back over my shoulder, my eyes scanning the empty hallway behind me for any sign of him.

Just because I don't see him doesn't mean he isn't close. And getting closer.

A sound echoes somewhere in the giant building, close enough that it ricochets through my body like a gunshot. I jump, my heart leaping into my throat as my pulse skyrockets.

I go still, listening.

The sound of insistent footsteps pounding on the same marble I just traversed spurs me into moving again. I skid to a stop at the end of the hallway, looking down the intersecting hall in both directions.

Which way? Which way?

Going for the exit would be the long way. The elevator is two halls away, and my movements can be tracked on any security camera. Especially when my boss, who started this multi-million-dollar tech corporation, is the man I'm running from now.

Oh, my God. I need to get home. I need to get to Decker.

Thinking of my sweet boy triggers a new surge of adrenaline inside me, and I leap forward, choosing to head right, toward the stairs. At least if I'm in the stairwell, I can hear anything coming above me or below me. All I'll have to do is get down fourteen floors to the lobby, and then I'm free.

Free. Free. Free.

Kicking off my shoes, I grasp them in one hand and break into a run. Crossing the short distance to the large double doors marked STAIRS, I push through them and allow them to latch silently behind me. Sucking in a deep breath, I start down the steps.

One flight at a time, Rayne. You can do this. You have *to do this.*

If Wagner Horton takes time to scan the security footage, that's even better for me. That gives me time to get out of this damn building, and get to my kid. The heel of my palm pounds against my head as I hurry downward. Over and over again. As if I could thump away the memory of the sight that got me into this mess in the first place.

Just work, the same work I've done every day for the past eight months. Only this time, being Wagner Horton's executive assistant gave me access to information I never wanted and wasn't supposed to see.

A sound from somewhere above me jars me back into awareness, back to the here and now. Step by step, I rush down the stairs. When I'm crossing the threshold to the seventh floor, the stairwell door below me opens and closes.

I freeze, holding my breath.

"Rayne? I know you're here."

Wagner's voice has never, ever scared me.

Until now.

I mean, he's a tech geek turned billionaire. I never considered him to be dangerous. But the look in his eyes tonight when he discovered me in the building after hours, working late . . . I shudder, remembering.

I close my eyes, willing him to *just go away.*

Silence from one floor below me.

Brrrrrrrrrng.

In my pocket, my cell phone rings.

Wagner's laugh floats toward me. "There you are."

The sound of his feet pounding up the stairs mingles with the quiet thump of my bare feet turning and heading up one more floor. Moving faster than I've moved ever, I throw myself through the eighth-floor stairwell door and into the hallway.

The only option I have now is to hide, or to get to the elevator before he gets to me.

I choose the elevator. Sprinting around the corner and into the hall where those heavenly golden doors lay waiting for me.

"Come, on, come on, dammit!" Stabbing at the button repeatedly, I glance over my shoulder again and again.

The elevator doors slide open as Wagner rounds the corner all the way down the hall.

"Rayne!" he screams.

The desperate sound reaches into my chest and squeezes my heart, stuttering the beats.

Frantic, I push the CLOSE button over and over again, jabbing it with such violence I'm sure to feel the pain later.

OhmyGodohmyGodohmyGod.

Please...close! Close!

My voice is silent as I yell at the elevator doors. They begin to slide shut and I sag against the back wall of the box, letting out the breath I'd been holding

And then Wagner appears, looming *right there.*

With a yelp, I press against the back wall of the elevator.

His face is a mask of hatred and fury. He goes to stick a hand between the doors, but it's too late. The doors slide shut.

With my heart in my throat, I ride the eight floors down to the parking garage. I know for a fact that, since only one elevator goes up to our offices, Wagner would have had to take the stairs. I have a decent head start, but I run anyway as soon as the elevator opens.

Straight to my car.

Police. I need to go to the police.

But the memory of a photo I saw on the wall in Wagner's office every day for eight months flashes in my brain. It's a picture of him and the chief of the Phoenix police department, smiling and shaking hands for the camera after Wagner's money built the department a brand-new, state-of-the-art headquarters.

I've never thought that having a chief of police in your pocket was a real thing, but that picture sends me reeling. There's no way I'm going there. Not until I know who I can trust.

Yanking the door open and thanking the heavens for key fobs, I start the thing and peel out of my spot. Pressing the car's Bluetooth button, I order the vehicle to call my babysitter.

"Payton? Yeah, I'm leaving work now. I don't have time to explain, but I need you to grab Decker, get in your car, and drive to the airport. Don't hesitate, Payton. Do it *now*."

I'll mourn the loss of my belongings later. Maybe I can send for them.

But right now? I have to get out of Phoenix. Maybe forever. I know now that what I saw was important.

Maybe important enough for him to kill me.

I'm going to have to do the one thing I *never* wanted to do.

For the first time in nearly nine years, it's time for my son and me to go home.

JEREMY

When my fellow team member Grisham Abbot strolls into the Night Eagle Security conference room a few minutes after I do, I lean back in my big, leather chair.

The seriousness and tension of the undercover mission I just led siphons off me, being replaced by the relaxed comfort of being home.

It's like I'm two different Jeremy Teagues: the one who kicks ass during a security or black ops mission or the laid-back jokester I tend to be when I'm not working. Sometimes they get in each other's way.

Sometimes they fight for supremacy.

Grisham eyes me, one hand shoving through his short blond hair as he comes to a stop across the table beside his usual seat. "You recover from whatever it is you think you saw at the airport this morning?"

Inhaling, I try not to flip back to that moment in the

airport. But the memory creeps in anyway, regardless of how hard I try to fight it...

We're just passing under the decorative model of a single-engine plane hanging overhead into the baggage claim area when a mane of long, raven hair catches my eye. My stomach flips, my muscles tighten, and my back teeth grind together.

Fucking hell. That hair.

She turns, her profile facing me, and everything inside me stills.

My steps stutter to a stop, and I'm pretty sure the air in my lungs does, too. Everything around me, the airport crowd, the noise, fades away, and it's like I'm staring through a tunnel of mist and fog and the only thing I can see at the end of it is her.

Because, swear on my dog, it's her.

I'd scoured the airport after that, my head swiveling left and right, my eyes roving. Searching.

There'd been rows of taxis lined up in front of the terminal, and that ghost could have disappeared into any one of them.

Or I could have just been losing my fucking mind. More likely.

Because I exorcised that ghost a long time ago. I don't need it to start haunting me again.

I snap back to the here and now as Grisham begins to lower himself into his chair. I ignore his question and lean forward. "Let's grab a beer after we debrief." I lift my brows, hoping he'll accept the invitation. I'm still feeling the need to unwind, let loose a little after our op.

He stares at me like I've lost my mind. "Man, I've been away from my fiancée for almost a week. There's no way in hell I'm going anywhere but home after we give Jacob the rundown."

I feign a heavy sigh, but I knew his answer before he'd said it.

"Whipped," I mutter.

"Damn right." Grisham's statement comes with a proud smile.

Jacob Owen strides into the room. "Let's debrief, gentlemen." His tone is wry as he sends me a pointed stare.

He leans over the low, rectangular table where, as a team, we use painstaking research to plan our missions. Clasping his hands together, he looks at Grisham and me in turn, holding our gazes as he assesses our reaction. His blue eyes, webbed with lines that are the only indicator of his middle age, stop on me.

"First black ops government contract. First time leading a Night Eagle mission. A lot of firsts for you in the last few weeks, and for the firm. Right, Brains?"

I nod my head and hold steady under his scrutiny. I'd give my left nut for Jacob Owen, pretty sure the whole team would. Adjusting to normal life again after Special Forces is difficult. For some of us, it's impossible. But Jacob gets it. And when he brings one of us into the fold at Night Eagle Security, we thrive.

Finally, he speaks again, this time addressing both Grisham and me. "You did good, boys."

Letting out a breath, I lean back in my seat and listen while Jacob fires questions at us about the intel we received that will bring down not just the Miami part of the arms ring, but the South American branch as well. He informs us that in a few months' time, we'll be leaving for Costa Rica on a second mission to first infiltrate, and then help the CIA eliminate, this nasty operation for good.

When our debriefing comes to an end, Jacob shakes both of our hands and glances at Grisham.

"Ghost," he barks.

Grisham "Ghost" Abbot leans forward, his elbows connecting with his knees as he locks eyes with his future father-in-law. The ex-SEAL earned his nickname with his uncanny ability to sneak up on enemy forces in the field. Grisham Abbot is the strategist of our group. He's a planner, an analyzer by nature, and that skill works to our advantage when it comes to nailing down the nitty-gritty details of a potential operation.

"Sir."

"Get home to my daughter. She's missed you." Jacob's lips twitch.

As we leave Jacob's office, I want to pump my fist in the air. I want to shout "Hell Yeah" now that I know for a fact that we're going black ops again.

I've been with NES for a little over a year. In that time, we've specialized in personal security for clients who can afford to pay the price for the best protection out there. In the past six months or so, Jacob has been in talks with some government agencies. His connections there have asked us multiple times to protect foreign dignitaries, their families, and other important international people who are working or vacationing close by, and we've excelled at every single one of those assignments.

This last mission, sending us to infiltrate the illegal arms organization in Miami, was not only the first time I've taken the lead on an op, but also the first time we've had an official "black ops" contract with Uncle Sam as a private contractor.

Deep cover, secret mission...everything that comes with it is my element. I fucking love it. The reason they call me Brains is because I have an obsession with techy gadgets for the field. I have a whole room dedicated to storing all of the tools and equipment we may need for a mission or an assignment, and I love stocking it up and keeping it up-to-date with everything current in the world of tech and gear. This job is in my blood, and I could never imagine doing anything different.

My adrenaline is still pumping from everything we accomplished, and I know when I get back to my house, the first thing I'll need to do is run.

Grisham and I file out the metal sliding door into the lobby.

Ronin "Swagger" Shaw claps me on the back as soon as the office door is closed. "Nice, guys. Heard you kicked some ass." I accept congratulations from the man who's been my teammate and best friend for years. First the army, then the police academy, then NES after we met Jacob while working on a kidnapping case.

Dare "Wheels" Conners, our other teammate and the man who can drive anything out there like a goddamn stuntman, follows suit with a fist bump.

When I'm in this office, in my city, with my people, I'm

home. There're no surprises, no unexpected bullshit the way there is when I'm on a mission. It's how I like it.

And it feels good to be home again.

But as I'm back in North Carolina, weaving through the Wilmington streets on my drive home, my brain drifts back to long, black hair, flawless, olive skin, and the endless sea of blue eyes I once almost drowned in.

It couldn't have been her.

About the Author

Diana Gardin is a wife of one and a mom of two. Writing is her second full-time job to that, and she loves it! Diana writes contemporary romance in the Young Adult and New Adult categories. She's also a former elementary school teacher. She loves steak, sugar cookies, and Coke and hates working out.

Learn more at:
  DianaGardin.com
  Twitter: @DianalynnGardin
  Facebook.com/AuthorDianaGardin

CPSIA information can be obtained
at www.ICGtesting.com
Printed in the USA
LVOW11s1508141217
559732LV00001B/125/P